Sidhera's

Revenge

Sleeping Beauty Overslept

Book Two

idhera's

evenge

Sleeping Beauty Overslept

Book Two

Joe Tompkins

Autumn Harbor Press

Atlanta, GA

Sidhera's Revenge

Sleeping Beauty Overslept: Book Two

Autumn Harbor Press

FIRST EDITION

January 2009

ISBN 978-0-578-00631-4

For more information about Autumn Harbor books, please visit our website @ www.autumnharbor.com

For **Lisa**, my real-life princess and true love, and for my **Mom**, who always inspires greatness.

Contents

Chapter One

Birthday

 orey was impossible to live with for most of the year, but when his birthday rolled around... it became so much worse. This was going to be his 15th birthday, and he talked about it incessantly for more than a month beforehand.

"Hey, Jasen!" he said one morning before school. "Got a joke for you. Ready?"

I sighed heavily as I poured milk into my morning cereal. "Alright."

Corey snatched the box of cereal and started to pour his own, spilling it over the top of the bowl and onto the counter. "Okay. Here goes... Knock-Knock."

"Who's there?" I asked.

"Thirty." Corey grinned.

"Thirty who?"

"Thirty more days 'til my birthday. Hope you got me something good." Corey laughed and laughed as if this was very witty, then started digging into his cereal.

He did the same thing every morning for a month, and each morning he laughed like it was the funniest thing he had ever heard.

When I had turned seventeen in July, Corey's present to me had been a crumpled half-sheet of notebook paper with the words "I.O.U. one present. From: Your brother Corey" scrawled across the front in purple crayon. I had considered just giving it back to him on his own birthday and telling him we were even.

Turned out, though, that I had already found a pretty cool present for Corey. What I was more worried about at that time was finding the right present for my girlfriend, who had a birthday just two weeks after Corey's. That one made me so nervous that I was having trouble sleeping at night. It was a big problem since Elayne was not only a princess who already had just about anything a person could need... but also that this was officially her first birthday in more than thirteen hundred years.

No pressure. No pressure at all.

I felt like I really needed to do something extra-special, but at the moment I was completely without ideas and the date was fast approaching.

"You broke an ancient curse, bro." Corey told me one day. "You defeated a terrifying fairy queen and even tangled with a dragon for her. You think she's really going to care if you buy her a box of chocolates or not?"

I knew that Corey was trying to make me feel better, but what he said actually made it much, much worse. It was true... no ordinary gift would do. It had to be something... extraordinary.

I was still mulling it over when the morning of Corey's birthday finally arrived.

It was a Wednesday... a school day. When I came downstairs for breakfast, still wearing an old tee-shirt and Snoopy pajama bottoms, I found the kitchen crowded and bustling with activity. Grandpa was there, clean-shaven and already dressed. He was setting the table with the help of his wife Liz (who was actually a fairy queen named Bridgette... but on mornings like this, when she looked altogether normal, that was something I could almost forget). Grandpa looked up at me and smiled "Mornin' sleepy head. We've got company for breakfast today."

I rubbed my eyes tiredly and looked around. Over by the stove, Emily stood flipping some pancakes. Her long dark-brown hair was pulled back into a ponytail. A year younger than Corey, the two of them had been officially dating now since last fall. She turned and looked at me with a crooked grin, her cheeks red from the heat of the stove. "Hey Jasen." she said as she turned another pancake. "Nice pajamas."

I smiled and rubbed my hand through my tangle of dirty-blonde hair. I was almost to the bottom step when I saw the last guest in our kitchen. She stood up from where she had been hidden from view behind the refrigerator door. It was Elayne. Her long blonde hair fell in soft rings around her shoulders. Although she was dressed in "regular" clothes, she looked every bit a radiant princess. When she saw me, her blue eyes lit into a beautiful smile.

I froze, my hand still caught in my tangle of messy hair. "Elayne! What are you doing here?"

The surprise on my face made her stifle a laugh and I could feel embarrassed heat rising in my cheeks. (*Man, oh, man! Why hadn't I at least gotten dressed before coming downstairs this morning?*)

"I'm here for Corey's birthday." Elayne said, pulling a pitcher of orange juice from the fridge.

"That's today?" I asked.

Emily, putting the last of the pancakes on a plate by the stove, let out a loud snort. "Yeah, RIGHT! As if he hasn't reminded us every moment of every day for a month!"

Elayne's eyes playfully darted to my tattered slippers with my toes poking out the fronts and I saw her smile widen.

"I'm just going to run up and get dressed real quick…" I started to say, but at that moment Corey came down the stairs behind me.

"Do I smell pancakes?" he called loudly.

Corey, of course, looked completely prepared. He was fully dressed and cleaned up, and it even looked like he'd made an effort to comb his mop of hair, which usually fell in a tangle over his eyes. As he stepped past me at the bottom of the stairs, he made a big show of looking surprised. "Wow!" he said loudly. "What's all this?"

Emily rolled her eyes. "Oh, brother," she mumbled. "Whatta ham."

Corey smiled broadly, looking at the big breakfast set out on the table. Liz stood with a gentle smile. "Happy Birthday, young Corey." she said.

Again, Corey managed a surprised, wide-eyed look. "Birthday? Wow, is that *today*? I had completely forgotten!"

Breakfast was delicious. Although I was still self-conscious about my messy hair and pajamas, I managed to relax and finally enjoy it. Elayne sat beside me, casting secret smiles at me when nobody was looking. When we were through eating, she moved her hand over to mine and held it beneath the table, and any embarrassment I had felt about my messy hair and tattered slippers completely melted away.

After breakfast, Liz produced two small, ornate boxes. (*Whether she had them hidden in her pocket or just conjured them out of thin air, I decided I didn't want to know.*) Each box was covered with blue-green gemstones and had delicate silver lines etched across the top. She handed one box to Corey and the other one to me. "I have a gift for you both," she said in her calm, even voice.

Corey took his box and looked over at mine. "Hey!" he said. "How come Jasen gets a present on my birthday?"

"It is something each of you should have. You may consider it a birthday present, but it is more than that."

Corey and I opened our boxes together. Inside, sitting on a plush blue-green cushion, was a beautiful ring made of fine-crafted silver with a small blue stone in the center. Along the edges wove the same carefully crafted pattern that covered the box. I recognized it as the symbol for water. When I looked over at Corey, I saw that his box held a ring identical to mine.

"Wow." I said. "This is beautiful, Bridgette." I had forgotten to call her Liz, but nobody seemed to take notice.

"Nice." Corey said. "I don't wear rings, though. They make my fingers itch."

Liz turned her solemn eyes to Corey. "You will wear this one." she said.

Corey blinked, obviously not sure how to respond to that.

"It is the royal ring of the Sylphs." Liz continued. "It is a symbol that you are royalty among my tribe and it is a sign of honor and respect among all fairies."

Corey blinked again. "Oh, well… okay then."

I looked up at Liz. "Thank you. This means a lot."

Emily leaned over and whispered to Corey quickly. "It's the ring of a royal prince, you moron. Tell her thank you!"

Corey looked up at Liz. "Oh, right! Thanks!" he said quickly. "Love it! Great gift."

We continued around the table, giving our gifts to Corey and watching the clock, knowing that we were going to be late for school. If it was okay with Grandpa, though, it was more than fine with us.

Elayne was next. She gave Corey his gift in a small pouch. He opened it excitedly, then looked confused, holding up a small, glassy yellow stone. "Oh, look!" Corey began hesitantly. "Elayne got me a…. marble?" He turned the pouch over, looking for more. "Er… are there more? Hard to play a game of marbles with just one."

Elayne laughed and told him to hold it up and look inside. When he did, we could all see a four-leaf clover inside the tiny yellow ball.

When Liz saw the gift, she nodded approvingly. "An excellent gift, Princess Elayne."

Corey seemed to like it, too. "Hey, yeah! Good luck charm. Nice!"

"Four-leaf clovers are more than good luck, Corey." Elayne said. "They allow you to see spirits and fairies that may have otherwise been hidden and unseen."

Corey rolled the tiny ball around his palm. "Well, very cool. Thanks."

I was next. I tossed Corey the gift that had been hiding under my bed all of these months. It was a small green glass bottle with a cork in the top of it. "Here you go. Happy birthday. I got it at a marketplace near Elayne's castle."

Corey looked at the vial with a grin, shaking it lightly. "Very cool! Magic potion, right? What's this one do?"

"It's pixie dust." I said.

Corey furrowed his eyebrows. "Pixie dust…" then he snapped his fingers. "Oh! Like Tinkerbell, right?" he looked at the vial again. "So, what? Thank happy thoughts and I can fly like Peter Pan?"

"Actually, real pixie dust makes you invisible." I said.

Corey's grin widened. "Cool present, bro! Thanks! Hey, maybe I can use this to get out of my science test next week in Mrs. Phee's class! One minute I'm at my desk and the next minute everyone's all like 'Hey! Where did Corey go?'"

Emily shook her head. "You're not doing that."

He turned to her. "And what did *you* get me for my birthday?"

Emily's eyes darted to the others at the table and her cheeks flushed pink. She handed him a small wrapped box and cleared her throat, trying not to look embarrassed.

Corey opened it and pulled out a small golden locket. Inside was a tiny picture of Emily and him smiling together. Corey squinted at the picture with a grin. "Hey, that's from homecoming last year, right?"

Emily's smile lit up. "You remember?"

Corey snorted. "Hard to forget. We got attacked by an evil fairy queen halfway through it."

Emily frowned. "That's all you remember about that night?"

Corey pretended to look confused. "I remember that the punch that the lunch ladies made was pretty good."

Emily narrowed her eyes at him.

He held up his hands. "Just kidding! I remember it was our first date. Don't give me the scary mean squinty look! It was a joke."

"It's time for you kids to be getting to school, anyway." Grandpa said suddenly, clapping his hands together.

Corey, Emily, and I all groaned together. We had hoped we could have gotten a little more time out of Grandpa before he noticed how late it was.

Grandpa smiled. "I do have my gift to give, though, before you go."

Corey's eyes lit up. "More presents?"

"Just one." Grandpa said with a small, secret smile that looked a lot like the one Liz always wore. "It's out in the driveway."

Corey shot up out of his chair so quickly that it clattered loudly against the wall behind him and Emily had to catch it before it fell to the floor. "A car?" Corey stammered. "You got me a car?"

"Not exactly…" Grandpa began, but before he could say any more, Corey was across the kitchen and had thrown open the door. The rest of us pushed our chairs out and shuffled out of the kitchen to follow.

The October air was already chilly, and I think that I felt it more than anyone since I was wearing only my tee-shirt and pajama bottoms. Out in the driveway sat the light-blue Grand Marquis that Grandpa had given me the year before. Beside it, covered with dents and peeling paint, stood a bright yellow motorcycle. I recognized it as a motocross bike, the kind they used for riding through the mud and pulling off stunts. This one looked like it was twenty years old and falling apart, but Corey stood beside it open-mouthed and staring with a look of pure adoration.

Grandpa chuckled at Corey's expression. "You like it?" he asked.

Corey was still speechless for a few moments, but finally answered breathlessly. "Like it? Are you kidding? It's *awesome*!"

"Well, I knew you were turning fifteen and getting your learner's license this year. I'm sorry I couldn't afford another car, but I thought that…"

Grandpa never got to finish. Corey cut him off with a big, smothering hug. Over his shoulder, I saw Grandpa smile happily to himself.

As I went back inside to get dressed, I smiled to myself, too. Now that Corey's birthday had finally arrived, I wouldn't have to hear his lame knock-knock joke anymore… at least not until next year.

Chapter Two

The Moonlit Clearing

 or a very long time, I had looked forward to my
senior year at Jacob's Rest High School. The tiny
town nestled in the Catskill mountains had been a
boring place to grow up for most of my life, and I
had often dreamed about finishing school and moving out...
starting out with college, probably in a big city, and moving
on to bigger and better things from there.

During my second-to-last year, though, so much had
changed. My eyes had been opened to a whole new world
(literally-- a whole different world separate from ours) that I
had never known existed. Now, my plans for beyond high
school weren't so clear anymore. Going to live in a big city
didn't seem quite as exciting as it once did.

During the school days, I found my thoughts drifting often.
I wondered what Elayne was doing in her castle, where she

was taught daily by scholars and tutors, learning subjects like the history of her world, the laws of social order, and how to read and write in the languages of the twelve fairy tribes. On the other hand, I sat in keyboarding class learning how to keep my fingers from wandering off of the home keys while I typed words like "fluffernut" and "fatterboodle" over and over again.

Occasionally, I would look up from the computer screen at the cracked plaster ceiling of my classroom. Many of the ceilings on the second floor of the school were still cracked like that, even though they had mostly fixed the roof during the summer. Their official explanation for the school roof collapsing was the weight of the snow from the big snowstorm we had last year. Corey, Emily, and I knew better, though. We knew that the roof had actually been crushed under the massive weight of the dragon Grendesh during our final showdown with Sidhera. It was there that we had finally broken Sidhera's spell on Elayne. Sleeping Beauty's legendary curse broken by true-love's kiss…

The bell rang, breaking me out of my reverie. When I looked away from the cracked ceiling and back at my computer screen, I saw that my fingers had been typing out "*kiss, kiss, kiss, kiss*" over and over again. Chad Wright, the football player who sat beside me, glanced at my screen and gave me a look like I was crazy before he got up and walked away. I quickly cleared off my screen and gathered my books.

As I was passing through the classroom door, I felt my shoe stick to the floor just inside the threshold. When I lifted my foot up, I found long, gooey tendrils of neon-green bubble gum stuck to the bottom of my shoe. Someone must've been trying to spit it into the nearby trashcan and missed. I did my best to scrape it off, but that only seemed to make it worse. I ended up just leaving it, and as I ran down the hallway to get to my next class, my shoes made a sticky popping sound with every other step.

After school, I was anxious to go visit Elayne, but Corey wanted to try out his new motorcycle first. While Emily and I sat on the hood of my car and watched, Corey straddled the cracked leather seat and strapped on a worn helmet.

"How do I look?" he asked. "Pretty cool, right?"

Emily rolled her eyes. "Yeah, yeah. Real cool, hotshot. Now start that thing up and give it a try. I want to get to the moonlit clearing before the sun goes down."

Corey savored the moment, though, running his hands over the chrome handlebars as if they were made of gold. "Alright," he said finally. "Ready?"

"We're ready!" I laughed. "C'mon! Fire it up and do a few laps around the block so we can go!"

With a big grin, Corey kick-started the bike and it gunned to life. It sputtered and shook for a moment, finally coughing up a big plume of blackish smoke before settling into an uneven idle. The sound of the old engine was loud enough to shake my teeth, and Corey threw back his head and howled with delight. Beside me, Emily started laughing.

As if he was about to put on a show for an audience of thousands, he waved to an invisible crowd and gripped the handlebars. "Here we go!" he yelled over the sound of the engine. He set his feet down, changed the gear, and pulled the throttle. The bike sprang forward like a wild animal, its front tire jumping high into the air. Corey was thrown backwards, arms sprawling, and landed hard on his back. The bike went almost twenty feet down the driveway without him before finally clattering to its side against the birdbath in the yard, where the engine went suddenly silent.

Emily and I shot up and ran over to Corey. I was already thinking that I would have to run inside and dial 911 for an ambulance. Emily moved even faster, and she was kneeling beside Corey in an instant, worry etched into the freckles of her face.

Corey lay there in his helmet, wide-eyed with shock. Even as Emily was kneeling over him, though, I saw the grin reappear on his face. "That…" he began, still staring up at the fading cloud of exhaust fumes… "was FREAKING AWESOME!"

Corey was still thrumming with adrenaline as we walked through the woods a half hour later. "So awesome!" he kept chanting. "So freaking awesome!" Every once in awhile he would hold his hands out like he was holding invisible handlebars and he would make a sputtering sound like an engine with his lips.

"You sure he's okay?" Emily asked, watching him sideways as we walked through the trees. "You don't think he hit his head too hard, do you?"

Corey was now pretending to ride a motorcycle in circles around the base of a big tree.

"Nah." I said. "He's always like this."

"I've got to be back for dinner tonight." Emily continued. "My parents got really mad last time I was late."

"Shouldn't be a problem." I said. "We'll stay at the castle for an hour or so, then head back."

"Did you see the way that bike moved?" Corey shouted. "It was like a lightning bolt! Man, the speed on that thing!"

"Right Corey. A big, sputtering lightning bolt with peeling yellow paint and a cracked leather seat. Now if you can just stay on it for more than a half a second, it would be even more impressive…" I turned back to Emily. "Hey… listen, I meant to ask you something. Elayne said that she had something really important to talk to me about. You wouldn't happen to know anything about that would you?"

Emily turned her eyes away and acted suddenly very interested in her shoes as they crunched through the fallen leaves beneath us.

"What?" I asked, "You do know something about it, don't you? What is it?"

Emily kept her gaze firmly down. "I can't say." she said quickly.

"I think I'm going to get some flames painted on the side of it. What do you think?" Corey called as he jumped up to snatch a leaf off an overhanging branch.

I ignored him, suddenly very worried at Emily's silence. "Is it bad?" I asked. I felt a lump rise in my throat. "Is she..." I found it suddenly hard to swallow. "Is she going to break up with me?"

Emily held up her hands. "Jasen, I'm not allowed to say, alright? It's something private between you and Elayne."

"If it's private then how come she told you?" I asked.

Emily looked at me sideways. "Duh... cause I'm her best friend."

I began to protest, but Corey started up again. "I should get some really cool sunglasses!" he said suddenly. "All great bikers have really cool sunglasses!"

"We're here." Emily said, sounding relieved for an excuse to avoid our conversation. I looked ahead and saw the charred remains of a huge tree stump.

I decided to drop the subject, but my mind was racing now. *Was it true? Was Elayne going to break up with me?*

I felt a pit of dread form in my stomach. Suddenly, I wasn't so sure I wanted to go to the castle anymore.

But ahead of me, Corey had already taken a running leap into the air and disappeared from sight near the blackened stump. Emily quickened her step and a moment later, she, too, had disappeared into thin air.

I stopped, honestly considering just turning around now and running back home. All of a sudden I didn't want to hear what Elayne had to say to me. I wasn't sure I could take it.

A moment later, Corey's head appeared, floating in midair as he peeked out through the invisible curtain. "Hey, bro! You comin?"

With a growing sense of unease, I started forward again and took a step across the threshold.

I stepped out of the cool October air and into the warm night of the moonlit clearing. In my next step, the crunchy forest leaves beneath my feet were replaced by thick, springy grass. The sunlight pouring through the branches overhead became the light from a huge full moon that sat forever resting against the treetops above.

The calm forever-night of the moonlit clearing had always been a special place for the four of us. It was the place between our world and Elayne's, hidden behind an invisible curtain. Often, we would meet Elayne here… sometimes for a picnic on the soft grass, or sometimes just to sit and talk beneath the warm night sky. It was a place of good memories for me.

Well, mostly good, anyway.

Here and there, scattered around the edges of the clearing, you could still see big chunks of broken stone and splintered wood… sometimes even glistening shards of colored glass, scattered like jewels in the grass. They were all that remained of the little stone chapel that had once sat on the edge of the clearing. The little building where we had first found Elayne, sleeping an enchanted sleep.

Now, there was only a slab of a stone wall sitting far back in the shadows where the back of the chapel had once stood. Behind it, the trees closed in densely into dark forest. In the center of the wall was an elaborately carved wooden door with a gold handle. The door to Elayne's world.

Corey ran up to the door as we had so many times in the past year. Without hesitation, he pushed it open and sunlight came pouring through from beyond. A bright green hillside could be seen, and a warm summer breeze blew through the doorway and ruffled Corey's hair.

Emily, perhaps trying to avoid more of my questions, hurried to catch up with Corey and a moment later they were both through the door. I took off my winter coat and laid it on the thick grass of the moonlit clearing. It was spring on the other side of that doorway and I knew I wouldn't need it. The seasons in Elayne's world were flipped from ours. Fall here, spring there. When we had gone to visit her on the hottest day in July, we had gotten snowed in for a week at the castle during a surprise blizzard. It was just one of the many odd and magical things we had grown accustomed to this past year.

Still fighting the dread in my stomach, I took a deep breath and stepped through the doorway.

I had to raise my hand to shield my eyes from the bright sun here. Even then, it took a moment to adjust.

I now stood on a grassy hilltop, set among rolling green fields beneath a bright blue sky. A warm breeze combed through the tall grass around me and moved across the distant hills like waves on an ocean. Behind me, the wooden doorway stood open in the face of a big stone wall.

Emily and Corey had already moved ahead to the other stone building on the hillside. It was a stable house, with two fierce-looking royal guards posted out front. When they saw us emerge from the doorway, one of them banged an armored fist against the door of the stable house to signal someone inside.

Immediately, a man came out and ran to us, smiling. He was dressed in bright wool clothing and had a long, thin nose. "Hello Lady Emily! Masters Corey and Jasen! How nice to see you all today!"

It was Keafer, the stable master. He took care of the horses here and got them ready for us whenever we visited. The king and queen had built this stable house after our adventure last year. Elayne's castle (which was formally called "The Castle of Lions" by the people in the kingdom) was a three-hour walk from this hillside, but only twenty minutes by horseback. It made our visits with Elayne much easier.

"How is Reese?" Emily asked Keafer immediately, referring to the horse she usually rode. Emily had grown up on a horse farm and loved horses. Corey, on the other hand, was the exact opposite. Even though we had been doing this for a long time now, horses still really creeped him out.

"Oh, Reese is doing just fine, Lady Emily." Keafer said quickly as he moved with her towards the stable. "I think he just had a summer cold. He seemed to sleep much better last night..."

As they disappeared into the stable to get our horses, I stood on the hilltop and looked out at the distant horizon to where I could just make out the four yellow pennants flying from the towers of the castle miles away.

Even then, I couldn't shake the growing feeling that something bad was about to happen. I felt like there were storm clouds gathering darkly overhead, but when I looked back at the sky again, there was nothing but clear blue for as far as I could see.

Chapter Three

The Red Room

 y the time we made it to the castle, I was almost sick with worry. In fact, I almost forgot to speed up as we crossed the drawbridge over the castle moat. When I was about halfway across the massive wooden bridge, a giant tentacle shot out from the dark waters beneath. It slammed down with a wet thud behind me, grabbing at my horse's legs. My horse jumped into a gallop and ran the rest of the way across as the huge tentacle slithered back into the water below.

Instead of trying to help out, the guards were laughing as I passed them.

"That monster truly hates you, Sir Jasen." one of them said. "In all my years, I've never seen it attack someone unprovoked, and yet it grabs at you every time you cross."

I stepped off my saddle and handed the reins to a waiting stable boy as Emily and Corey pulled up beside me.

Emily was also obviously trying not to laugh at my startled expression. "I thought he would have forgiven you by now," she said. "I guess that giant, man-eating leviathans really hold a grudge!"

"He's definitely after you." Corey laughed. "Hey! Maybe you can get him to swallow a big ticking clock like the alligator that was always after Captain Hook."

Emily giggled, handing over her horse to another waiting boy. "It might just be playing with you, Jasen. It probably just enjoys giving you a scare."

I rolled my eyes. "Yeah, right. Ha-ha. What a kidder. Like that time it almost ate me--- TWICE. Funny stuff. Good times."

Emily and Corey really cracked up laughing then, although I hardly saw anything funny about it. A moment later, I noticed that the guards standing around us all suddenly straightened to rigid attention.

A gentle voice called from behind us. "What's so funny? What did I miss?"

We turned to see Elayne standing there watching us curiously, a smile tickling her lips. When I saw her, I instantly felt the dread return. *She's going to break up with me.* I thought. *What other 'important thing' could there be for her to talk to me about?* I wished now that the leviathan in the moat actually had gotten me this time and dragged me under. At least I wouldn't have to face having my heart broken.

Emily looked at Elayne, then back at me again quickly. The smile dropped from her face and she took Corey's arm. "Um… hey, Corey. Let's head up to Elayne's suite and wait for them there."

"What? No way. I was hoping to head to the kitchen to see if they still had some of that pudding that they made last week."

"The plum pudding?" Elayne asked. "I believe they do, Corey. Tell the head cook that I sent you."

"We're outta here." Corey said and they started down a side corridor. Before they disappeared, I saw Emily look back and exchange a significant look with Elayne. I couldn't tell what it meant, but it made me even more nervous about what was coming.

Elayne turned back to me. Her face was pale and she looked very nervous all of the sudden.

"Hi." she said. I saw that her hands were clenched awkwardly in front of her as she stood facing me.

"Hi." I said back, feeling the stares of the guards all around us.

"We... um. We need to talk about something." Elayne said carefully. Her blue eyes darted to the ground and she chewed on the corner of her lip nervously.

I swallowed a lump in my throat. "I know." I said, my voice cracking a little.

Elayne's eyes widened. "You know?"

"No." I said quickly. "I mean, I don't KNOW. I just know that you wanted to talk, but I don't know what it's about."

"Oh." Elayne said, and her eyes darted around nervously, as if she, too, were suddenly aware of the guards all around us. "Well, um... let's go someplace where we can talk."

I swallowed hard. "Lead the way."

Elayne led me through a side passage that I had never been down before. It took us to a wide hall with a huge marble staircase. Up the stairs and around several other side passages, we arrived finally at a gilded gold door with three huge guards standing at attention outside. When Elayne approached, the one closest to the door pulled an iron key from his belt and unlocked the heavy door, then stepped aside and pulled it open for us. Feeling more nervous and wary by the moment, I stepped inside behind her.

Everything was red.

The walls were painted a bright, crimson red and the high ceilings were painted a lighter shade of red. The floor was covered in a red carpet so thick that my shoes almost disappeared into it.

In the center of this room stood a marble pedestal in the shape of a huge lion. Sitting on top of the pedestal was a glass case. There was nothing else in the whole room.

Elayne led me through the thick carpet and stopped beside the glass case. Inside the case was a red cushion, and upon it sat a delicate silver-leaf crown. I recognized it immediately as the one Elayne's mother often wore when she had to greet guests in the throne room.

Elayne, looking paler than ever, wouldn't even meet my eyes now. I had never, in all of the time I had known her, seen her so nervous. It made the pit of dread in my stomach even worse to see her like that.

The huge door slammed closed behind us, making us both jump. The heavy air of the room closed immediately around us. In the sudden silence, my own fast heartbeat sounded very loud in my ears.

Elayne, standing with one foot digging nervously in the thick carpet, seemed suddenly too nervous to speak. The awkward silence stretched out to a long minute. Finally, I cleared my throat and turned to the crown beneath the glass beside us.

"That looks like your mom's." I said.

Elayne, seeming stunned that I broke the silence, looked up at me, then averted her eyes quickly to the crown. "Oh! Yes. It is. The Crown of Lions." Elayne cleared her throat and seemed to turn her attention wholly to the crown, thankful for the distraction. She started reciting as if reading from a history book. "It was crafted by dwarves thousands of years ago and has been worn by the rulers of this world ever since. It is imbued with the magic of all twelve fairy tribes. First worn by the goblin queen Kara Mia in the year 131 B.E."

Still nervous, I swallowed to keep my throat from going dry. "It's magic?" I asked.

Elayne nodded. "Yes. One ruler passes it down to the next in a coronation ceremony. Once crowned, the subjects of the kingdom are magically bound to obey the wearer."

Momentarily forgetting my nervousness, I was startled to hear what Elayne was saying. "Whoa... what? What do you mean 'bound to obey'? You mean that it forces everyone around them to do whatever they say?"

Elayne shook her head. "Not exactly, no. It's complicated. People can't be forced to do something they wouldn't normally do. It just makes them... want to follow."

I looked closely at the crown behind the glass. "So the people of this world are all under this crown's spell? Whoever wears the crown they have to follow?"

Elayne nodded hesitantly, confused by my shock. "That's right, but don't make it sound like a bad thing. This crown is the reason our kingdom has been at peace for thousands of years. No one has ever tried to overthrow the monarchy."

"Because they're under a spell!" I said. "That doesn't seem right. Sometimes the monarchy needs to be overthrown."

Elayne looked startled by this. "Jasen!"

"Seriously. You read the history books in my world. Some of the greatest nations in my world have come about by overthrowing a bad ruler."

Elayne shook her head, looking confused by my sudden anger. "Jasen, it is a great responsibility to carry. My mother would never abuse its power."

I looked at the crown, realizing now why they needed so many guards outside the door. "So what if someone bad got hold of this crown and put it on? What would happen? Would they be able to control everyone in the kingdom?"

Elayne shook her head. "No, Jasen. The magic can only be passed willingly from one ruler to another through a coronation ceremony. When my mother was seventeen, she was coronated with this crown by her mother, so now the power is hers. It will remain with her until my mother places it on the head of the next ruler of the kingdom. The crown by itself does nothing. If someone came in here and put it on, it would not work for them. The magic is in my mother right now and the crown is a way to pass it to the next person."

I looked at the crown again, still very creeped out by the idea that it could control so many people. "Okay..."

Elayne, wringing her hands in front of her, continued nervously. "So, as I was saying, the eldest daughter of the king and queen is coronated on her seventeenth birthday." Here, Elayne paused, looking at me significantly.

My mind was still buzzing nervously, and I realized that she was looking at me expectantly. "What?" I asked, confused.

Elayne's eyes darted to the red carpet, then back up at me. "Jasen, I'm trying to tell you that I will be crowned in fourteen days, on the day I become seventeen."

I looked up at her and the nervousness that I had been feeling before was suddenly forgotten. "You... you're what? You're going to be queen?"

Elayne's blue eyes watched mine closely. She still bit her lip nervously, and nodded.

"Wow! Well that's... wow."

Elayne closed her eyes. "And there's something else." she said, keeping her eyes closed as if too terrified to look at me.

Here it comes. I thought. *The breakup.*

But... of course, right? What did I expect, after all? She's going to be queen. She can't be going out with a nobody like me. There was no other way. I swallowed hard. *Don't cry, Jasen. DO NOT CRY.*

"On the day of the coronation ceremony," Elayne said, "I have to announce my intentions to betroth." Elayne's eyes locked on mine suddenly and she watched me, terrified.

I felt like I had just missed something. "What? Say again?"

Elayne's blue eyes watched mine steadily. "I'm supposed to choose a husband." she said carefully. "I have to announce who I intend to marry, and I have to be married within one year of the coronation."

I felt like I had just been punched in the stomach. Not only was she breaking up with me, but she already had someone else lined up. Despite trying my best to hold it in, I couldn't help my voice cracking when I finally spoke again. "Who?" I asked. "Who is he?"

Elayne's intent gaze faltered for a moment, then her eyes widened. "No! Jasen! You misunderstand. It is you. It is you that I want to name."

In the silence of the big empty red room, I felt my heartbeat stop for a moment. It took a long time for the spinning emotions in my head to slow down enough for me to realize what Elayne was saying.

"Are you... are you asking me to marry you?" I said in a small voice.

Elayne rushed to answer. "It is just an announcement of intention." she quickly explained. "We would not have to actually get married for another year."

I probably should have hidden my shock and disbelief a little better, but my mind was numb at that moment. Without realizing it, I had started pacing the thick red carpet and running my hands nervously through my hair.

Elayne stood in silence, rooted to the spot and watching me closely. It was several minutes later when she finally burst out "Jasen, if you do not say something soon, I'm going to explode!"

It was then that I turned my attention back to Elayne and saw how terrified she looked. I realized that as shocking as this had been to hear, it must have been absolutely terrifying for her to tell me. I stopped pacing and moved over to her. "I'm sorry." I said. "This is all just so..."

"What?" Elayne asked quickly, her eyes still watching mine. "Tell me what you're thinking." Elayne waited for me to finish my sentence, but I didn't know how to.

"You don't have to answer right now." Elayne said at last. For some reason, she seemed suddenly as if she was about to cry herself. "Just think about it." she said. "Just... if you do decide to accept, we will need to talk to my parents. There would be lots that would need to be done before you can take the throne."

I looked up at Elayne sharply. "What? What throne?"

Elayne hesitated. "Well... I mean... if you do decide to accept, then you would be king by my side, of course."

"What?" I almost shouted, and Elayne flinched a bit. Remembering the guards just outside the door, I lowered my voice to normal again before continuing. "*King*? Are you crazy? I'm not even from here. I hardly know anything about this world, and you want me to be king?"

Elayne took my hand in hers and looked at me steadily. "Jasen, it's alright. I've thought about this and talked with my parents about it. They know you and trust you. They think that you would be an excellent king… and so do I."

But I was near panic now. "Elayne! I'm… I'm not even through high school yet! I haven't even decided what I want to do *after* high school. You're asking me to change my whole life here."

Elayne lowered her hands from mine and her eyes looked stricken.

As much as it hurt me to see that look in Elayne's eyes, I found that I couldn't stop now. "I can't, Elayne. I'm sorry. I'm not the guy for this. I'm just… I'm nobody. I'm not a king. I would mess it all up."

This time, a tear did escape from the corner of Elayne's blue eyes as she looked at me. "Jasen…"

"No." I said firmly, suddenly wanting to get away. I seemed to be sinking in the thick red carpet at my feet. The blood red walls of the room seemed to be closing in on me.

I turned and ran to the heavy door and banged on it. "Let me out!" I yelled to the guards outside.

"Jasen! Stop. Please…" Elayne was crying behind me, but at that moment the door opened and I could feel a rush of fresh air from outside. I pushed past the guards and into the corridor.

I started out walking fast, then sped up to a run. I wasn't sure where I was running to, but I knew that I had to get away.

Chapter Four

Sudden Storm

 hat evening, I lay in my room as the sun's fading light filtered through my window. The grey October day had given way to the shadows of dusk, and now I could just make out the familiar shapes of my room. The desk in the corner that had once belonged to my father. The old radio that Grandpa had pulled out of the attic for me when I was ten (it only got two stations… and one of those was full of static… but I loved it anyway). The bookcase against the wall that was so full that books were stacked in it sideways and overflowed into piles on the hardwood floor around it.

I heard the slosh of running water as the radiator heater along the baseboard filled to start heating my room. As it heated up, I heard the familiar pops and plinks of metal that reminded me of so many cold nights sitting and watching the snow pile up outside.

All of my life, my world had seemed so small. There had been times that I would imagine that there was only my small, comfortable room, with nothing else beyond. Things had gotten so… complicated now.

I heard Elayne's cries in my mind over and over again, and it twisted my gut to remember them. I had run because it had all been so suddenly overwhelming. It had been too much to take in at once.

I had imagined my adult life before, but it had never been anything very clear or certain. I had once thought I might like to be a writer. Maybe write for a small newspaper somewhere. Other times, I thought I could maybe be a college professor at some big university. I had never been sure what exactly my future held for me, but I had always thought that my uncertainty was fine. I had plenty of time to decide what I wanted to do with my life. What was important, though, was that I could be anything I wanted.

Now, I felt caught in a huge trap. I loved Elayne. I was sure of that without any doubt. I had never stopped to consider, though, how that would fit in with my life plans. Even now, it was all still sort of new and magical. She was a princess… but until just then I had never realized what that truly meant. I had never considered how that title would shape Elayne's life, and possibly mine with it.

I was sick about the way I had run out of that red room. I had faced a dragon and more for Elayne and had never considered running from any of it. Somehow, though, those things seemed less scary than any of this.

As the darkness came, there was a quiet knock on my door. Without waiting for me to answer, the door opened on squeaky hinges and Corey stuck his head in carefully.

"Jasen?" he called into the darkened room.

"Yeah, I'm here." I answered sullenly.

Corey pushed the door open some more and flicked on the light switch, making me squint into the sudden brightness.

"You just disappeared, bro." Corey said, still speaking in a quiet tone that was so unlike him. "I was wondering where you'd run off to."

I sighed as Corey stepped over to the bed beside me. "Sorry. I had to get out of there."

Corey sat down and looked at me carefully. "Yeah... I heard what happened. Elayne was in pretty bad shape when we left. She had locked herself in her room and wouldn't stop crying."

My stomach cringed and I put my pillow over my head. "Unghh! I hate myself."

"No, man. Don't. I know where you're coming from. I would have run screaming from the castle, too."

"I wasn't screaming." I said.

"No, I know. I mean I would have, though. I would have been running and screaming all the way home. Then, I would have locked myself in my room and kept on screaming. It would have been a scream-fest. All night."

I clenched my fists. "It just caught me by surprise. Did you know? Did Emily tell you about this beforehand?"

Corey snorted. "Ha! There's no way Emily would have trusted me with a secret that big."

"I just wish I had reacted differently." I said. "Now everything is all messed up."

Corey scratched his mop of blonde hair (which had returned to its normal tangled mess since this morning). "Well... now that you've had some time to soak it all in, do you feel any different about it?"

"Which part?" I asked. "The part about getting married next year or the part about becoming king for the rest of my life?"

Corey shrugged. "Both. Either."

I sighed. "I don't know. The getting married part isn't so

bad. I know that mom and dad were only eighteen when they got married. I know I love Elayne and I thought that maybe someday we probably would, but…"

"But not so soon." Corey finished for me.

"Right. Exactly."

"And… the other thing? Being king and ruling the kingdom?"

I let out a deep breath. "THAT is the part that makes me want to hide under my bed until it all goes away."

Corey grinned. "I did that for a big math test one time. Didn't work. The teacher just made me take it when I came in the next day."

I laughed. "Yeah, well… good lesson, there, I guess. Math test, becoming king… those are almost the same thing."

Corey grabbed a nearby pillow and smacked me on the side of the head with it, then got up and started to leave again.

When he was almost to the door, I called after him. "Hey, Corey!"

He turned in the doorway and looked back at me.

"Knock-knock." I said.

He grinned a bit. "Who's there?"

"Three hundred and sixty-five." I said.

"Three sixty-five who?"

"Three hundred and sixty-five days until your next birthday." I smiled.

Corey chuckled and disappeared out my bedroom door.

And fourteen more days until Elayne's birthday… and coronation. I thought to myself. Two weeks to decide what I wanted for the rest of my life.

The next day was one of those grey, cloudless days that hinted at the approaching cold of the New York winter. I sat beneath the cracked ceilings of my classrooms, looking out the windows at the chilly wind combing leaves from the trees outside. I was lost in my own faraway thoughts, interrupted only by the bell that ended each class period to send me shuffling to the next.

After school, Corey and Emily were silent on the drive home. They had said nothing more to me about what had happened yesterday at the castle, and I was thankful for that. After I dropped them off at Emily's house, I drove to the place that would lead to the shortest path to the invisible curtain. I left the car parked on the gravel shoulder of the road near the woods and started walking before I could begin to have second thoughts.

I still wasn't completely sure what I was going to tell Elayne. I just knew that I had to talk with her. I had to let her know that I still loved her, no matter what. The thought of her hurt was almost more than I could bear.

When I stepped through the doorway from the moonlit clearing into Elayne's world, I was startled by the sudden flash of lightening and boom of thunder. A strong gust of wind grabbed the heavy wooden door from my grasp and threw it with a loud bang back against the stone wall. Fat raindrops pounded the stone and soaked me instantly.

Giles appeared from the gloom, struggling to hold a tarp over me to keep me dry. "Sir Jasen!" he shouted over the rain and wind. "Good to see you. As you can see, we're having some unpleasant weather today. If you can wait a little while in the stable house, I can have the carriage hooked up for you to carry you to the castle."

I shook my head, flinching as lightening flashed close by. "I don't want to wait." I said. "I'll just take my horse. I don't care if I get wet or not."

Giles looked shocked. "But... Sir! It's miles in the pouring rain and..." he trailed off.

And you're not such a great rider I finished for him silently. I knew it may have sounded crazy, but at that moment I only wanted to get to Elayne as fast as possible.

Without another word, Giles disappeared into the stable to saddle up my horse. Thunder boomed so suddenly and loudly overhead that I saw one of the guards flinch before straightening back up again.

I looked out towards the castle, hoping to catch a glimpse of the distant towers, but all I could see was pouring rain beneath black clouds.

My horse seemed more terrified than I was to be running through the torrential storm. She ran at an unsteady gallop the whole way, cringing several times when lightening would flash nearby or thunder shook the air. When we finally hit the big wooden drawbridge, she must have been excited to see the end in sight, because she ran full-speed across it. I was already through the portcullis and into the main courtyard when I heard the heavy "thump" of the leviathan's tentacle grabbing at me from the moat. This time, we were well out of reach.

I was soaked. I grabbed a handful of my thick hair and wrung out the rainwater, watching it splatter to the cobbled stone at my feet. The clothes I had worn to school were plastered to my body. When I took a step, I realized that even my shoes were full of water.

In front of me appeared a tall, thin man dressed in a blue coat. I recognized him as Dwayne, one of the castle workers. He instantly produced a towel for me, which I took thankfully and dried my face. He made a small bow and gestured towards a side corridor. "If you come this way, Master Jasen, I have some dry clothes awaiting you."

I almost said no, since my need to see Elayne was still stirring so strongly inside of me, but when I took another step and water sloshed out of the tops of my shoes, I decided that it probably would be best to get dry first. I followed Dwayne's direction down the corridor.

As I walked down the hallway, my mind was still a confused mess of emotions and I tried to decide what exactly I was going to say when I saw Elayne. I still was not ready for the responsibilities of being married or (especially) being king, but I wanted to let her know that I was sorry for the way I reacted yesterday.

When I looked up, I was at the door Dwayne had pointed to. As I opened it to go inside and change, another woman was coming up the hallway from the opposite direction. She was a large woman, dressed in a maidservant's uniform. She had an uneven tangle of wiry black hair on her head and a fat, pasty white face with a large black mole on one cheek. Just as she was about to pass, the woman looked up and saw me. There was an instant when something like surprise flashed over her face, then her eyes locked on mine and she scowled. In the second that it took for her to walk past, I felt such a wave of hatred and anger pass from her that I stood stunned for a moment.

She never slowed down, though. A moment later, she had passed and I was left with nothing but an uneasy prickle on the back of my neck and the thought of her hateful eyes glaring at me. I turned to watch her, but she was already far along the corridor and she did not turn back.

"I love you Elayne, but I've decided that I can't marry you. I can't be king."

Those were the words I had decided upon as I finished changing my clothes. Although I had considered this for a long time and thought it to be a good decision, I saw that my hands were shaking as I tried to brush back my wet hair in the big jeweled mirror.

I took a deep breath and found that my stomach was even more nervous than it had been the day before.

"Maybe it wouldn't be so bad." another part of me answered. *"I mean, after all… who doesn't want to be a king? Aren't you crazy for not wanting that?"*

I took another heavy breath and started pulling on the soft leather shoes that Dwayne had laid out for me.

I had one shoe on when I first heard the noises from the hallway outside. Banging and yelling, then the heavy clanking of armored guards running. I froze, listening. In all of my time at the castle, I had never seen any guard run for anything. The guards always stood there, looking mean and scary… but they never ran.

I pulled open the door and stuck my head out in the corridor. I heard more yelling and shouting. When I looked to the left, I saw a big group of huge guards running down a side passage. Their swords were drawn and their commander was barking orders at them as they ran.

As I started to step out into the hallway, another group of guards came sprinting up the narrow corridor and I had to dive back into the room to avoid being trampled. I heard the grind of machinery and the walls and floor around me started to shake. There was a huge echoing "boom!' that sounded like thunder and I realized that it was the sound of the huge castle drawbridge being closed.

Seconds later, Dwayne came running up the hallway, his face white with terror. I grabbed his blue coat as he ran past. "What's happening?" I yelled. "Where are all of the guards running to?"

Dwayne, who was usually calm and mannered, looked at me wide-eyed.

"It's the princess!" he cried. "She's been attacked!"

Chapter Five

After the Attack

 had never run so fast in all of my life. The hallways and corridors of the castle became a blur to me. When I reached the staircase, I flew up the huge stone stairs five at a time. I was only wearing one shoe, and when I came around the last corner I slipped and fell hard on the stone floor, but I was up again in an instant and kept running.

There was a mob around the door to Elayne's suite. It seemed as if every guard in the castle was there, all with swords drawn and ready to fight. When I came flying around the corner, several of them raised their swords, ready to attack. When they saw it was me, they relaxed a little—but kept their swords raised.

"It's Sir Jasen!" one of them shouted. "Let him through. Open up! Let him through!"

The guards parted and formed a narrow opening so I could slip through into the suite. When I was past, they formed up again instantly behind me.

The main sitting area of Elayne's suite was full of guards, too, but I didn't see Elayne anywhere. I was starting to panic now, imagining Elayne dead or dying, breathing her last breaths. "Elayne!" I shouted into the chaos.

A moment later, I heard a man's voice. "Jasen! In here."

It was Elayne's father, King Lionheart. The voice had come from Elayne's bedroom, where another group of guards stood blocking the door.

"Let him in." I heard him say, and the guards outside the bedroom stepped aside as I ran past.

The first thing I saw was the broken glass. It lay shattered in jagged pieces beside the door. Forgetting that I only had one shoe on, I ran on anyway, scanning the room frantically for Elayne.

She was there, sitting on the edge of the bed with her mother holding her hands. The sleeve of Elayne's dress was torn and there was an ugly red mark on her wrist where it looked like someone had grabbed her, but otherwise she looked unharmed.

When Elayne saw me, she moved away from her mother and ran across the room, throwing her arms around me. I hugged her tightly. "Are you alright? Are you hurt?"

Elayne pulled away and shook her head. Her eyes were red as if she'd been crying. "I'm not hurt. I'm okay."

I ran my hands through Elayne's hair and held her face up to mine. "Are you sure?"

Elayne nodded. "Yes. I was lucky. It could have been much worse."

"What happened?" I asked.

It was the king who answered, standing in the corner among another group of guards. "Here," he told me. "It was one of the castle maidservants."

I moved closer to the far corner of the room where they all stood and saw a white, pulsing glow coming from the center of the group. As I got nearer, the guards parted and I could see that they were all standing around a woman lying on the floor. Around her was a white, glowing bubble.

"We have her trapped for now," the king explained, scowling down at the woman through his thick brown beard. "She must be Sidhera. There is no other explanation. We knew that she would be back someday. She is so twisted with evil and rage that she would never have left Elayne to live her life after she was defeated."

I looked at the brightly glowing bubble. "What is that bubble? What does it do?"

"It is something my wizards have conjured up to hold her," the king answered. "She is out cold now, but even when she awakes, she will find herself unable to speak or move. She will not be able to use any of her magic to escape."

I shivered, looking down at the body faintly visible in the bubble.

Was it really Sidhera? I had not seen her since she had fled from the roof of the school a year ago. I had woken up to many nightmares about her since that night. I had jumped at many shadows, always fearful that she was just around the corner and ready to take her revenge. Even now, seeing her lying face-down beneath the swirling bubble, I felt scared to be this close to her.

As my eyes adjusted, I could make out the pasty white, fat arms of the body and the wiry black hair. Even without seeing her face, I recognized her instantly. "I saw that woman downstairs just before the attack." I said.

The king nodded solemnly. "Yes. She was dressed as a servant, but nobody recognizes her as anyone who works here. She was able to come right into Elayne's suite without anyone even noticing."

I looked down at the body again, remembering the look of hatred the woman had given me as she passed.

I should have known. I thought to myself. *I should have recognized Sidhera immediately. I may have been able to stop her.*

"What's going to happen to her?" I asked.

"We're going to get rid of her once and for all." Elayne answered, where she had appeared again by my side. She looked down at the body in the bubble with a dark and angry look on her face.

I was shocked. "Really? I thought you told me that you can't kill a fairy."

The king scratched his beard. "We can't kill her, true, but there are things we can do. This witch has a lot to answer to for everything she has put my family through." He motioned to the guards. "Carry her to the dungeon. I want twenty guards watching her at all times. She needs no food or water, and NO ONE is to remove that bubble from her... no matter what. That will keep her until we can decide what to do with her on a more permanent basis."

The guards jumped in to action immediately, forming up in a circle around the woman on the floor. Elayne and I moved aside to let them do their work. Outside the bedroom windows, I saw that rain was still coming down hard, but the thunder at least seemed to have died down.

Elayne's mother and father had surrounded her again. The queen, with worry lines pressed into her beautiful face, put her arm again around Elayne. "Are you sure you are unharmed?" she said quietly.

"I'm fine." Elayne answered. "Just shaken up a bit."

"What did she say?" the king asked gently. "What did she do?"

Elayne held her hands up. "It all happened so fast. I'm not even sure anymore. I was sitting on my bed when she came in. I asked her who she was and she told me that she had brought me a gift from Jasen."

The king and queen turned to look at me.

I shrugged. "I never gave her anything to give to Elayne. The first time I saw that woman was when I passed her in the hallway downstairs."

"It was a perfume bottle." Elayne continued. "She wanted me to put some on, but I told her to leave it on the bedside table instead. She kept insisting that I try some, though, and she opened the bottle and ran at me with it."

The king looked at the shattered glass beside the door and scowled. "Some sort of poison." He murmured darkly. "Guards!" he commanded. "Have that cleaned up immediately. Use caution, it may be deadly."

The queen, looking more worried than ever, looked at the shattered glass with disgust. "Did it get on you? Did she touch you?"

Elayne shook her head. "No. I swatted the bottle away and it flew from her hand where it shattered on the floor. That seemed to enrage her and she threw herself at me, screaming and tearing at me. She was... she was like a wild animal or something."

The king's eyes looked so angry that I thought for a moment that he was about to attack someone himself. "How DARE her!" he bellowed. "How dare her come into our home... our castle, and try to harm our daughter again!"

The queen, perhaps sensing the growing rage in him, laid her hand on his gently. "Be calm, Stephen. The witch is captured. She will not harm our family again."

The king's eyes flashed to where the guards were carrying the woman's still-sleeping body out the door. "You can set gold to that. She will *never* harm our family again. I'll see to it."

I never did get a moment alone with Elayne that day. After the King and Queen were gone, servants arrived to tend to the scrape on Elayne's arm and to get her cleaned up.

"Elayne, I was hoping that we could talk." I said, stepping aside quickly as another servant scurried past me.

Elayne, surrounded by people tending to her, looked up at me. "It will be like this for hours, still." she said with an apologetic sigh. "Can we... can we maybe wait until tomorrow?"

Standing there in borrowed clothes and one leather shoe, I remembered my frantic ride in the rain to get here.

"Sure." I said. "Of course, I understand."

"Thanks." she said.

As I turned to leave, she called out to me again. "Jasen?"

I turned back to see a woman in a nurse's outfit dabbing greenish liquid on the red mark on her wrist. Elayne put on a smile for me. "I'm glad you were here." she said.

I smiled back, feeling a glad warmth spreading through my chest.

By the time I left the castle, the sun had broken through the clouds once more.

I found Corey still at Emily's house when I returned, and the sun was just setting over the edge of the valley. They couldn't believe it when I told them what had happened. They listened, stunned, to every word of the story until I had finished, then bombarded me with a thousand questions.

"They got Sidhera? They really captured her?"

"What was in the bottle? Was it poison? An evil magic potion? Would it have killed her or made her go back to sleep?"

"How did they make that magic bubble? Will it really be strong enough to hold Sidhera?"

"What are they going to do to Sidhera? They can't kill her. Are they going to trap her in a magic bottle like a genie in a lamp? Is the king going to have her tortured first?"

They wanted to go immediately to see Elayne and make sure for themselves that she was okay, but I told them that she had asked us to wait until tomorrow.

"Even me?" Emily asked. "Doesn't she need someone there with her right now?"

I shook my head. "She is mobbed right now. We need to wait until things calm back down a bit."

Emily looked sullen, but didn't say anything more about it.

When Corey and I got back to our house, it was after dark already. The house was empty, and the kitchen light was on. We found a note on the kitchen table.

Jasen and Corey,

Liz and I have decided to finally take a long-overdue honeymoon. We'll be gone at least two weeks. Corey: Jasen is in charge. Listen to your brother and you two stay out of trouble. There are groceries in the fridge and some money to get take-out food on the table in the foyer.

We'll call if we can, but it sounds like they won't have phones where we're going. Stay out of trouble!
Love, Grandpa

I couldn't help but smile a bit. I was glad that Grandpa finally got a chance to get away. Ever since Corey and I were small, we had never had enough money to go on a real vacation. The farthest we'd gotten was the Jersey shore when I was twelve, and that had just been for the weekend.

Two weeks! I thought. *Good for you, Grandpa!*

Corey was frowning, still looking over the note. "Did you notice here that he says 'Stay out of trouble' twice?"

I smiled, patting Corey on the back. "Yup. That was for you, Corey."

Corey frowned. "I know... but one time would have been enough, don't you think? I mean... c'mon. How bad does he think I am?"

Chapter Six

The Elephant

hen Corey, Emily, and I arrived at the castle the next day, we found the drawbridge still pulled closed and guards on horseback circling the moat. As we approached, they surrounded us and led our horses through a gate around the other side of the castle. Once inside, they made us stand in the courtyard while they searched us for hidden weapons.

Corey looked shocked as the guards roughly patted him down. "Do you know who we are?" Corey demanded. "We're the people that saved your frozen behinds and broke the curse on your princess! If it wasn't for us, you all would still be a bunch of statues!"

Emily tried to calm him down. "It's alright, Corey. They're just doing their job. They have to be careful. Elayne was attacked yesterday by someone who looked like a normal serving-woman. They need to check everyone."

"But they caught her!" Corey said. "She's in the dungeon!" Corey hesitated, then tuned to the nearest guard frightfully. "She *is* still in the dungeon, right?"

The guard nodded. "Aye. The witch is still locked up good and tight. I was on duty last night when she finally woke up and opened her eyes, but of course she couldn't move a muscle in that bubble they got 'er in. We all wanted to kill 'er after what she did to the princess... but the king gave us orders not to touch her. Seems he has something else in mind for her."

"Something good, I hope." I said under my breath.

The guard heard me. "Oh, it'll be good alright. I've never in all of my years seen the king so angry. He's going to do something terrible to that fairy hag, that's for sure!" the guard turned after he had finished searching us. "Oy!" he called. "This lot is clear. Let 'em pass."

A nearby iron gate rattled up and the guards in front of it stepped aside to let us enter. The three of us walked together through the archway, and as we moved down the long corridor, we heard the rumbling of the heavy gate closing again behind us.

There were more guards posted outside of Elayne's suite... and another search for hidden weapons. "C'mon, Barry." Corey was saying to the guard. "You *know* me for goodness sake."

The guard looked a bit embarrassed, but continued patting down Corey's shirt. "Sorry, Master Corey. King's orders."

Even after we were searched, we had to wait as another guard went into Elayne's suite and announced our arrival. It was several minutes later before we were finally allowed to pass into the suite.

Surprisingly, there were no more guards to be seen once we were inside. In the large central area of the suite, there was no sign that there had been almost a hundred people in here the day before. Everything was pristine and in place. Even the thick carpet beneath the center table looked freshly vacuumed… or whatever it was they did to get the carpets cleaned in this world.

Elayne stepped out of the doorway to her bedroom and greeted us.

Hi, guys!" she said with a smile.

She looked much better today than when I had last seen her. The red was gone from her bright blue eyes and her blonde hair was radiant in soft curls around her shoulders. She wore a long blue dress that I had never seen her in before. She looked beautiful.

Emily ran over to her and gave her a hug. "We're glad that you're okay." Emily said. "We were so worried when we heard what happened."

"The guards around here have gotten a little too touchy-feely if you ask me." Corey said.

Elayne laughed a little. "Sorry about that, Corey. All of the extra security is my father's doing. I've tried to tell him that the danger is passed now that Sidhera is locked away, but he can be a bit overprotective sometimes."

"Who can blame him?" Emily said.

"We'll I don't like it one bit!" Corey said. "I was going to try to get some munchies from the kitchen, but the way things are now, I'd have to go through twenty stop-and-searches just to get there! It's crazy!"

Emily rolled her eyes. "It's always about food with you, isn't it, Corey?"

Corey managed to look offended. "Hey! I'm a growing boy here…"

Emily poked him in the stomach. "Yeah, you'll be growing *outward* if you keep eating so much."

Elayne giggled and I took the opportunity to step up to her. "Elayne, do you think that we could talk? I mean--- privately, just for a moment?"

Elayne furrowed her eyebrows at me. "Um... sure, Jasen. That would be fine. We can step into my room for a moment."

Emily and Corey, sensing the sudden awkwardness, quietly started to move towards the door that led to the terrace outside. As Corey passed me, he took my arm and whispered "Don't make her cry again."

"Thanks, Corey." I muttered. "I'll do my best."

My heart started pounding as I stepped into Elayne's room. Just like the other room, this one had been cleaned spotlessly since yesterday. There was no sign of anything out of place.

Elayne stood just inside the door, her hands clasped in front of her, and her eyes watching me expectantly. Wiping my sweaty palms on my pants nervously, I took a deep breath. "You sure you're okay?" I began. "I didn't really get a chance to talk to you yesterday."

Elayne smiled warmly. "Aw, Jasen. It's so sweet that you're worried about me. I'm really fine, though. It could have been bad, but everything turned out okay."

"I'm sorry I wasn't here." I said. "I really wish I had been here."

Elayne shook her head. "You can't always be there to save me, Jasen. I am a big girl, you know."

"Oh, I know." I said quickly. "I just... well, I'm glad that you're not hurt."

Elayne smiled and stepped forward to take my hand. "Is that all you wanted to talk to me about?" she said. "Come on, let's go join Corey and Emily on the terrace outside."

I held on to her hand and stopped her. "Wait. Actually, I wanted to talk about our discussion the other day."

The expression on Elayne's face was unreadable. "Oh?"

I took a deep breath. "I'm really sorry. I wanted to tell you that I love you."

Elayne hesitated. "I know that you love me. You broke my spell, remember? Only true-love's kiss could do that."

"Right," I said. "I just wanted to tell you again. I know I reacted badly to our conversation."

Elayne bit her lip uncertainly and pulled her hands from mine. "Right," she said, stepping back. "That was... surprising."

"I know." I said. "It just all caught me off guard, you know?"

Elayne nodded, her hands once more clasped in front of her. "Right." she said again. An odd expression played across her face. "Hey, Emily and Corey are waiting for us. Let's go out and join them."

I glanced out the window to the terrace and saw Emily and Corey on the far side, sitting at the small table out there in the sun. I turned back to Elayne, confused. "But... I think we really should talk about this, don't you?" I said.

Elayne, her eyes darting to the window, then back at me, shuffled her feet uncertainly. "No. I don't want to talk about this. Not now."

I remembered what Corey had said. *Don't make her cry again,* and I started to get the impression that her odd behavior was her way of showing that she was getting upset.

I took a deep breath. "Alright," I said. "I understand. You had a hard day yesterday. I need to talk to you about this, though. We can't leave it unfinished. I'll try to come alone tomorrow."

Elayne's eyes looked at me flatly, then finally she took a deep breath and rolled her eyes. "Oh, this is *ridiculous*." she spat. "Why am I even bothering?"

I stood, shocked and still, unable to understand her sudden change in demeanor.

"What?" I stammered, confused.

Elayne took a flustered breath, reached up and grabbed her left sleeve, and pulled hard. There was a sound of ripping stitches and a moment later, Elayne's dress had a big tear across it.

"Elayne, what are you..."

But before I could even finish, Elayne picked up a heavy jade elephant figurine from a nearby table and brought it down hard and fast across her face. A bloody gash appeared on her cheek and I stumbled forward in confusion, trying to stop her. She threw the jade elephant at me and took a step back.

She watched me for an instant--- a cold, terrible instant that I will always remember--- and a small smile played across her lips. Then she drew a deep breath, and before I could even begin to react, she started screaming. "Guards! Guards! Ahhhh! Get off of me! Help! He's attacking me! He's attacking me!"

I stared in confused terror at Elayne as she screamed, her hands clenched into fists, blood streaming down her cheek. There was a crash as the door in the outer room was thrown open and in that instant, Elayne threw herself to the floor at my feet.

Guards ran in, swords drawn. They stopped at the bedroom door and saw me, standing there frozen and terrified, with

Elayne on the floor bleeding by my feet. She started crying then, clutching her bleeding face and writhing in pain.

I didn't have time to even think before they were upon me. Something heavy clubbed me hard on the head while strong hands threw me to the floor. Somewhere, an alarm bell sounded and I could see Elayne being lifted up and away. I caught one final glimpse of her before she was gone, her eyes locked on mine and something like a bitter smile flashed across her lips.

Then, one of the huge armored men holding me down pressed a heavy boot against my neck and a blanket of darkness fell over my eyes.

When I awoke, I could feel a soft pillow under my head and warm blankets wrapped around me. Sunlight was hitting my eyes, making everything too bright to see.

"He's waking up." I heard a voice say quickly.

(Corey's voice? Was that Corey?)

"He's waking up!" somebody repeated from a little further away. "Get the king. He wanted to know when the prisoner awoke."

That made my heart jump.

The prisoner?

I tried to move my arms and heard the loud rattle of chains. When I pulled, I found that I couldn't lower my hands. Something cold and metal was clasped around each of my wrists.

"Take it easy, Bro." I heard Corey whisper by my ear. "They've got you chained up for right now... but don't worry. We'll get this sorted out."

Sorted out? I thought, blinking into the bright sunlight. As my eyes adjusted, I moved my legs and found that those, too, seemed to be shackled with chains. I was lying in a big bed. It looked like one of the guest rooms in the castle. I recognized it as the room I had stayed in when we were snowed in last July.

I opened my mouth to say something, but I found that my jaw hurt badly and my throat wouldn't work.

"Water." I heard Emily say from somewhere close by. "Get him some water."

A moment later, Corey lifted a glass to my lips and I drank it thankfully. An ache shot through my neck when I swallowed, but when I tried to speak again, I found my voice.

"What happened?" I asked weakly.

"That's what we'd like to know." Corey said under his breath, glancing at the guards by the door. "Elayne is saying that you attacked her…"

My eyes grew wide as the memory came rushing back to me. "Elayne!" I croaked hoarsely. "Where is she? Is she okay?"

"Elayne is fine." A voice said from the doorway. Corey moved aside and I saw King Lionheart standing there. His face was unreadable, but I didn't see the hateful fury on his face that I'd seen after Sidhera's attack. He stepped into the room and closer to the bed. He was dressed in a loose, informal robe and wasn't wearing his crown. There seemed to be dark circles under his eyes and for the first time, I noticed flecks of grey in his beard.

"How are you feeling?" he asked me after a moment's pause.

I tried to clear my throat and found that it was dry again. I think I remembered a guard stepping on my neck…

"Where is Elayne?" I asked again.

The king's eyebrows furrowed. "She is safely under guard once more." he said, watching me closely as if I might try to go after her again.

"Something's wrong with her!" I said quickly. "I think that Sidhera may have gotten some of that magic potion on her after all. She's not herself."

The king frowned. "No, Jasen my boy, it's you that are not yourself. You may not remember, but you attacked Elayne in her suite."

"But I didn't!" I said, a little too loudly. Pain shot through my throat. The guards at the door leaned in to make sure I was still in my chains.

"You're under an enchantment," the king said sadly. "You say that Sidhera passed you in the corridor yesterday. She must have done something to you."

I blinked, shaking my head. "No. No! That's not what happened."

"It's alright," the king continued. "I know that you are not yourself right now. You love my daughter. I've seen that, and I know that you would never intentionally hurt her. Please understand though, that we have to keep you locked up for her protection and your own until we can find a way to break the spell that is upon you right now."

I was stunned. "No! I'm not... that's not true."

"Corey and Emily can stay here at the castle with you as long as they like. Unfortunately, we don't know what nature of enchantment is upon you yet, so we will have to leave the chains on."

I looked up to my hands and saw that they were shacked to the heavy wooden bedposts. My heart started beating faster. "No! I have to see Elayne. Something is wrong."

The king's face grew stern. "You will not be allowed near Elayne until this matter has been resolved. I've instructed the guards to use whatever force is necessary to protect her. You came away with only a few bruises this time, but you may not be so lucky again."

He seemed to realize that he was almost yelling and forced himself to calm down. "We have our best people working on it." he said. "I've also sent a messenger back to your house to bring Bridgette."

"They're on their honeymoon." Corey and I said at the same time.

The king looked disappointed. "Oh… well. She was our best hope for now, but we will keep working. Don't worry. We'll find out what is wrong with you."

He hesitated as if he was about to say something more, then took a deep breath and just shook his head. "I'll come by later to see how you're doing." he said.

A moment later, he was gone. I turned to look at Emily and Corey, who watched me in silence.

"Am I… do you think I really have a spell on me?" I asked fearfully.

Corey shrugged. "I dunno. I mean, I haven't seen you kick any puppies or shoot green fire from your hands or anything. When you attacked Elayne it was the first---"

"I didn't attack Elayne." I said quickly. "She was acting crazy. I was trying to talk to her about the whole marriage proposal and king-for-life thing and she started acting all funny. All of the sudden, she ripped her own dress, smashed herself in the face with an elephant, and started screaming that I'd attacked her."

"She smashed herself in the face with an *elephant*?" Corey asked, startled.

"A little statue thingy on her table. Not a real--- listen! I'm not crazy here, alright?"

"Why would she do that?" Emily asked evenly. "That doesn't even make any sense."

"Maybe she was afraid you were going to break up with her. She just went gonzo." Corey said.

"She wouldn't go 'gonzo'!" Emily snapped. "She may have been upset about the way Jasen treated her, but that wouldn't make her go crazy like Jasen is describing."

"The way I treated her?" I asked. "I was trying to apologize! And I don't even think I did anything wrong in the first place, while we're on the subject."

Emily crossed her arms and looked at me. "If you don't think that you did anything wrong, then why were you apologizing?"

I started to answer, then looked at Corey for help. Corey just rolled his eyes. "Ignore her. She gets all girl-power like this sometimes."

Emily smacked him hard on the shoulder.

"Ow!" Corey yelled. "Hey! You'd better watch it! I'll call the guards in here and tell them that you're attacking me!"

I clenched my teeth. "Listen, guys. This is serious. Something is wrong with Elayne. I'm fine, but Sidhera did something to her."

Corey looked at the guards by the door uncomfortably and lowered his voice. "No offense, bro... but isn't that exactly what you would say if you were under a spell? How can we even believe you?"

"I need to see Elayne!" I said, pulling on the chains.

Corey sat back. "And that's also what you would say. There's no way we're getting anywhere near Elayne, bro... even if we did believe you."

I pulled at my chains in frustration. I felt helpless and desperate to get to Elayne.

I forced myself to calm down and took a deep breath. When I looked back up at Corey and Emily, they were watching me expectantly.

"Alright." I said calmly. "Okay. If I can't see Elayne, then I want to go down to the dungeon and see Sidhera."

"*What*?" Corey gasped. "Now I *know* that you're under a spell. That's just crazy talk right there."

"I'm not crazy and I'm not under a spell, Corey. It's me, Jasen. Your brother. I'm the one that taught you how to catch a ball with a mitt. I'm the one who helped get your head unstuck from the stair railings when you were five. I'm the one who never told anyone that you wet your pants on that roller coaster when---"

"Whoa!" Corey jumped in, clapping a hand over my mouth and looking at Emily mortified. "Alright, big brother. I believe you." He laughed nervously, looking suddenly red in the face.

"Yup. You're Jasen alright. Got your head on straight. I believe you."

Emily watched me worriedly, and I could see that she, too, was starting to believe me. She took a deep breath. "I don't know. I guess Corey and I could go down there and…"

"No!" I said. "I want to go."

Corey's face looked pained. "How? There are chains on your arms and legs and big, scary guys with pointy swords outside the door."

I hesitated for a moment, then whistled loudly to get the guards' attention. One of them pushed his head in through the door, looking annoyed.

"These chains are killing me!" I said. "Any way you can take them off?"

The guard grunted. "Sorry. King's orders. It's either the chains or the dungeon."

"Fine!" I said quickly. "Unlock 'em. Let's go!"

Chapter Seven

Into the Dungeon

 had been all over the Castle of Lions and seen the royal suites and the hidden passages and everything in between. In all of that time, though, I had never once been to the dungeon.

I could now understand why.

In the movies, dungeons always looked a certain way. Dark and creepy, sure, but in a neat, sort of mysterious and spooky way. I had always imagined that they would be an interesting place to explore.

This was nothing like a movie dungeon.

Oh, it was dark and cold and wet. That part was true enough. In the movies, though, you can't smell the disgusting smell of rotting food, vomit, and who knows what else. In the movies, you can't feel the slimy filth that coats the walls and drips down into piles of stink and mush on the floor. I felt like

I couldn't breathe and I gagged every time my arms brushed up against the thick slime on the walls.

I saw the soft white glow immediately. It filled the dungeon and pulsed slowly against the uneven walls.

My cell was like a dark stone closet. Rough, wet walls that oozed with that same foul-smelling slime and an uneven cobbled floor with a handful of moldy straw tossed in one corner. The cell door was built of rusting, crooked iron bars. Directly across the dank corridor, I saw another cell with two guards sitting in front of it. From the cell behind them, I could make out the pulsing unnatural light of the magic bubble, floating a few inches above the dark stone floor.

These two guards looked fierce, and on the way into the dungeon we had passed a group of nearly twenty others guarding the dungeon's only exit.

I pressed my face against the bars, watching the silent bubble intently. Sidhera was awake. She was still dressed in the maidservant's uniform. A pudgy, pale woman with that ugly black mole on her cheek. She floated there in the light, like a fish in a bowl of water. She was not moving, but was facing my direction. My stomach clenched when I saw that her eyes were locked on mine.

"Ugly thing, innit she?" one of the guards outside her cell said.

I was still watching her eyes. "What? Oh… yeah." I looked at Sidhera's face with a shudder. "She looked much different when I last saw her."

The guard snorted. "Yup. That's the way them fairy folk are. Always changing shape. Never know where they'll show up."

The guard may have wanted me to answer, but I was mesmerized at that moment by Sidhera's gaze. Her mean-looking, ugly face was motionless, but those eyes followed me even as she bobbed up and down in the magic bubble. I had expected the same hateful glare she had given me as she had passed me in the hallway the day before, but her expression now was unreadable.

Although I felt a grim satisfaction that she was captured and that the king had something terrible planned for her, the look in her eyes looked almost... desperate. Pleading. It was not what I had expected.

It's a trick. I thought to myself. *She's an ancient, evil fairy queen, remember? When she was disguised as Ms. Locke for all of those years, she seemed like one of the nicest people in the world. Corey even had a crush on her. It's what she does and she's a master at it.*

I knew that she was a snake just waiting to bite, but those eyes...

After awhile, as all guards on night watch seem to do, both guards fell asleep. When I had watched them snoring soundly for a good fifteen minutes, I finally whispered into the darkness. "Corey? Emily?"

"Hey, bro." Corey's voice whispered right in my ear, scaring me so badly that I jumped and hit my head hard against the bars of my cell door.

"Right here." Emily's voice came from the darkness.

I smiled. "Awesome. I see that pixie dust really does make you invisible, huh?"

"Worked like a charm." Corey's voice said. "We snuck in here right behind you. Thought that chatty guard there would never go to sleep!"

"I think I stepped in something dead over here!" Emily said, disgusted. "These shoes are totally ruined."

I watched Sidhera closely, and at the sound of Corey and Emily's voices, her eyes darted around, looking for them.

"Good." I said. "She can hear us."

Corey shuddered. "Ugh. You weren't kidding, bro. Sidhera picked one ugly face to hide behind this time! Look at the size of that mole on her cheek! I think it's actually got hair growing from it!"

Emily's voice appeared from close by. "So, now what? Even if she can hear us, she won't be able to answer any questions. She can't move or speak, remember?"

"She can blink." I said. I looked over at the pudgy face floating in the light. "Can't you?"

There was a moment's pause, then she blinked her eyes, watching me steadily.

The guards snored on.

"Alright." I said, gripping the bars of my cell door and fixing a steely look at Sidhera. "This is how it's going to work. We're going to ask you some questions. To answer, you will blink once for yes and twice for no. Got it?"

Another hesitation, then Sidhera blinked once.

"Good idea, bro." Corey whispered. "Ask her what she did to Elayne."

I thought about how to word the question. "Alright." I said. "Does Elayne have some kind of magic spell on her?"

Sidhera's eyes seemed to quiver, then she blinked once.

"She said yes!" Emily gasped quietly. "You were right, Jasen."

I felt an anger stirring in my chest as I looked at Sidhera, but forced my voice to remain calm and steady.

"What is it?" Corey asked. "What kind of spell?"

Sidhera's eyes watched me intently, unmoving. "It's got to be a yes or no question." I murmured. This was going to be hard. "Do you have a way to remove the spell from Elayne?" I asked finally

Sidhera's eyes hesitated again, then blinked twice.

"She's lying." Corey said instantly. "She's got to know how to undo her own spell."

This was frustrating. I wished she could talk. It was going to take forever doing it this way. I glanced at the sleeping guards nervously before continuing.

"Alright." I said carefully. "When you attacked Elayne, did you—"

Sidhera blinked twice quickly.

I shook my head. "Let me finish the question. You don't even know what I was going to ask. When you attacked Elayne---"

Again, two quick blinks.

"Why do you keep saying 'no'?" I asked, feeling the anger stirring inside of me. "When you attacked Elayne…"

Blink. Blink. She blinked twice, very hard and very deliberately.

I gritted my teeth. "No? Why do you keep saying 'no'? Are you saying 'no' that you didn't attack Elayne?"

Blink.

I hesitated, and there was a long moment where I struggled to understand what she was trying to say.

"So… you *didn't* attack Elayne?"

Blink.

"You can't believe her." Emily said quickly. "She's going to lie. We knew that."

I was getting angrier by the moment. I had the feeling that Sidhera was just playing with us and if she could move, then she would have a big, smug smile on her face right now.

"Sidhera, you are only making this worse…"

Blink. Blink.

Her eyes looked frantic now.

"No? No what? You're not Sidhera.?"

Blink.

I paused, uncertain. There were times that I truly hated ever getting involved with fairies. One thing I had learned from experience: Even if they told you the truth, they never really told the *whole* truth.

"You are trying to tell us that you are not Sidhera?" I asked again, almost sarcastically.

Blink.

"This is ridiculous, bro!" Corey mumbled in frustration. "A total waste of time."

I looked at the woman silently. Her eyes were locked on mine. They looked so desperate and pleading.

Maybe she's just a woman that Sidhera put under a spell. I thought. *Maybe she really is just a maid and when she attacked Elayne, she was under a spell.*

I decided to play along. "So you're just a person?"

One blink was her reply.

"Jasen..." Emily warned. "Why even continue? You know she's lying."

I knew that Emily was probably right, but I wanted to see where Sidhera was going with this. "Did Sidhera put you under a magical spell?" I asked.

This time, the woman blinked hard. When she opened her eyes again, there were almost tears.

One of the guards snorted loudly and his arm fell by his side, but he continued sleeping soundly a moment later.

I swallowed uncertainly. If she was telling the truth and she wasn't Sidhera, then that would mean that the real Sidhera was still loose somewhere and Elayne was still in danger.

I looked at the woman's eyes, begging me to ask the right question. "So... you're actually just some maid that works in the castle?"

Blink. Blink. Two blinks. No.

Corey exhaled with disgust. "See! She's just going around in circles."

I had to agree. This was getting more mixed up by the minute. "So, you're not a maid, and you're not a fairy. You're saying that you didn't even attack Elayne, yet Sidhera has you under a spell."

Blink.

There was another long moment. I stared through the bars at the woman floating in the white bubble in the other cell. Her eyes were locked on mine with such a quiet desperation that I started to believe that what she was saying might actually be true.

There was a tickling in the back of my mind as I considered this, and in that moment, a slow, terrible realization came over me.

I stared intently into the strange woman's eyes before I spoke again. When I did speak, it was in a fearful, hushed whisper.

"Elayne?" I asked. "Is that you?"

Instantly, tears began pouring from the woman's eyes. Steadily, she closed her eyes and blinked one.

Yes.

Chapter Eight

Escape

here was a stunned moment of silence in the dark dungeon in which the only sounds to be heard were the steady breathing of the sleeping guards.

Emily finally spoke. "Jasen… it could be a trick." she said, but her voice sounded uncertain as she looked at the woman floating in the bubble.

"Test her." Corey said quietly. Then he spoke up. "Did you give me a pencil for my birthday present?" he asked her.

The woman blinked twice.

"How about a pair of socks?" Corey asked.

Blink. Blink.

"A four-leaf clover?" he asked.

This time, she blinked once.

I could hear Emily clear her throat. "Alright. Where were we when Jasen asked you to homecoming last year? Were we in the castle?"

Blink-blink.

"How about the moonlit clearing?"

Blink.

Tears were pouring from the woman's eyes now. Her eyes never left mine.

"I have a question." I said quietly. Nobody would know this but Elayne. Everyone had heard the story of our famous kiss on the school rooftop. Sidhera herself was there, but she wouldn't know this one.

"Where was our first kiss?" I asked, watching the woman's eyes.

"Was it on the school rooftop?"

Blink. Blink. Two blinks. *No.*

"In the moonlit clearing?" I asked.

Two blinks.

"Beside a waterfall on the way to Brightwest Mountain?" I asked finally.

Blink.

I watched her eyes steadily for a long moment, feeling suddenly terrified. "Elayne." I said in a hushed whisper.

She blinked once as more tears fell from her eyes.

"This is... this is crazy." Corey said.

"If this is Elayne," Emily said, "then who is that up in Elayne's suite?"

My heart jumped.

"Sidhera." I said with a cold chill.

"She's switched places with Elayne!" Corey yelped.

From where she floated in her bubble, Elayne blinked once in confirmation.

"We've got to tell the king and queen!" Emily said.

"Where's the proof?" I said. "They already think that I'm under a spell because Sidhera faked that attack on herself today. If you go to them with this story, they will think that you two are crazy, too."

"Well what other choice do we have?" Emily asked desperately.

"You have to escape." one of the sleeping guards mumbled.

I froze and Emily and Corey fell silent. Even Elayne's eyes moved questioningly to the sleeping guard who had just spoken.

The guard yawned and stretched, slowly scratching his beard. After a moment of silence, he blinked his eyes and looked around.

"What?" he said gruffly. "You didn't think I was really sleeping, did you?"

My heart jumped. What would he do? Would he call in the other guards to grab Emily and Corey? If he had overheard our conversation, maybe he actually believed us.

He looked at my wide-eyed expression and burst out laughing. He laughed so loud that I thought for sure that the other guard was going to wake up, but he kept snoring soundly.

The laughing guard looked at the guard sleeping beside him. "What? You worried I'm gonna wake him? Ah, don't worry about it. He's out like a light."

As if to prove his point, he pushed the sleeping guard over where he clattered loudly to the floor. We all watched as the fallen guard continued snoring with his face against the slime-covered stone floor.

I looked up in confusion. "What... how?"

The bearded guard started laughing again, really howling. "Oh man, oh man! You should see the look on your faces. Corey's eyes look like they're about to bug out."

I stood up quickly. "Hey! How did you know Corey's name? Wait... how did you even *see* Corey?"

"Aw, pixie dust is the oldest trick in the book." the guard said. "I learned how to see through that stuff a long time ago!"

The guard was still grinning broadly when he looked again at the bewildered expression on my face. "What?" he asked. "You still don't recognize me? Ah... humans! Here, maybe this will help."

As we watched, two horns suddenly popped up through the top of the guard's head and a long, snakelike tail slithered out of the back of his pants. In the glowing white light of the magic bubble, we saw fur pepper his upper body where his uniform had been a moment before.

"Dryan!" Corey sputtered. "How did you... when did you..."

Dryan grinned his sharp, yellow-toothed grin at us. "I've been down here ever since I heard what happened to the princess." he said.

My mouth dropped open. "You knew that was Elayne? Why didn't you say something?"

"Fairies, kid!" Dryan said. "Remember? I'm not allowed to interfere. I had to let you knuckleheads figure it out for yourselves before I could say anything. Took you long enough, too. I was about to grab you and shake you if you didn't figure it out pretty soon."

I was speechless. Dryan just smiled his toothy grin and clapped his hands. "So, as I was saying, it sounds to me like an escape is in order. Let's get you kiddies out of here before the king comes down in the morning and does something really terrible to his own daughter."

"You can help us escape?" Emily asked. "That's not bending the rules?"

Dryan pursed his lips. "Ehhh... technically it bends the rules, but it doesn't break 'em. Sidhera's never been one to play totally by the rulebook herself, so I figure a little nudge can't hurt."

He started to scratch his beard. "Alright, where do we start?"

"How about getting Elayne out of that bubble?" I said quickly, seeing the tears still pouring from Elayne's eyes (although the way she was looking at Dryan, they may have been tears of joy).

"Right!" Dryan said. He made a clicking sound with his tongue and the glowing white bubble burst with a soft *pop!*

Instead of falling hard to the floor, the woman in the maid uniform floated gently down to a rest. She let out a tearful sob, then stood up uneasily on her shaky white legs.

When she spoke, her voice was hoarse and strange. "I have never been so glad to see anyone in my life. I kept praying you guys would come, but I was beginning to think it was hopeless." She sobbed again, but this time she was smiling tearfully.

"Are you alright?" I asked quickly.

Elayne, with the strange woman's voice, answered. "Yes! Now I am. Yes." She pushed on her cell door and it opened easily. When I pushed on mine, I found it was also unlocked.

Elayne rushed forward and hugged me with her short, plump arms. Any doubts I may have had vanished in that instant. I knew I was holding Elayne in my arms, no matter what she looked like.

"Aww. Ain't that sweet." Dryan crooned. "Now if you two are done with the mushy reunion, it's time to bust outta this joint."

I took Elayne's hand in mind. Her fingers were rough and cold, but it felt great to have her by my side. "Alright." I said. "Well, now we take a hundred guards with us, go upstairs, and confront Sidhera. We'll make her change Elayne back…"

Dryan snorted. "Ha! You just don't learn your lesson, do ya kid? Don't you remember who you're dealing with here? You can't force Sidhera to do anything she doesn't want to do."

"We'll go to my parents, then." Elayne said in that rough voice. "We can explain it to them."

Emily's voice came out of the darkness from where she stood invisible nearby. "But look at yourself, Elayne. Your parents think that you are Sidhera right now. Even if the guards didn't kill you first, they would never listen to you."

"We need some time to come up with a good plan." I said quickly, "and we're not going to be able to do it here. The morning shift of guards will be coming in soon and if they catch us here, then it'll be game over real quick." I thought for a moment. "We need to go somewhere and regroup. Someplace where we can figure this all out."

"We need to get back to our world." Corey said.

I nodded. "Yeah, I think so too." I turned to Dryan. "Alright. Let's go."

Dryan stood, looking at me. "What?"

I wiggled my fingers at him. "You know. Poof! Do your fairy magic thing. Take us back to our world."

Dryan crossed his arms. "Poof nothing. My work is done here. Like your invisible friend over there pointed out, I can bend the rules, but that's about it. I gotcha outta your cells and the guards outside are asleep… for now. You're on your own for the rest of it. If you make it back to your house, I'll meet you there."

With that, Dryan tipped an invisible hat at us and faded into a wisp of smoke.

"I hate that guy." Corey mumbled from the darkness.

I gritted my teeth in frustration. This was why I really hated dealing with fairies.

"You got any more of that pixie dust with you, Corey?" I asked.

"Yeah. I've got a little."

I took a deep breath. "Alright." I said. "Let's get out of here."

Pixie dust itches. That's something they never talk about in the stories. It itches all over. And another thing: being invisible is not as easy as it sounds.

Corey used up the rest of his pixie dust on Elayne and I, and the four of us snuck out of the dungeon and past the soundly sleeping mob of guards outside.

Once we were back up on the first floor, though, things got tough. Since it was three in the morning, I expected most people in the castle to be asleep. Turns out, though, that time is right when most of the servants get up to do their chores. The hallways were packed and we soon discovered that it is really, really hard to walk down a hallway when the other people can't see you coming. People hurried by, carrying mops and brooms, buckets of water, and crates of food. Several times we had to backtrack quickly just to dive into a side corridor and let someone pass so they wouldn't bump into us.

I led the way. Elayne held my hand, Emily held her hand, and Corey came up behind holding Emily's hand. I was terrified of letting go since we couldn't see each other and I didn't want us to get separated.

Sometimes Elayne would tug on my hand to guide me down a side corridor that I hadn't known was there. One time, she even led us to a narrow secret tunnel that was hidden behind a tapestry. That took us almost halfway to the main courtyard without meeting anyone.

We had to wait until the iron gate was opened for someone before we could run through it. Even then, it closed so quickly behind us that I was almost worried that Corey may not have made it out.

Once in the main courtyard, we had to dodge patrols of soldiers and horses, too. One time, a soldier practicing with his sword swung so close to my invisible head that I felt the wind of his blade on my cheek. Luckily, we were able to hurry past unharmed and in one piece.

Ahead, we could see the drawbridge, which was thankfully down as the night-watch guards were coming in and the new guards were going out to take their places.

The distant horizon was tinted orange now and there was enough light in the predawn air to see clearly. The ground was still wet with muddy puddles scattered about from the torrential rain the day before yesterday.

Between horses and marching soldiers, we made a break for the drawbridge. It was a dangerous and scary run. Once I actually bumped into a passing guard, and he looked around quickly, but kept moving. There was almost no room to move on the crowded drawbridge. Horse hooves pounded on the wood and clattered in the morning air, mixed with the sharp ringing of shields knocking against armor.

A passing horse had just knocked me in the shoulder hard when I suddenly heard some of the guards around us start to cry out in alarm. The ones closest to me all scattered suddenly and I had just enough time to hear Elayne shout "Jasen! Look out!" before something huge and wet smacked me in the side and sent me sprawling.

"It's the leviathan!" some of the guards were yelling. "Look out!"

A moment later, the huge tentacle found me again and batted me into a group of nearby guards. They yelled out in surprise when I hit them, and some of them fell to the ground. I landed with a splash in a puddle of mud just off the far side of the drawbridge.

I heard some men gasp and there was a sudden tense silence around me. I looked up and saw the surrounding soldiers looking right at me.

When I looked down, I saw that patches of me were no longer invisible. As the muddy water sloshed down my face, it washed away the covering of pixie dust.

"Is... is that Sir Jasen?" one of them asked in a rumbling voice.

I froze, terrified. My mind raced for a way out of this.

"I heard he was locked up." a soldier with a big red mustache said, holding his sword by his side.

At that moment, a bell started to ring from inside the castle. A bellowing voice from the other side of the drawbridge boomed "Alarm! Alarm! Prisoners have escaped!"

The gathered guards all turned their attention to the castle for a moment and in that second, I felt invisible hands grab my shirt and yank me up.

"Time to go!" Corey said in my ear.

When I started to run, I heard the soldiers behind me yell out and some of them leapt after me. I had gone no more than twenty feet before the fastest soldiers were right behind me.

From behind the pack, two horses appeared, galloping fast and without riders. The charging horses knocked the soldiers aside and as they were running past me I heard Emily's voice yell "Corey! Jump on!" just as another invisible hand grabbed me and pulled me up onto the other horse.

Steadying myself behind the saddle, I reached forward and felt the invisible rider. "Hang on tight." I heard Elayne say in that hoarse, unfamiliar voice.

Before long, the castle was falling into the distance. When I looked back, though, I could see soldiers jumping on their own horses to give pursuit.

As the sun rose over the distant hills, we galloped through the morning mist at full speed, always managing to stay just ahead of the guards thanks to Emily and Elayne, who were both better riders than any of our pursuers. The damp fog in the air clung to our skin as we rode and by the time we reached the white bridge that arced across the river, the pixie dust had washed off and the four of us were visible again (except for Corey's left foot, which remained invisible... making it look like his leg ended at his knee.)

By the time we reached the hilltop with the stable house and the doorway, the sun was visible over the distant hills to the east and the fastest soldiers on horseback were starting to catch up. I kept bracing myself, expecting to be shot with an arrow in the back, but apparently they were still under orders to bring us back alive,

Keafer, hearing the approaching thunder of hooves, was just stepping out of the stable house with sleepy eyes and a hesitant smile. When he saw us approaching at full speed and the legion of soldiers with raised swords behind us, he dove back into the house and quickly slammed the door. The two guards that were posted there looked up at us in confusion, their hands going to their swords, but before they could react, we were past them.

Before the horses even came to a stop, we were all four on the ground and running. We made it to the wooden door just as the soldiers reached us, their huge horses surrounding us. "Stop!" they ordered. "In the name of the king! Stop at once and return the foul witch Sidhera! You are under her spell! Do not let her turn you all into traitors!"

But we didn't even hesitate. Corey was through the door first, pulling Emily by the arm fast behind him. As Elayne ran through the door, one of the soldiers actually threw an axe, and it smashed into the wooden door just inches from Elayne's crooked nose. I gave her a sudden push and she was through, then I grabbed the door and slammed it closed just as the soldiers scrambled to climb down from their horses.

There was no way to lock the door behind us, so we just ran. We ran through the moonlit clearing and dove through the invisible curtain without slowing. Moments later, we were in the woods and running fast through the trees, kicking up piles of fallen October leaves from the ground beneath our feet.

It was only seconds later when I heard the shouting of the soldiers in the woods behind us. I felt a sudden panic swell inside my chest. There was something unnaturally terrifying about having the soldiers pursuing us here, in the woods of Jacob's Rest.

"Over here!" one of them bellowed through the trees, and there were more shouts and then they were closing in on us once more. Emily and Corey were a little ahead of us, and I pushed harder to keep up with them. When I looked back, though, I saw Elayne struggling to keep up. Her bloated white face was mottled red and her stringy black hair was plastered to her skull with sweat. She was straining to move her body's legs as fast as they would move, but it was a losing battle.

I fell back and grabbed her by the hand. "Come on!" I said. "They're catching up!"

Elayne was struggling to breathe. "I can't." she said. "These legs are not strong enough. This body can't make it. You go. Escape with Emily and Corey. Find a way to reverse the spell and stop Sidhera."

The soldiers were crashing through the trees behind us. I could see them with their swords drawn, running hard. They hadn't seen us yet, but they were getting closer.

"Go." Elayne whispered again, slowing down as she gasped for air.

I gritted my teeth, looking around frantically. Corey and Emily were far out of sight now.

"Don't go back to the farmhouse." I said quickly. "They know where Corey and I live. Get to Emily's house. It should be safe there for now."

Elayne's pudgy white face looked up at me in startled surprise. "What are you doing Jasen? Don't…"

But before she could finish, I started yelling at the top of my lungs. "Woo-hoo! Hey! Over here, suckers!"

The guards instantly jumped to attention and looked my way as I backtracked towards them. "This way!" one of them yelled. "Go around! Cut them off!"

"Catch me if you can!" I yelled, taking off through the trees and leading the soldiers away from Elayne and the others, silently praying that they would follow and take the bait.

There had been a time, over a year ago, that Corey and I had gotten lost in these woods. Since then, they had become a second home to me as I had traveled to visit Elayne each day. I knew right away where I needed to go, and I knew without hesitation the way to get there.

"Over here, solider-boys!" I yelled out wildly from time to time. It wasn't necessary any more, though. They had definitely taken the bait. There were at least twenty of them behind me now, and they were catching up fast, clanging loudly through the trees and shouting orders.

I was struggling for breath myself now. I knew I had run nearly a mile since leaving the moonlit clearing. My lungs burned with every breath I took of the cool October air. Terror kept me moving, though. The sounds of the soldiers getting ever closer pushed me to find more energy and run harder.

I saw it through the trees ahead. Right where I had parked it on the gravel embankment beside the road. I had never been so happy to see my beat-up old car.

I ran up the embankment and to the side of the car. The soldiers were right behind me. I could see the bearded face of the closest one, scowling at me as he ran with his sword high.

My hands shaking badly, I fumbled in my pants pocket for my keys. My heart froze when I couldn't feel them. The closest soldier was less than fifty feet away now.

There! In my other pocket. I yanked my keys out, turning my jeans pocket inside-out as I struggled to get the key up to the lock.

My trembling fingers would not keep the key steady and I missed the lock three times before it finally slipped in and turned with a click. I dove in the car and pulled the door shut just as the soldier behind me caught up. The sound of his heavy mail crashing into the side of the car was jarring, and the whole car shook as I fumbled again with the keys to get them in the ignition.

The other soldiers had caught up now, too, and they surrounded the car. Some kicked at it, putting their angry faces up to the windows and shouting for me to come out. The one closest to my door pulled on the handle and started to open my door. In a panic, I grabbed the door back and slammed it closed, throwing down the lock.

When the car started, some of the soldiers took a step back in surprise, not sure what to expect. I didn't hesitate any more. I threw it into gear and slammed on the gas. The tires behind me threw up gravel and some of the soldiers jumped back, yelling and cursing, as the car shot forward.

I saw one of them bring his heavy sword down hard on the back of the car as it pulled away. Some of them started to run after me, but in seconds they were left far behind in a rolling cloud of dust.

I was a mile down the road before I remembered again to breathe.

Chapter Nine

Sidhera's Revenge

 drove up the long dirt driveway that led to the horse farm where Emily's family lived. My heart was still racing and my head buzzed like someone had kicked a beehive inside it. Before I got to the house, I veered off the driveway and drove into the open barn.

Killing the engine, I closed my eyes and took a deep breath. In the sudden silence, I tried to calm my panicked heartbeat. I had finally taken a long, deep, shuddering breath, when I caught a glimpse of movement from outside.

There, down the long driveway, three figures were moving, hunched low and keeping close to the bushes. A smile spread over my face and I felt my tense muscles finally relax a bit.

I had run halfway towards them when they saw me and one of them broke from the bushes and ran to meet me. It was

Elayne. Her pale body in its torn and disheveled maidservants dress hobbled towards me with a growing smile spread across her face. When she reached me, she threw herself into my arms, apparently forgetting about the extra weight her new body carried. I was thrown to the ground hard and pinned beneath her.

Even as I was gasping for air, she was kissing me. "I was so worried!" she rasped, breathing hard. "You shouldn't have done that! You should have left me!"

"You know I would never do that." I said, smiling even as my legs were crushed beneath hers.

"Alright, Elayne. Looks like my brother is having a hard time breathing, there." I heard Corey say. I looked up to see Corey and Emily, sweaty and out of breath, but smiling now that we were all safe and in one piece.

Before Elayne had come into our lives, Emily was the only girl we had ever really known well. We had grown up down the road from her all of our lives and to me, at least, she was very much like a little sister.

We had always felt welcomed in her home. During a huge blizzard when I was ten, the pipes had frozen in our farmhouse and Grandpa, Corey, and I had spent a few days with Emily and her parents as the storm piled over four feet of snow outside.

Her room had changed quite a bit in that time, but every inch of it reflected Emily's personality. There were a lot of horse things, obviously. Posters and framed pictures, some of which I recognized as her own horses (although honestly, they all looked alike to me). She had some trophies and blue ribbons on display, all of them also having to do with horses (except one that said it was for first place in the hundred-yard dash during Field Day in Second Grade). On her dresser was a framed picture of me, Corey, and Emily from a time we'd gone hiking a few years ago.

Emily walked immediately over to the window and peered outside to see if we had been followed. A moment later, we heard a startled gasp and looked up to see Elayne, standing in front of the dresser mirror, her hands covering her mouth.

I realized that it was the first time she had been able to take a good look at her new face.

"Yeah. You went from being Sleeping Beauty to the Ugly Duckling." Corey said wryly as he collapsed on the bed.

"Corey!" I snapped.

"What?" Corey shrugged. "She can see it for herself. No point in lying to her about it. Sidhera did quite a number on her."

"You can say that again!" a rough voice snarled from somewhere in the room. It was Dryan's voice. It took me a moment to find where it was coming from. Finally, I saw his reflection in the dresser mirror, standing beside Elayne. He wasn't in the room with us, he was in the mirror.

"Oh, Dryan!" Elayne said when she saw him. "What has she done?"

The image of Dryan in the mirror scratched his rough beard. "Well, as you have already figured out, she's gone and switched places with you. The thing is, she hasn't done it the way most fairies would have done it. Most fairies would have put an ugly spell on you, then made themselves look like you.

That is the easy way. Fairies can make themselves look like anybody they want, so it would have been a piece of cake.

Our girl, Sidhera, though, being the sweetheart that she is, never seems to do things the easy way. No, what she's gone and done is actually *taken your body*. Her essence is now firmly glued inside your old body and she's kicked you out to live in the body you are in now."

Elayne looked stunned. I moved closer to her to put my arm around her. Emily and Corey had moved up behind us now, and we were all gathered around the dresser mirror to hear Dryan.

"It's actually a beautiful plan." Dryan admired. "And quite an impressive bit of magic. Very hard to undo. If she had just *disguised* the princess, it would have been a piece of cake. Witches and fairies have been doing it for as long as I can remember." A smile curled his lips as if he was remembering some happy thought. "In my day, they would turn princes into toads all the time. Great spell, really. I miss those days."

Dryan paused thoughtfully, rubbing his beard with that same wistful smile. A moment later, he seemed to snap out of it. "The thing is, though, the good old standby… 'true love's kiss' can undo most of those spells. Sidhera knows this and she wasn't about to make that same mistake again."

"So what can we do?" I asked with growing alarm. "There's a way to undo it, right?"

Dryan guffawed. "Oh yeah. It's the law of magic. Anything done can be undone. It just ain't gonna be easy."

"Yeah, yeah." Core said impatiently. "We beat Sidhera before and we can do it again."

Dryan, looking annoyed, gritted his sharp yellow teeth. "The last time you bested Sidhera," he growled, "it was little more than blind luck, if you remember right. Also, she pretty much sat back and watched last time since she didn't think you were much of a threat. You can bet that she will not be making that same mistake again."

Corey looked like he was going to respond, then stopped himself. Dryan glared at him for a moment longer, then continued. "Another thing is the time restraint you have."

I didn't like the sound of that.

"What time restraint?" I asked carefully.

"Well, you must've figured it out by now." Dryan grumbled. "Sidhera's timing here was no accident."

Realization spread across Elayne's face. "The coronation!" she gasped.

Dryan nodded. "The coronation."

"When my mother places the Crown of Lions on my head on my seventeenth birthday, she will be transferring its power to me." Elayne said, shocked.

Emily's eyes grew wide. "You mean that crown you were telling us about that makes everyone obey?"

"Your mother will think she is crowning you." I said. "She'll give its power to Sidhera without realizing what she is doing."

"Sidhera's already bad enough." Corey yelped. "If she becomes the ruler of your whole kingdom, she's going to be…"

"Unstoppable." I finished for him.

"Yep." Dryan said. "You've got to give the old witch credit. She's certainly got style."

"We've got to get my body back before my birthday!" Elayne said firmly. "We cannot let Sidhera wear the Crown of Lions."

"Alright." I said. "That gives us eleven days." I squeezed my hands into fists nervously. "Man, I *hate* these time limits!"

"Let's have it." Corey said. "How do we get the princess here back into her own body? Or—let me guess--- you aren't allowed to tell us?"

Dryan grinned at Corey. "I can give you some clues. You know that us fairies just love cryptic clues. It's a great way to bend the rules a bit without breaking them."

Dryan produced something in his hands and tossed it to me. It came through the mirror with a spark of orange and I caught it in my hands.

It was a round chip of wood. It looked like a slice of a thick tree branch, about four inches wide, with rough bark around the edges. On the face I could see light rings in the wood, like the rings on a tree trunk.

I looked at it doubtfully. "This is the clue?"

"Think of that like a guidebook." Dryan said. "Tell it what you want and it will tell you what you need."

I turned the piece of wood over in my hands, studying it carefully. *Tell it?* I thought. *Are you kidding? It's a piece of wood!* But I kept my mouth shut. Dryan's clues had proven to be useful in the past, even if they were odd.

"What about Elayne's father?" I asked. "He thinks that we freed Sidhera and his soldiers are still after us. They're not going to stop until they find us."

Dryan pursed his lips thoughtfully. "Oh, right. Well, after you escaped into this world, the king called his soldiers all back. You won't have to worry about them anymore."

"Sweet!" Corey said triumphantly.

I knew, though, that there was something very wrong with that. "Why would he do that?" I asked suspiciously.

Dryan scratched his beard absently. "Well, I think they've got the feeling that you won't be back anytime soon."

Oh, boy. I *really* didn't like the sound of that. "Why would they think something like that?" I asked carefully.

Well," Dryan said, almost uneasily. "They sort of closed up the doorway between your world and theirs."

I didn't understand. "You mean the wooden door in the moonlit clearing? They locked it somehow?"

"Not exactly." Dryan said. "I mean that the portal is closed completely. Sidhera almost certainly had something to do with it. Anyway, that way to Elayne's world is gone. You guys are going to have to find another way to get back."

It wasn't that we didn't trust Dryan, it was just… well… alright: I didn't trust him. I had to see for myself if what he was saying was true. As evening approached, we made our way with rising panic through the woods and to the place with the invisible curtain. As we had done so many times over the past year, I stepped past the threshold that would lead me into the moonlit clearing…

And nothing happened. I was still standing there in the woods of Jacob's Rest.

Just to be sure, I took another few steps forward, expecting at any time to feel that familiar little dropping sensation of passing into the clearing… but I had just shuffled forward a few feet through the fallen leaves on the forest floor.

Corey, disbelieving, took a running jump past me. He fell and skidded on the leaves close to the charred remains of the nearby tree stump. When he saw that he was still with us, he jumped up and dove forward again with a frantic yell, landing hard on the forest floor.

Elayne's face looked stricken. "It's gone!" she whispered, terrified. "The way back is truly gone."

"This makes it impossible to do what we need to do." I said in disgust. "If there is no way back to your world, then we'll never be able to get to Sidhera in time."

"What did Dryan say, exactly?" Emily asked. "He said '*that* way to Elayne's world is gone'. He didn't say that we *couldn't* get back. There must be more…"

"What about Bridgette?" Elayne asked. "She may be able to help…"

"There's no way to reach her." I said helplessly. "She's gone with my Grandpa."

"How about your rings?" Elayne asked. "Can you use them to reach her?"

I looked down at the bright blue ring that I wore on my finger. "If they are magic, then I don't know how to use them." I said. Just to be sure, I held the ring up to my mouth and called "Hello? Bridgette? Can you hear me?"

"She wouldn't be able to help anyway." Corey said, brushing the leaves from his clothes. "She would just pull that same 'Laws of magic' garbage that Dryan always pulls when we need his help. It's ridiculous."

I tried to swallow down the overwhelming feeling of hopelessness that was crashing down on me. This seemed impossible. I looked over at Elayne, trapped in that strange body, and saw her fighting back tears herself.

"Okay." I said, running my hands through my hair. "Alright. We've got eleven days here. We *cannot* let Sidhera win this one."

Corey took one last pass into the air just to convince himself once and for all that the invisible curtain really was gone. "That evil fairy queen really gets on my nerves." he mumbled.

We turned and started heading back to Emily's house in the fading evening light.

Chapter Ten

Broken

he next morning, we gathered in Emily's room, sitting in a circle on the round Indian-print throw rug on her floor. The "magic" piece of wood sat on the floor between us.

Think of it like a guidebook. Dryan had said. *Tell it what you want and it will tell you what you need.*

"This is crazy!" Corey said. "I'm not talking to a piece of wood."

"Good." I said. "Let me do the talking. First, though, we need to decide what exactly we want to ask it. I know from experience that with fairies, every word counts. If they get the chance, they will find some way to twist the meaning of what you're saying."

Elayne nodded. "Jasen's right. We need to be careful."

"We just tell it what we want, right?" Emily said. "What we want is a way back into Elayne's world."

"Ok." I said. "So how should we ask…"

Before I could finish, Corey shouted out. "Hey! Freaky scrap of wood! We want to get back to Elayne's world!"

"Corey!" I snapped furiously.

Corey shrugged. "What? I told it what we wanted, right?"

We all looked at the wood, waiting for something to happen. Waiting for some voice to appear with guiding words of wisdom. Waiting for… something.

The piece of wood sat still and unmoving between us.

"This is lame." Corey said.

I looked nervously around the group, then leaned forward and spoke again as if the wood held a microphone and I needed to speak up. "We want to find an open portal that will lead us back to the world where Elayne was born."

There. I thought. *That should do it. Certainly there was no way to misconstrue those words…*

But still, the piece of wood lay silent.

Corey threw up his hands in frustration. "Hey! Wood! You are about two seconds from ending up in the fireplace!"

"Corey!" Emily said, shocked. "Don't make it mad!"

"Make it mad? Are you kidding me? It's a freaking piece of wood!"

"We're not asking it right." Elayne said finally. "We should be looking at the final goal. The portal is just one stumbling block in our way. What we really want is to find a way to stop Sidhera's plan and return me to my body before she can take the Crown of Lions."

I nodded. "That's true, I guess, but…"

"Look!" Emily shouted suddenly. "Something is happening!"

I turned to look at the piece of wood and saw that indeed something was happening. The light brown rings that made up the grain of the wood had begun to spiral and turn. A moment later, they shifted and broke into little tiny dots that marched across the face of the wood like an army of ants. When they settled into place, the surface of the wood grew still again and the wood grain now spelled out a message in a scrawled, spidery text.

You need the flame that forever burns...
brandished by Washington's Dark Rider.

We all read the message silently.

"Why can't they ever just come out and tell us what we need to do?" Corey said finally. "Is that really so hard?"

"Washington's Dark Rider?" I asked quietly. "What in the world?"

"I don't get it." Emily said. "This doesn't tell us anything. How are we supposed to use fire to get Elayne back in her own body?"

"Maybe we can set Sidhera on fire..." Corey said hopefully.

"She's in Elayne's body." I reminded him. "We're not trying to kill her, we're trying to get Elayne back inside and Sidhera out."

"With fire?" Corey asked. "How?"

I shook my head. "I have no idea."

"Maybe it will tell us once we get the flame." Elayne said.

"What's the point of even trying to figure it out if we can't get back to your world?" Corey asked.

"This actually may not be something in Elayne's world." I said carefully.

Emily agreed. "Yeah. I was thinking that, too. 'Washington's Dark Rider'. The name Washington isn't too common in your world, is it, Elayne?"

"No." Elayne said. "It's not a name from my world."

"Okay, but what does George Washington have to do with magic or fire?" Corey said sarcastically. "Are you saying that the father of our country was a magical fairy?"

"It doesn't actually say it's him." Emily corrected. "It's his 'Dark Rider'."

I thought for a moment. "Washington fought in the Revolutionary War, right? Wasn't there some famous rider who rode through the dark to warn about the British coming?"

"Paul Revere." Emily said.

I snapped my fingers. "Right! Paul Revere. That could be 'Washington's Dark Rider'!"

"Paul Revere?" Corey asked doubtfully.

"Well, if he carried this magical fire, maybe it was in his lantern somehow." I said. "Or maybe his lantern is in a museum somewhere."

"We need to go to the library." Elayne said.

A moment later, I had pocketed the piece of wood with the cryptic clue and we were heading out the door.

The Jacob's Rest Public Library was an oddly comforting and familiar place. Living in the secluded valley, there had never been too many choices for entertainment growing up. Corey and I had occupied great amounts of time hiking in the miles of woods around our house, we had seen every movie that came to our one-screen theater each week, and we had spent countless hours roaming the shelves of that musty library.

There was a reading nook with couches and tables covered with magazines. The small alcove jutted out into a floor-to-ceiling window that overlooked the woods behind the library. We made ourselves at home here, spreading out in the shaded light pouring in through the glass wall. Occasionally, the wind would blow the trees outside and a kaleidoscope of shadows would dance around us.

On this Saturday afternoon, the library was empty except for us and the one librarian, a stern old woman who was the stereotype of what a librarian should be. She kept busy out of sight in a back room and left us undisturbed.

Corey was spread out on the couch. He had pulled a bunch of books about George Washington and the Revolutionary War from the children's section. Most were picture books, but he thumbed through them, tossing each aside in his vain attempt to find something mystical about our first president.

Emily sat at a table with a computer on the other side of the nook. She was pouring through some biographies of George Washington that she had pulled up on the internet (searches for "Washington's Dark Rider", of course, brought up nothing helpful. That would have been too easy...)

Elayne and I sat facing each other across a table in the center of the nook. We had pulled out every book in the library that had any words from our clue in the title and they were stacked in a pile on the table between us..

I was looking at some of the weird pictures in a book about dreams called *Dark Dreams: Your Guide to What They Mean.*

I was flipping through it quickly, knowing that it was not at all what we needed. Still, I stopped at a few pages to read some of the crazy things it was saying. "Hey, did you know that a dream about a milkshake means you have a dangerous adventure ahead of you?"

"Oh, yeah." Corey called from the couch, "Milkshakes are creepy and dangerous. Everyone knows that."

I laughed.

"Hey!" Corey said. "I dreamt that I drank three gallons of orange juice the other night. What does that mean?"

I flipped through the book and quickly found something. "It says that you will soon die a watery death."

Corey laughed. "Man! Even orange juice is bad? Wow. Next time I'll try to dream about chocolate milk instead."

"I'm not finding anything!" Emily called hopelessly from her computer. "There is nothing mystical about George Washington."

"Try the state of Washington or Washington D.C." I suggested.

Emily looked surprised. "Hey! Good idea!" She started typing immediately.

Elayne laid another book aside and reached for the next one on the pile. I saw her rub the black mole on her face absently, then her eyes caught mine for a second and she looked away quickly.

"Um, Jasen…" she began carefully.

"Umm hmm?" I asked, looking for "Fire" in the dream book.

Elayne hesitated for a moment as if trying to figure out what she was about to say. "We… um… never really got to finish talking about what I had discussed with you the other day in the red room."

I felt my stomach clench. I carefully kept the book up in front of my face and pretended that I was still only half-listening. "Mmm?" I said.

I heard Emily stop typing and knew that she was listening closely.

Elayne seemed to be aware of the sudden silence. Although she lowered her voice, her words still were very loud in the silence of the alcove. "There are things that we still need to talk about. Important things... about our future."

I avoided her eyes uncomfortably. "Didn't we talk about this the other day in your suite?" I asked.

"That was Sidhera you were talking to." Corey interjected.

I cringed. "Oh... right."

Elayne looked startled. "You talked with Sidhera? What did you say?"

I cleared my throat. "Well... um..."

"Not much." Corey said again from his place on the couch. "Before he could get too far, she got freaked out and started beating herself with an elephant."

Emily snapped from the other side of the nook, "Corey! Zip it!" She made a show of starting to type again, but I knew that she was still listening intently.

Elayne slid the pile of books aside and leaned across the table towards me. "Listen," she said quietly. "I understand your reaction. It was wrong of me to spring it on you like that. I'm sorry."

I looked at her hesitantly, still not used to looking at her strange pale face and hearing Elayne's words in a stranger's voice. "Thank you." I said. "Apology accepted."

Elayne watched me closely for a long moment, waiting. The silence stretched out. I could see Emily squirming in her seat by the computer across the alcove as if she was dying to say something but was forcing herself to stay quiet.

"Are you going to say anything?" Elayne asked me softly.

"What do you want me to say?" I asked. "You're right. You shouldn't have sprung it on me like that."

Elayne swallowed. "Okay. And what about the way you reacted?"

I closed the dream book in my hands and leaned forward. "Elayne, I know that this may not be what you want to hear... but everything I said the other day was true. The way I said it may have been a bit... abrupt... but that doesn't change anything. I'm not finished with high school. I haven't decided what I want to do with my life yet, and I can tell you that being king was definitely never in my plans."

"Well, what did you think, Jasen?" Elayne said, with a spark of anger flashing across her eyes. "I am a princess. You've always known that. What do you think that means— just that I live in a castle and have pretty dresses? Have you never stopped to consider what that meant for my future? I was born into the royal family. I am the heir to the kingdom. You knew that I was going to be queen. What did you think was going to happen? Have you really not thought about any of this?"

I was quiet for a moment. I guess that it was true that I had not really considered these things. Part of me, that quiet part of me that I would never admit to, had held a small hope that Elayne may have come into my world to live... maybe go to college with me. When I thought about it now, it seemed absurd.

Elayne's eyes looked uncertain. "You love me."

"Yes." I said quickly. "You know I do."

"Well," she said, looking like she was trying hard to keep herself composed. "It's been a year. Have you given any real thought to our future?"

"Yes!" I said defensively. "Well, no. Sort of. I thought we would date for awhile. Get engaged for a year or two. I guess that I always knew we would be married someday..."

Elayne moved forward and took my hands in hers on the table in front of us. "If you knew that we would be married, then what does it matter if it's next year or five years from now?"

I pulled my hands away, flustered. "It matters!" I said. "It matters because marrying you takes away all of my choices! If we get married then I'll have to be a king in a country that I know almost nothing about. I'll be stuck for the rest of my life!"

I heard Emily draw a sharp breath from where she was trying to pretend that she wasn't listening to us. I saw that Corey had grown suddenly very silent and was hiding behind a picture book called *George Washington Never Chopped Down a Cherry Tree*.

Elayne pulled her empty hands back slowly, looking stricken by my words. Her eyes looked at me with a mix of anger and sadness. "I'm sorry that you think of our relationship as a 'trap'... I never knew you felt that way."

"Elayne, I don't. That's not what I meant. I just..."

"Jasen, this is the way my life is." Elayne interrupted. "I have no choices. When I was born, it was decided that I would be queen." She paused here, straightening her shoulders and looking into my eyes intently. Even in this unpleasant body, she managed to look royal and commanding. "If you love me, Jasen," she said with a tone of finality, "then that is the life you must choose as well."

There was a long breathless moment of silence in that library nook while Elayne looked across the table into my eyes. The wind rustled the trees outside and the shadows shifted across her face.

I cleared my throat quietly, my heart pounding fast in my chest. Finally, I raised my head again and looked at her.

"I'm sorry, Elayne." I said in a low whisper. "I can't."

The long terrible silence that followed was worse than anything that had come before it. Elayne's eyes, still locked on mine, and still watching me firmly, began to tear up, but her gaze never left mine and her expression remained firm.

"That's it, then." she said at last.

I felt my own throat constrict as I forced myself not to look away. "That's it." I said.

Another long moment, then Elayne turned her eyes from mine and pushed her chair back from the table carefully. She got up slowly and walked out of the shadowed reading nook. Instantly, Emily was up and following after her.

When I finally looked at Corey, he was staring at me, wide-eyed, his mouth hanging open in shock and the book in his hands forgotten. "What... what just happened?" he asked slowly.

I took a long, slow breath. "I think Elayne and I just broke up."

Corey looked like his world was falling apart unexpectedly around him. "But... what...how..." he turned to look in the direction Emily and Elayne had disappeared.

"Let them go." I said tiredly, running my hand through my hair.

Corey blinked, still looking lost and confused. "So... what about Sidhera?"

I picked up another book from the stack in front of me. "Oh, we're still going after Sidhera." I said. "This doesn't change that at all. That evil fairy is going to be real sorry that she ever messed with us."

I focused all of the pain and hurt and confusion inside of me and turned it into a passionate anger towards Sidhera. I was flying through books now, looking for any words that would give us insight to the wood chip's stupid clue.

Emily and Elayne never returned to the nook, although Corey pretended to excuse himself to the restroom one time and came back to report that the girls had moved to a table on the other side of the library where they, too, had dove back into books.

"How did Elayne look?" I asked carefully.

"Ugly as ever." Corey said quickly. "I really hate that big black mole on her..."

"That's not what I mean!" I snapped.

"I know what you meant." Corey said. "I'll tell you the same thing that I told her: I don't want to get in the middle of it."

"What? She asked about me, too?"

Corey shrugged. "She may have asked how you were."

I sat forward. "What did you say?"

"Same thing I told you." Corey said. "Ugly as ever."

Before I could snap at him, he had disappeared into the shelves to gather another stack of books.

Chapter Eleven

Our Haunted Valley

he next day was Sunday, October 29th.
Corey and I, feeling that it was safe to return home since we knew the soldiers were gone, had spent the night in our empty farmhouse alone. Although I lay in bed all night, I hadn't slept a bit. I was angry, frustrated, and felt like a huge empty hole had opened inside of me. My conversation with Elayne played through my mind in a hundred different ways. When the morning light finally colored my window shade, I felt beaten and exhausted.

I met Corey for breakfast downstairs. He looked tired, too, but much better off than I was. We ate our cereal in the chilly morning silence of the kitchen. When Corey finally spoke, he had his mouth full of corn flakes.

"You look terrible." he said, milk dripping from the corner of his mouth.

"Thanks." I smiled. "That's a real pick-me-up, Corey."

"Any new ideas?"

I sighed and shook my head. "Nope. You?"

Corey shook his head. "Nope. What's the plan for today?"

I rubbed my bloodshot eyes. "I guess we'll meet up with the girls."

Corey stopped chewing for a moment and eyed me. "You gonna be okay with that?"

I shrugged, my head pounding tiredly. "I guess I have to be, don't I?"

Corey paused a moment longer, then turned his attention back to his bowl of corn flakes.

Emily's parents had gone out again for the day. They had left that morning for the outlet mall in Central Valley, leaving Emily and Elayne to themselves. Emily met us at the door and led us into the kitchen where Elayne sat at the table, looking at some kind of atlas. It was still an unnerving sight to see her in that odd and misshapen body.

She had cleaned up a bit and changed clothes. Her thin tuft of wiry black hair looked freshly washed and still wet, and her pale scalp could be seen showing through in patches. She didn't look up when we entered, so I couldn't tell yet if her eyes were as bloodshot and exhausted as mine felt.

"We think we may have an idea." Emily said.

Even though Corey had just finished three bowls of cereal at our house, he went straight for the cabinets in Emily's kitchen and pulled out a box of Pop Tarts.

"What do you have?" I asked, forcing myself to look away from Elayne.

"Well, it's not about the clue, exactly. It's about finding another way back into Elayne's world."

I nodded. "Alright. I'm listening."

Emily turned to Elayne. "You want to tell explain it to them?" she asked.

Elayne, keeping her face down as she turned the pages of the atlas, shook her head. "No. You can tell them."

Emily cleared her throat uncomfortably and turned back to me. "Well... Elayne was telling me that fairies cannot actually travel between the worlds using magic alone. They need to use portals, just like we did."

I was surprised to hear this. "Really? I didn't know that."

Emily nodded. "Right? So that one... the one behind the invisible curtain in the woods... that one was sort of a special one that not too many fairies knew about. It had been hidden by Dryan and Bridgette and had been guarded by Albero all of those centuries while Elayne slept."

"Ok..." I said.

Emily glanced at Elayne again. "So, anyway, Elayne was saying that most of the portals between the worlds probably would be much more...active."

I considered this. "You mean that there would be fairies coming and going through them all of the time?"

"Right." Emily said. "Exactly. They would still be in odd, out-of-the way places, but there would be lots of fairies around."

Corey, with his mouth full of Pop Tart, rested his elbows on the kitchen counter. "So we're looking for a fairy hotspot. Like a pixie disco or a goblin nightclub."

Emily scrunched up her nose. "Sort of. I mean, when you think about it, there aren't really too many places to hide anymore, right? With cities and roads and all. There are spells that they can use to cover things up, but if you get enough fairies moving in and out, then sooner or later people are going to find out about it."

I thought about this. "Right. They would think..." I hesitated. "Well, with all of the freaky things they might see and hear, they would probably think that that spot is..."

"Haunted." Emily finished for me with a triumphant smile. "Exactly." She pointed at Elayne, who held up the atlas she was reading so we could see the cover. It was called *Our Haunted Valley*. "That's a book my dad had on his shelf. It talks about our area, the different legends around here, and the places that are supposed to be the most haunted."

Corey froze, his mouth full of food. "Haunted?"

Emily nodded. "Yeah! You would be amazed at how many ghost stories have come from around here. People have been seeing strange things around Jacob's Rest since long before the town was even here. The Iroquois Indians used to call this place 'The Whispering Hills'. They would pass through, but never stay long. They said the trees talked."

I snorted, remembering the huge talking tree Albero that we had run into last year. "Well, that one we know is true." I said.

Corey's face looked pale. "Our valley *is* haunted! We used to see a ghost-beaver," he said seriously, turning to me. "Didn't we, Jasen?"

I sighed, remembering Corey and his terrified claims of seeing a giant ghostly beaver outside of his window when he was eight. "I remember." I said.

Elayne looked up and spoke for the first time. "Most supernatural things that people claim are ghosts are most likely magical creatures or fairies that are visiting from my world." she said.

Corey made a face. "You have any beaver-demons with beady red eyes and huge buck teeth?" He stuck his teeth out to imitate a fierce-looking beaver.

A smile broke across Elayne's lips at Corey's crazy expression, then her eyes flicked to me and her smile vanished quickly. She looked down at the book again. "There are lots of supposedly haunted places around Jacob's Rest." Elayne said. "We can go to some of these and investigate... see if any of them can lead us to a portal back to my world."

Corey's face dropped. "We're going to go purposely looking for the most haunted places in Jacob's Rest? Two days before Halloween?"

I nodded. "It's a good idea." I said. "Where should we begin?"

Emily and Elayne exchanged a look.

"What?" I asked.

Emily cleared her throat. "Well... we marked a couple of places in the book that we can check out. But you'll never guess where one of the most haunted hot-spots of the valley is."

"Where?" I asked.

Elayne held up the book to a faded black and white picture of a family swimming in a big beautiful lake. "Lake Sorrow." she said.

Emily, Elayne and I drove together up the secluded mountain road that led to Lake Sorrow. Corey, seeing the opportunity to get some much-needed driving practice while Grandpa was away, decided to ride his motorcycle. We drove slowly and he followed, jerking from side to side every now and then. To his credit, he only fell once... but he had dozens of close calls, including a time he veered off into the roadside ditch.

We finally made it to that familiar overgrown track beside the road, marked only by a dented and faded blue sign that read "Lake Sorrow."

Even before we got out of the car, I knew that this was going to be the place. It was just too much of a coincidence. This once-beautiful lake and vacation getaway was now a vast crater of brackish mud. This was where Sidhera had hidden one of the magic vials that could have broken Elayne's curse. I still had nightmares about Corey and I running through the snow, chased by a legion of rabid mud golems.

Corey pulled up beside the car with his sputtering motorcycle. Smoke poured from the exhaust of his bike, and he was covered from head to foot in mud and brambles, but he had a huge smile on his face.

"I really think that I'm starting to get the hang of it." Corey called over the engine. "I almost missed that last tree back there. Another six inches to the right and I wouldn't have even hit it!"

"Good job, Corey." I said as Emily moved towards him and began examining his injuries worriedly.

A little while later, we made our way down the weedy trail and to the edge of the massive muddy field where the lake used to be. It didn't look like it had changed much at all. We knew from experience that the mud in the lakebed was almost like quicksand, and would pull you under fast if you were foolish enough to try to walk out on it.

We all stood on the bank for a long quiet moment, looking around.

"What are we looking for again?" Corey asked at last.

"Ghosts." I said. "Spirits. Fairies. Two-headed turtles. Talking caterpillars. Anything out of the ordinary."

"We've definitely come to the right place." Elayne said at last.

We all turned to her. "Why do you say that?" I asked.

She pointed her stubby finger towards the lakebed. "Fairy tracks." she said.

We all turned and looked down at the muddy ground. They were crisscrossed with random scratches and plastered in places with soggy leaves, but I couldn't see anything that resembled any type of footprints or tracks.

"Really?" Emily asked. "Where?"

"Everywhere." Elayne said. "They're all around the lakebed and on the bank here."

Corey shuffled his feet and looked at the grass he was standing in. Finally, he shrugged. "I don't see it."

"It's something we're taught to look for in my world." she said.

Corey looked around uncomfortably. "Are there..." he swallowed and lowered his voice. "Are there any fairies here right now?"

Elayne looked around and nodded. "Most likely. But they are all hidden. If we want to see where the portal is, we will have to come out here at night and watch them as they come and go."

Corey winced. "I knew that was coming."

Just to make sure we didn't miss anything important, we spent the rest of the afternoon checking out some of the other "haunted" locations in Jacob's Rest. One was a junkyard that was supposed to be haunted by people who had died in terrible car wrecks. We certainly saw lots of wrecked cars, stacked up high with weeds growing out of their engines... but nothing that we considered "unusual". We were chased out by a really mean-looking junkyard poodle that snarled and yapped after us as we jumped the fence to escape.

There was a pasture (close to Emily's house, actually), that was supposed to have been the scene of a bloody Revolutionary War battle. The book said that people had heard shots and screams and seen flashes of light from the haunted field on the anniversary of the battle (which was in June). On this day, we saw nothing but a dozen grazing cows who watched us boredly as they chewed. Corey shouted at one of them just to make sure it wouldn't talk back to us. We didn't get so much as a "moo" in response. Just your average cows.

There were other places mentioned in the book, too. Many were places we knew (like the duck pond outside of town or the small restaurant that had been built in an old red barn on Glasser Street). These were places that we knew well and didn't think were likely locations for a hidden portal to another world.

After we had checked all of the places off of our list, we were sitting in the car trying to decide where to go next. Emily said. "Well, that's it then for our Haunted Tour of Jacob's Rest. I guess that right now Lake Sorrow is our best bet."

Corey flipped through the *Haunted Valley* book in his hands. "Huh? You mean they didn't even have the Kasner house in here?"

Elayne looked up from the back seat. "What is a Kasner? Is that some sort of beast?"

Emily laughed. "No. Kasner is a person's name. The house is an abandoned house over on Lakes Road. The kids have been telling stories about it for as long as I can remember."

"That's because it's a real haunted house!" Corey said earnestly.

I rolled my eyes. "Corey. C'mon. You don't really believe that, do you?"

"You bet I do!" Corey said. "You heard about Ernie Johnson, right?"

I sighed. "Yeah, but…"

"What happened to Ernie Johnson?" Elayne asked curiously.

Corey turned in his seat to look back at her. "Some kids dared him to go into the house and just stay in there for five minutes. He went in, the door closed behind him, and he didn't come out. They sent the police in and they found him lying there on the floor in the den. He was never the same again. His family had to move… and I hear that Ernie is still in a hospital somewhere. He said that he heard voices talking to him in his head."

Elayne's eyes were wide. "That's horrible!"

"Oh, please." I said. "Ernie Johnson's family moved away, but he did not go insane and he is not in a hospital somewhere."

"Is too!" Corey protested.

Emily looked at her watch. "We still have plenty of time before dark. We might as well go and check out the Kasner House."

"Fine." I sighed. "Let's go."

The way to the house led us down a little dirt road in a wooded area. A stone mailbox out front had a metal plaque bolted to it with the word "Kasner" in tarnished green letters. It wasn't your typical-looking 'haunted house'. In fact, the house didn't look more than twenty years old. It definitely looked abandoned, though. The grass and flowerbeds had been swallowed by weeds and a gazebo out in the yard was falling apart. All of the windows of the house had been covered with big pieces of splintering plywood.

After we parked, I led the way and we walked up the cracked and weedy front sidewalk. Corey kept looking behind us as if he expected a monster to erupt from the yard and swallow us. Posted on the front door was a fading "No Trespassing" sign. Just in case the place was not as deserted as it looked, I knocked and we waited for a moment. When there was no answer, I tried to turn the knob.

"It's locked." I said. "Oh well, we tried."

"Amen!" Corey said, and he was already moving towards the car.

"Hold on," Emily called. "Let's go check around back."

Corey looked like he was about to protest, but decided to follow. We walked around the back of the house and found a beautiful brick patio there with crumbling white statues and fountains spread around it. There was also a big swimming pool.

"Ick." Corey said.

We followed his gaze and saw that the pool was filled with water that was as black as ink. There were a few scattered leaves floating on its surface and what looked to be the bloated dead body of an unfortunate squirrel.

The black pool, sitting amid the cracked and vine-choked statues, definitely gave the whole area a creepy feel. I understood now why the kids in the town had started thinking the place was haunted.

On the back of the house, all of the windows and even the back door was boarded shut. There was no way in.

I took one last look around. "Creepy," I said. "But no sign of any fairies." I turned to Elayne. "Right?"

Elayne was looking at the black water in the pool. "There is an Urisk living in the pool." she said, "but there don't seem to be any other fairies close by."

Corey took a startled step back from the pool. "What's a Urisk?"

"Water fairy." Elayne said. "Not always too friendly. It's probably best if we keep our distance."

Corey didn't have to be told twice. He took another ten steps back from the pool.

"Hey guys, over here." Emily called. We looked up and saw that she was standing near the house beside one of the boarded-up windows. She had pulled up one corner of the plywood and was looking behind it. "I think I found a way in."

When we reached her, I looked behind the plywood and saw a darkened window. A little pull showed me that the window was unlocked.

"I'm not going in there!" Corey said quickly.

Emily, still holding up the plywood, rolled her eyes. "Aw, c'mon you big baby. We need to check it out. If we don't find a portal back to Elayne's world then we have no chance at all of stopping Sidhera."

Corey crossed his arms. "I'm not going to go insane like Ernie Johnson!"

"I'll go." Elayne said quickly. "I know what to look for."

I hesitated, looking at the dark window beneath the flap of plywood. "I'll go with you." I said.

Elayne stopped and looked at me. For a moment, I thought that she may say that she didn't want me to come, but she remained quiet and turned instead back to the window. A moment later, we had it open and we had both squeezed inside.

The house was dark and had a dusty smell to it. It wasn't old or run down, though. In fact, it looked like a normal, everyday house that had just been abandoned. As we walked though the shadowy hallway, we saw bedrooms with neatly made beds, a study with papers still lying on the desk, a play room with toys and dolls scattered on the floor, and even toothbrushes with an opened tube of toothpaste lying near the bathroom sink. In the kitchen, we opened the cabinets to see canned foods and boxes of cereal. When I looked in the refrigerator, it was empty and the power was off.

"Look." Elayne said.

On the kitchen table was a folded newspaper. I squinted at the date in the darkness and saw that it was from nine years ago.

"That's probably the last time anyone lived here." I said. I put the paper down and looked around. "You see any sign of fairies?" I asked.

Elayne had an odd look on her face. "Not exactly..." she said slowly. "But..." She turned quickly towards the kitchen doorway, as if hoping to catch someone sneaking up on her. The doorway appeared empty. "Did you see that?" she asked tensely.

I got a little prickle in my spine. "What?"

She looked at the doorway uncertainly. "I'm not sure. I thought I saw something out of the corner of my eye."

I stared at the kitchen doorway. "It's got to be the shadows." I said. "The light is so dim in here that it's messing with your eyes."

Elayne jerked her head again quickly toward the doorway, and watched it closely for another moment. "Maybe..." she said, then she closed her eyes and put her finger up to her forehead.

"Hey guys, let's go!" We heard Corey call from somewhere in the house. "I want to get out of here before this freaky thing in the pool decides that it's hungry!"

"Yes, let's go." a voice said.

"Okay, let's go." Elayne said.

I turned and looked at Elayne. "Fine, you don't have to tell me twice."

Elayne cast a puzzled look at me, but started walking back towards the bedroom with the window where we had come in.

A few minutes later, we were outside again. Corey looked at me with wide eyes. "You guys okay?"

"We didn't go insane like Ernie Johnson, if that's what you mean." I said sarcastically.

Emily let go of the flap of plywood once we were outside and the window was closed behind us again. "Anything unusual?" she asked.

"Just an empty house." I said.

Emily looked disappointed. "Well, ok. At least we still have Lake Sorrow tonight."

When we were back at the car, I was unlocking my door when I saw a shadowy flicker of movement from the corner of my eye. I looked up towards the mailbox with the tarnished sign, but didn't see anything there.

I paused a moment, uncertain.

"What's wrong?" Corey asked, waiting for me to unlock the car door.

After another second, I shook my head. "Nothing. I think that my sleepless night is just now catching up with me."

I unlocked the car and we all piled in.

Chapter Twelve

The Lake at Night

 ince it was still daylight, we went back to the library to work. I ended up falling asleep on the couch in the reading nook while the others poured over books and maps. The overwhelming exhaustion from the night before had finally caught up with me and I fell into a deep and dreamless sleep.

When I woke up, the library was lit by lamps and the fading evening light was deepening the shadows outside the big window.

"'C'mon Rip van Winkle!" Corey prodded as I tried to open my eyes. "The librarian is kicking us out."

I pulled myself up, my head still heavy with sleep, and tiredly rubbed my messy hair. Emily and Elayne were waiting by the door. Corey stood above me, watching me with a big, expectant grin.

"What's so funny?" I asked, yawning and looking at Corey's amused grin suspiciously. I ran my fingers through my hair. "What did you do? Put spitballs in my hair while I was asleep?"

Corey shook his head. "Nah. We're all just laughing because you've been dancing like a circus monkey for the last few hours, that's what."

I squinted up at him. "What are you talking about?"

Corey laughed. "You were moving in your sleep. You kept moving your arms up and down, up and down. One time you even talked."

I looked at him doubtfully. "I talked in my sleep? What did I say?"

"You were waving your hands in circles and you said 'this is so cool!' and then you went 'Weee! I have hands! Weee!'" Corey burst out laughing again.

"No I didn't!" I said, shocked.

"Yes you did! Ask the girls."

I looked up at Emily and Elayne. They both nodded. Emily was suppressing a giggle.

I frowned. "Man. I guess I was more exhausted than I thought."

Corey clapped me on the back. "Don't worry about it, bro. We all enjoyed the show. Now let's go explore the creepy haunted lake."

On the way to the lake, Corey sat in the front seat beside me and the girls rode quietly in the back. Darkness had fallen quickly and it was already black outside. I drove carefully up the tiny winding road that led towards the lake.

In the silence of the drive, I thought about the crazy things Corey had said I was doing in my sleep. "What was it that you called me when I woke up?" I asked Corey.

"Rip van Winkle." Corey said. "Remember that story from when we were kids? Grandpa would read it to us before bed."

I did remember. I even remembered the pictures from the old tattered storybook he would read from.

"We know the tale of Rip van Winkle even in my world." Elayne said from the back seat. "He was enchanted by pixies as he slept under a tree and when he awoke, a hundred years had passed."

Emily chuckled. "Sound kind of familiar? Was he awakened by the kiss of true love or..." Emily seemed to catch herself and grew suddenly quiet.

Nobody spoke again for the rest of the trip.

Something tickled the back of my mind, though. Something that I knew was important, but stayed just out of reach. *Rip van Winkle.* I thought. *There's something about the story of Rip van Winkle that could help us with all of this...*

Then, I saw the ghostly lights in the road ahead and all other thoughts were forgotten.

After a day of searching Jacob's Rest's "Most Haunted Places" and coming up empty-handed, I think that all of us still half-expected to come to the lake that night and see nothing but an empty lakebed and maybe a raccoon or two.

The moment we crested that final hill, though, we knew that this was going to be something different.

What we thought at first was the light of a swinging lantern crossing the road, turned out to be a bobbing white light that disappeared when the headlights crossed its path. It reappeared again a moment later, joined by two others, a little way down the overgrown path that led towards the lake.

"Will-o-wisps" Elayne whispered as I parked the car and shut off the lights.

"Willa who?" Corey asked, staring with wide-eyes at the floating lights bobbing down the trail and out of sight.

"Will-o-wisps," Elayne repeated. "Ignis Fatuus. Swamp lights. They are lesser fairies found around swamps or bogs."

"Or giant muddy lakebeds." Emily murmured.

Elayne nodded. "Yes. They are cruel creatures. They will lure hapless travelers into the swamp where they watch them drown."

I shuddered. "Is it safe to follow them?" I asked.

Elayne opened her door. "Yes. As long as we stay together we should be okay. If you notice that one of us starts to fall into a trance, though, shake us awake immediately."

The path was treacherous at night and I felt really stupid for not remembering to bring a flashlight. We all stuck together, though, and moved carefully through the weeds towards the lake. As we neared, we saw more will-o-wisps moving ahead of us, bobbing eerily in the silence. Occasionally, we would also hear something rustle the grass nearby or flutter through the tree branches overhead.

When we finally broke from the trees and came to the wide-open lakebed, the moon overhead lit things with a silvery glow and the wind blew against our faces and rattled the trees behind us.

"Holy moly!" Corey gasped, looking out at the lakebed.

"There it is." Elayne whispered. "Just as we suspected."

I followed Elayne and Corey's astonished gazes and saw…

Nothing.

I squinted into the darkness. There was one lonesome, silent will-o-wisp floating nearby as if just begging one of us to step into the muddy lakebed… but I didn't see anything else at all.

Emily seemed just as confused. "What?" she whispered tensely. "I don't see anything."

Corey guffawed loudly. "Ha! Yeah right. Man, I have never seen so many fairies in one place. It looks like the circus is in town! Just look at that freak show."

"There's a group of hobgoblins that just crawled out of that hole there." Elayne said, pointing. "That must be where the portal is. Look! See. A phouka just stepped into it."

I looked to where she was pointing. I saw only the empty lakebed under the silvery moonlight.

Emily looked exasperated. "You guys are kidding, right? There's nothing there." she said.

"I don't see anything, either." I said in the darkness.

Corey turned to me, surprised. "You guys are serious? You don't see all of this?"

I looked out across the empty lakebed. Even the ghostly will-o-wisp had disappeared now. I turned back to Corey. "No. Nothing."

We looked at Elayne. She looked confused. "Well, I can see them because it is one of my birth-gifts."

"Your birth-gifts carried over to your new body?" I asked, surprised.

Elayne looked offended. "Of course! They were gifts of spirit, not of body."

"Except for your gift of Beauty, obviously." Corey snorted.

Emily poked him in the ribs and he cried out.

Elayne sighed, looking down at her pudgy fingers with their yellowed and cracked fingernails. "Well, that's true. MOST of my birth-gifts are still intact."

I shook my head. "Alright, but Corey doesn't have any birth-gifts. How come he can see them and we can't?"

Elayne looked at Corey, confused. "I'm not sure." She thought for a moment, then her eyes grew big. "Corey, are you holding my birthday present?"

Corey thought about this. "Hey! Yeah. That's right. The four-leaf clover." He dug into the pocket of his jeans and fished out the tiny four-leaf clover globe that Elayne had given him.

"Let me see..." I said, and Corey slipped the small ball into my hand. Immediately, the world around me jumped into sharp focus and I saw what Elayne and Corey had been talking about.

First of all, the lakebed was lit up with what looked like hundreds of will-o-wisps. They bobbed up and down all across the lake like carnival lights playing in the breeze. Moving among them were creatures of all shapes and sizes. Walking, crawling, even flying. Most were just shadowy forms flitting between the lights. Sometimes, though, I would catch a glimpse of a bearded face or some tattered clothes. Once, I saw something carrying a big silver axe walk close by.

I handed the clover to Emily and she looked out at the lakebed and gasped.

We each took turns, passing the tiny amber ball around once more as Elayne pointed out the spot where she thought the portal was. It was close to the lake's edge, under an overhang of trees. It did indeed look as if the creatures were coming and going through some sort of hole in the ground.

"That's probably what happened to all of the water in the lake all those years ago." I said thoughtfully. "A portal opened up and drained it… but nobody could actually see the hole."

Emily shuddered. "It's creepy to think about all of these things walking around Jacob's Rest at night and nobody can even see them."

I agreed completely.

"You can only see about half of them with the clover. You should see what I see. It's a real parade of storybook freaks."

"Really?" I asked Corey.

Corey turned to me. "Really what?"

"You said that you can only see about half of them with the clover. Is that true?"

Corey shrugged. "I didn't say that."

"That is true, though." Elayne said. "The clover will only let you see most of them. Some of the stronger fairies cannot be seen if they do not want to be seen."

I hesitated, still looking at Corey. "Well, then who said…"

"We should go." Elayne continued. "As the moon gets higher, some of the nastier fairies will start to appear and we probably shouldn't be around when they do."

That got us all moving. Silently, we crept away from the edge of Lake Sorrow and made our way back towards our parked car.

Chapter Thirteen

Washington's Dark Rider

 hen I woke up the next morning, light was already pouring brightly through my window. I looked at the clock on my bedside table and saw that it was past 10:00 already.

My muscles were sore… I guessed from running from the soldiers a few days ago. I was still exhausted and I felt like I had had a restless and odd night. Also, my stomach was aching. It felt bloated and full for some strange reason.

When I stretched and turned, I heard an odd rustling beneath my covers; the crackle of paper and plastic. Curiously, I reached down and pulled the sheets aside. I was stunned to see the bed was full of trash. Wrappers and crumbs, bits and big chunks of food filled my bed. There was a bag of potato chips that I remembered seeing in the pantry downstairs.

There were no less than three empty bags of microwave popcorn and seven empty cans of coke.

I stared at the pile in disbelief, my heart pounding fast.

How had this happened? When I looked down at my fingers, I saw that they were smeared with grease and salt. With growing alarm, I realized that I had somehow done this. While I was sleeping, I had done this.

My stomach turned again. It was really starting to ache now.

At that moment Corey walked in, already in jeans and a sweatshirt. He started to say something, then took a double-take at the pile of trash in my bed.

"I was going to ask if you wanted some breakfast." he said, "But looks like you've already eaten."

After I got dressed, I cleaned up the mess and changed my sheets. My mind was still frantically wondering what had happened to me last night. Was it stress? Was I sleepwalking (and sleep eating) because deep down I was so upset about my breakup with Elayne? Was it because I was so tired and had not slept the night before? Even more frightening: Had one of the fairies at the lake last night put some sort of spell on me? It certainly sounded like one of the mischievous spells a fairy would enjoy. I had to remember to ask the others if anything strange had happened to any of them last night.

Thinking about "mischievous spells" and fairies also reminded me of something else. I went over to my closet and rummaged around until I found an old cardboard box in the back. I grabbed it and dragged it out into my room. Scribbled letters in black magic marker on the top spelled out "Old Books".

Inside were a bunch of books I had put away, either because I hadn't liked them or had outgrown them. I dug through them, smiling at a few that I remembered hearing as bedtime stories when I was little. *Little Toot, Wacky Wednesday...* the covers were tattered on some, but I could have probably still recited some of them by heart.

Finally, near the bottom, I found what I was looking for. A tattered, light-blue picture book called *Rip van Winkle*.

The picture on the cover showed an old man sleeping against a tree. He had long white hair and a white, tangled beard that snaked on the ground all around him. There were tiny creatures laughing and dancing all around him as he slept.

Looking at the picture gave me a chill. The tiny creatures were obviously fairies of some sort. Looking at the old man with his long cartoon beard, I couldn't help but wonder: *Was he real?*

That would have sounded like an absurd question to me a little more than a year ago, but now I knew the truth. Some fairy tales *are* real.

I shuddered, looking at the front of the book again. Then, I noticed something:

Rip van Winkle was in big blue letters across the top of the cover. Then down below, at the bottom of the faded, peeling picture, was the author's name in yellow letters: *Washington Irving.*

Emily and Elayne were already downstairs, sitting in the den with Corey and eating sandwiches.

"There he is!" Corey announced when I entered. "The amazing human eating machine!"

Emily was stifling a laugh, but Elayne avoided my eyes altogether, as she had been doing for the last day and a half.

"Thanks for telling them, Corey." I said grumpily. "I'll be sure to remember that next time you do something embarrassing."

I tossed the book down in the middle of the coffee table and it landed with a loud "pop!" that drew everyone's attention.

"Hey!" Corey said. "You found that book you were looking for!"

"Look at the author's name." I said.

Emily's eyes grew large as she looked at the book. "Washington Irving!"

Elayne sat forward. "Is this the one? Does this Washington have ties with fairies or magic?"

I pointed to the creatures on the cover. "This story has fairies in it."

Elayne picked up the book and thumbed through it. "But I don't recall the tale of Rip van Winkle having any 'dark riders' in it... unless this writer has told the story differently from the way I heard it in my world."

I shook my head. "No. You're right. There's nothing about a dark rider."

Emily finished the sandwich she was eating and took the book. She flipped to the back and started looking at the last page. "Let's see. Washington Irving. Born in New York in 1783. First popular American author. Wrote stories and essays. His most famous tales are *Rip van Winkle* and..." Emily paused, her eyes growing wide.

"And what?" Corey prompted with his mouth still full of food.

"*The Legend of Sleepy Hollow*." Emily said.

I felt a cold prickle in my aching stomach.

"Huh?" Corey asked, confused. "What's that?"

"Washington's Dark Rider." I said, feeling the rising fear in my chest. "The Headless Horseman."

Corey actually jumped, spilling the drink in his hand. "What?" he cried. "Are you serious?"

Elayne, watching Corey's reaction, looked a bit wide-eyed herself. "What is this Headless Horseman?" she asked. "I don't know this tale."

Still in shock, I shook my head to try to clear it. "Um... well. I don't know the whole story, either. People usually tell it around Halloween... about a headless ghost that rides a horse at night, mostly trying to cut off people's heads, I think."

Emily glanced at her watch. "The library should be open by now. Let's go see what we can find."

We found a lot.

First, we found a big, illustrated copy of Washington Irving's *The Legend of Sleepy Hollow*. On the cover was a terrifying headless man riding a blazing-eyed horse. Before we started reading the story, Emily turned to the back of the book to read the information there.

Sleepy Hollow in Irving's story was in a valley in the Catskill Mountains of New York. The short biography in the back of the book said that the name of the real town was Tarrytown... which was the town just north of us. We used to go shopping at the Grand Union there before they built a Shop-Rite in Jacob's Rest.

"That's here..." Corey gasped, "In our valley!"

"If these are real places that he's writing about," I said quietly, "then the rest of the story could be real, too."

"Let's hear it." Elayne said, and Emily settled on the couch and began to read aloud.

The story was about a schoolteacher name Ichabod Crane that taught in Sleepy Hollow in the 1800's. He was a very superstitious man and believed in ghosts and goblins and loved spooky tales. In the story, he falls in love with a wealthy farmer's daughter... but the author gives the impression that he was more interested in her money than her.

Also in love with the farmer's daughter was a rowdy country boy named Brom Bones who liked to play practical jokes on people. One night after a party, Ichabod was riding home in the dark and he met up with the Headless Horseman, who was supposed to be the spirit of a Hessian soldier killed in the Revolutionary War. Supposedly, he carried his head on the saddle in front of him and chased the school teacher, scaring him badly and finally throwing his head at him to knock him off his horse.

At the end of the story, we find out that it was probably Brom Bones pretending to be the Horseman and it had been a pumpkin (and not a head) that had been thrown. Still, the schoolteacher was scared off and ran to live in some other town.

Corey looked cheated when Emily was finished reading the story aloud.

"He was a fake!" Corey protested. "The Horseman wasn't even a real ghost!"

"That's true," Elayne said, "but in the story they talked about the legend of the *real* Headless Horseman. Those are the parts we need to pay attention to. They talk about a churchyard where the Horseman was most often seen, and a bridge nearby that led to a road with trees that closed in overhead."

"That sounds like Tulip Bluff." Emily said thoughtfully. "Isn't there an old church and graveyard up there near a stream?"

Corey nodded. "Mrs. Miller took us for a field trip there in second grade." he said. "Some kind of nature hike. I remember a little wooden bridge up there, too."

"Alright." I said. "Let's split up and see if we can find any more books on Washington Irving or the Headless Horseman. We'll come back together in a few hours and share what we learned."

Corey, Emily, and Elayne nodded and we split up and got to work.

That evening, we sat around the kitchen table in our empty farmhouse, finishing a late dinner of hot dogs and potato chips. Corey had just gotten up to turn on the heat, and the radiators along the floorboards began to pop and crack as they filled with hot water.

Elayne sat across from me and avoided meeting my eyes. It was awkward and uncomfortable. I couldn't help but remember Corey's birthday breakfast only days before when Elayne had secretly taken my hand in hers under the table. I missed that closeness with her so badly that it made my stomach twist in knots.

Emily was the first to get out her notepad and read.

"Well," she began. "I went back and looked more closely at Washington Irving's story to see what I could find out about our friend the Headless Horseman." She licked some ketchup off her fingers as she flipped through her notes. "He is described as 'riding on the wind'. He can ride across the countryside in moments... supposedly on a ghostly black steed." She paused here and turned to Corey. "That's a horse, in case you were wondering."

Corey, his mouth full of hotdog, looked indignant. "I know what a 'steed' is!"

Emily smiled and gave him a playful wink. "I'm just saying 'cause I know you're afraid of horses."

Corey rolled his eyes. "More worried about the evil headless ghost in this case, but thanks for your concern."

Emily returned to her notes. "That bridge definitely seems to be important. In the story, he can't cross it. There is a legend about the Horseman chasing one rider to the bridge. The rider got across safely and the Horseman, furious that he couldn't follow across the bridge, exploded into a flaming skeleton."

"How sweet." I commented wryly.

Emily smiled. "Right? That's what I thought, too."

"I got some better stuff." Corey said, taking a swig of Coke before grabbing up the crumpled paper where he had scrawled some notes. "This one book I found on old legends says that the Headless Horseman has been seen in the valleys around here for over two hundred years. Lately, though, he seems to have gotten a bit shy. Nobody's reported seeing him since 1942. I guess he's embarrassed about not having a head and all."

Emily giggled and Corey took another hot dog and started to load it up.

I rubbed my eyes. "Well, my books said a lot of the same things. I did find this one story by a guy who claims to have actually seen the Headless Horseman and survived. He was chased right down that same road that all of the stories talk about... the one leading up to the bridge by the old church. He says that the dark rider moved like the wind and swung at his head with a flaming sword."

Corey paused in the act of putting ketchup on his new hot dog. "Flaming sword?" he asked carefully.

"That could be the 'flame that forever burns' that the clue talks about..." Elayne said.

I nodded. "Yeah, that's what I'm thinking, too."

Elayne watched me for a moment, thinking, then she cleared her throat. "The way this Horseman is described, he doesn't actually sound like a fairy or a beast from my world." She took a deep breath here and paused, considering. "I think that what we're dealing with is a phantom. A vengeful spirit who haunts a specific place... probably the place where he was killed."

Corey swallowed the bite he had been chewing and his eyes were growing fearful.

"That would match up with the stories of him being the ghost of a fallen Hessian soldier." Emily said.

"If it's just a spirit, then it can't hurt us, right?" Corey said hopefully. "It's like Casper, right? If he tried to grab us, his hands would just go right through us... right?"

Elayne furrowed her bushy black eyebrows and shook her head. "No, Corey. Phantoms are extremely dangerous. It's true that a phantom's image is like a shadow... if we tried to touch it, we would pass right through it just like you say. But that sword. That flaming sword with the fairy magic of fire burning on its blade. *That* is deadly. If the phantom were to touch someone with that sword, their death would be instant and painful."

Corey's face had turned a chalky white. We all sat in stunned silence around the table, our appetites lost.

"Well, then how is this going to be possible?" I said finally. "Sounds like the Horseman hasn't come out for over fifty years... and even if he was nice enough to show up for us, then we can't hurt him or even touch him. This isn't like Old Man Wembly trying to scare off the tourists in an episode of Scooby Doo. We can't toss a net over him or catch him in a sheet. I mean... how do you catch a shadow? Plus, if he can move like the wind and is swinging a flaming sword around... then even if we could find him, we don't stand a chance against him, right? Are we just going to ask him super nicely if we could take a little smidgen of that magic fire from his sword?"

There was a long silence as everyone looked around the table uncertainly at everyone else.

Corey shrugged. "If we asked him pretty please with sugar on it, he might consider..."

I gritted my teeth. "Corey, be serious..."

Elayne's eyes grew wide. "Corey! You're a genius!"

Corey looked even more stunned than me and Emily. "I... I am?" he asked, trying to decide if Elayne was being sarcastic.

"It's not sugar, though." she said. "It's salt."

Corey looked confused. "Huh? Pretty please with salt on it? I don't think that's really an expression, is it?"

Elayne shook her head. "No. I mean that salt will paralyze a spirit... trap it in place momentarily."

"Really?" Emily asked.

Elayne nodded.

I sighed. "Problem still remains, though. How do we get him to even appear for us?"

We all grew silent for another long moment, then finally Elayne spoke up again. "A phantom is most likely to be seen on the Night of the Converging Stars."

We all blinked at her.

"The what of the whosits?" Corey asked.

"The Night of the Converging Stars." Elayne continued. "It is a time once a year in my kingdom where the barrier between our world and the spirit world is the thinnest. A night when ghosts and spirits are most likely to be seen."

"You're talking about Halloween." I said slowly.

"Yes!" Elayne said. "When is that? Isn't it coming soon?"

Corey leaned back and looked at the calendar on the front of Grandpa's refrigerator. At the same time he spoke, I seemed to hear another voice, close by, say the same thing at the same time: "It's tomorrow."

Chapter Fourteen

Charlie

he next morning, I awoke to find myself lying backwards in my bed. It was a strange and disorienting way to wake up, and when I finally realized why things seemed so turned around, I realized something else: I had my tennis shoes on.

No pants or shirt. Just my underwear and my tennis shoes.

Early morning light was filtering in through my window. As I struggled to understand my strange position and blink the sleep from my eyes, I realized that my muscles were also aching as if I had just finished running a marathon.

I sat up and looked at the untied tennis shoes on my feet.

Did I have those on when I went to bed last night? I don't remember...

I shook my head and tramped tiredly down the stairs. It was still early. Corey wasn't even up yet. I walked across the kitchen and reached into the cabinet for the cereal. That was when I first saw the smoke.

It was a black, greasy smoke filling up the front yard outside the window. Forgetting about my lack of clothing, I ran to the door and out into the cold morning air to see what was on fire.

What I saw there made my jaw drop open.

My car was sitting in the front yard, its front smashed up where it had run into the heavy marble bird bath there. The windshield was gone. The driver's door was wide open... and the engine was still running. It was sputtering and churning, belching out plumes of black smoke into the morning air.

Shocked, I stood for a moment, trying to understand what I was seeing.

Corey! I thought angrily. *Corey snuck out last night and took my car for a drive! He must have gone over to Emily's!*

Angry heat rising in my face, I tramped across the dew-covered grass to where the car door was open. The front seat was empty and I found my keys in the ignition. I turned off the car and the engine immediately fell silent in the cold morning air.

"Sorry. I guess I can't drive as well as I thought."

I spun around at the sound of the voice, ready to yell at Corey... furious that he had stolen my keys in the night and taken the car behind my back.

My angry words died in my throat as I spun to see the empty yard behind me.

I turned from side to side, still ready to lash out, but I couldn't see anyone. The voice had been right beside my ear...

"Corey!" I yelled.

"He's sleeping." the voice said wryly. "Hey, did you know that your car can go about one-fifty even though the speedometer only goes up to a hundred and ten? It really starts to shake once you pass ninety, though."

I walked to a nearby bush and bent it aside roughly, expecting to see Corey hiding there. "Where are you, Corey?" I demanded.

"Your brother is sleeping right now. You can blame him if you want, though. In fact... Aw, man! I should have kept quiet and let you blame him! That would have been fun to watch."

Now I was starting to get a bit leery. "Where are you?" I asked out loud.

I walked around to the other side of the car and bent down on the wet grass to look underneath. There was nothing there but pieces of the smashed birdbath.

"I'm a voice in your head."

That made me pause, my stomach clenching tightly.

"In my head?" I asked slowly.

"Yup. Oh! Hey. Car coming in thirty seconds. You probably don't want to be out in your front yard in just your boxers and shoes."

I glanced down the long empty road that passed in front of our house. It was empty both ways.

"Who are you?" I asked again. "Is this a spell? A fairy trick?"

The voice seemed to chuckle. "Always so easy to blame the fairies, isn't it? Naw, not a fairy. I did find it real interesting that you're so wrapped up with fairies, though. I really didn't expect that when I hopped onboard."

I was still looking around the empty front yard warily. "Uh-huh. You say you're not a fairy. So... what are you?"

"You can call me Charlie for now."

I stood motionless for a long moment. "You're a voice in my head named Charlie?"

At that moment, a car came over the hill and I didn't have time to move before it was driving past. Even as it slowed, I saw some girls gawking at me from the windows of the passing car. I think I recognized them from school.

Although I should have been embarrassed beyond words, I stood, rooted to the spot, stunned that I was talking with a voice in my head.

"Told you a car was coming." the voice said.

I looked up the empty road. "How could you have heard that so far in advance?" I asked carefully. "Lucky guess, right?"

The voice (Charlie) laughed again. "Let's just say that from my position I can see things coming from a little farther away… time-wise, that is."

"You can see into the future." I said doubtfully.

"Yup. Just a little. Oh… and I knew you were going to say that, by the way."

I hesitated for a moment, considering the situation. "You're doing something while I sleep."

"And thank you for that!" Charlie said. "I've been having the time of my afterlife. You don't mind, do you? I figured your body is just lying there, going to waste at night anyway. Might as well get some use out of it."

I felt a shiver go up my back. "You are the reason my bed was full of food yesterday morning." I said slowly.

Charlie sighed longingly. "Oh, yes. And what a glorious feast it was. Do you know that it has been years since I've had ice cream and mustard?"

My stomach turned, although not at the thought of eating ice cream and mustard. I was realizing with growing terror that I really may be going crazy.

"You're not going crazy." the voice said matter-of-factly.

I held my breath. "You can read my thoughts?"

This time Charlie laughed out loud. "No… I could just see it in your expression."

"This can't be happening." I muttered. "I am going crazy."

"Nah." Charlie said. "Although you do talk in your sleep sometimes about that woman Elayne. Were you really in love with her? I gotta tell you… you're not so great looking yourself, but you could probably do much, much better than that wiry-haired marshmallow."

"Don't talk about her like that!" I snapped instinctively.

Charlie gave a slow whistle, an eerie sound in the empty morning air. "Wow. I take that back. You didn't used to love mole-face... you STILL love mole-face. Man, that's just gross. Well, everybody has got their own tastes, I guess."

The voice paused for a moment, as if considering. "I will say this about her, though." Charlie continued. "She's got quite a cocktail of magic inside of her. When I tried to hop into her head back at the house, all that magic rolling around inside her was like a tidal wave throwing me back."

Back at the house...

"Wait a minute." I said suddenly. "What house? You mean the Kasner house that Elayne and I went into?"

The voice was suddenly silent.

"Was that you... that shadow that she thought she saw in the kitchen?"

A long pause. Nothing.

"Hello?" I asked.

Another car passed as it drove along the road in the front of the house. I didn't even bother looking this time.

The voice remained silent.

"Charlie?" I asked again into the silent morning air.

No reply. Just me, standing beside my wrecked car in my front yard.

Fine. I thought. *Be that way. Good riddance.*

I decided, for the time being, to keep the voice in my head a secret from the others. I still was not completely convinced that I wasn't just overtired and sleepwalking… and I didn't want to sound crazy by bringing it up.

I had to make up some story about the car slipping out of gear and rolling down the driveway at night to crash into the birdbath. Corey looked shocked, but didn't question it too much. The car was still drivable, although it now smoked like a chimney and it wouldn't go much faster than forty-five miles an hour. By the time we picked up the girls, the sun was high and it was a cold, clear day.

Tulip Bluff was actually a nice place in the daylight. The trees there were big, old trees that arced up high overhead and were covered with mossy vines that hung down and swayed gently in the breeze. The sunlight was almost blotted out by the high-reaching branches, and the uneven dirt road that led to the bluff was a long, shadowy stretch.

At the end of the wooded road was a creek and a small plank bridge that was only about ten feet across. After the bridge, the ground sloped upwards onto a green hillside. At the top was the abandoned shell of an old church surrounded by the crumbling ruins of a small cemetery.

"Creepy." Corey declared.

The four of us stood on the dirt road that led to the bridge. This was the place that the Horseman was most often seen in the old legends.

"It's not creepy." Emily said, looking around the quiet woods. "I think it's nice."

Corey rolled his eyes. "Right. The cemetery view is just lovely."

"We're close to the far bank of Lake Sorrow." I said. "I think it's just about a mile through the woods there."

Elayne looked at the small bridge in the sunlight at the end of the long shadowy road. "So that's the bridge that the Horseman cannot cross?" she asked.

"Right." I said. "That's home base. If the Horseman comes after us, then we just have to run to the other side of that bridge and we'll be safe."

Corey nodded. "But there won't even be a chase, right? If we see him, we'll toss some salt on him and freeze that sucker. Should make things a piece of cake, right?"

I looked to Elayne for confirmation, but Elayne was silent, looking at the bridge.

Corey turned to her. "Um… no chase will be involved… right, Elayne?"

Elayne was biting her lip thoughtfully. "Well…"

I didn't like the sound of that one bit. "Well, what?" I asked.

"Well, it's true that salt will paralyze most spirits... temporarily."

Corey crossed his arms and leveled a look at Elayne. "Temporarily? What does that mean exactly? How long?"

Elayne shrugged. "It depends on the spirit. Could be hours… minutes."

"Minutes!" Corey exclaimed

Elayne looked down guiltily. "Maybe seconds."

"What?" I jumped in as Corey's mouth dropped open in silent shock. "Seriously? You're saying that if we toss some salt on him that he may only be stunned for a few seconds?"

Elayne nodded. "But that's all we need, right?" she said quickly. "A few seconds to get some fire from his sword and then we can get to the bridge. Just freeze him by the bridge and be ready to run across it."

Emily shook her head. "But we have to meet the Horseman here." she said, pointing to a huge elm tree nearby. "The stories say that he appears by a giant elm tree where he was probably killed." She turned and pointed to the distant bridge.

"The bridge is way down the road there and he 'runs like the wind', remember? We won't be able to outrun him."

"Can't we just keep throwing salt on him to stun him for longer?" Corey asked.

Elayne shook her head. "No. If it works, it will only work once."

"What do you mean 'if' it works." I said. "You told us that salt would work."

"Well, salt on a spirit or phantom *will* stun them. We're assuming that this Headless Horseman is really a phantom and not... something else."

I narrowed my eyes. "Something else... like what?"

Elayne looked exasperated. "I don't know! Even I can't name every type of beast or ghoul in existence! It could be anything!"

I clenched my hands in frustration. "So what you're saying is that IF this is a spirit and IF we can get close enough to toss some salt on him, then he MAY be stunned for a few seconds... during which we are supposed to somehow get some fire off of his deadly flaming sword, and then run a half mile to the bridge while the scary headless ghoul who can move as fast as the wind is chasing after us?"

The pudgy brown eyes in Elayne's face flashed angrily at me. "Yes, that is the plan! If you have a better one Mr. Know-It-All, then feel free to say so at any time!"

"Whoa! Okay you two." Emily jumped in. "Time out. Take it easy. I know we're all a little freaked out right now, but we need to just calm down."

Elayne continued to glare at me and I clenched my teeth, biting back my angry response.

"You guys keep talking about 'getting some fire off of his sword'." Corey said. "What the heck does that even mean? Are we going to just get a stick and light it on fire from his sword? Then what? We run with it like the Olympic Torch all the way to Sidhera?"

Elayne, still glaring at me angrily, shook her head. "No, Corey. We will need something to hold the fire in. Some magic container."

"A magic container?" Corey said sarcastically. "Do they sell those at Jamesway? What isle would they be in? Is it like Tupperware?"

I took a deep breath. "We've got a magic container." I said. "in fact, we still have two of them."

Corey looked puzzled. "What are you talking about, bro?"

"The vials." Emily said with realization. "You mean the vials that held Elayne's wake-up potions last year."

I nodded. "I'm thinking that one of them should be just what we need."

Elayne nodded in agreement. "Yes. That might work."

Emily took a deep breath. "Alright. So if the Horseman shows up tonight like we hope, and if we can stun him and get some fire, we still need to run back to that bridge before he can separate our heads from our bodies."

"We can't run." Corey said. He was looking down the long shady lane to the distant bridge. "We'll never make it. You're right. We can't outrun something that can ride like the wind."

My eyes followed his gaze to the distant bridge. "What are our choices? The car is smashed up. You saw. It barely moves now. I'm surprised it even made it up here without falling apart."

"What about horses?" Emily asked "We could ride horses. Try to outrun him."

Corey scratched his head. "But in the stories, aren't the people always riding horses and doesn't he always catch up to them pretty easily?"

Emily nodded. "Yeah, but what else do we have?"

Corey considered for a moment. "I've got my motorcycle."

There was a moment of uneasy silence as Emily, Elayne, and I exchanged glances. Finally, I was the one who had to speak. "Er... Corey. I hate to tell you this, but... you really can't ride the motorcycle too well, can you?"

Corey looked at me indignantly. "What! I can too! You saw me that last time I rode it."

Emily winced. "That's the problem, Corey. We all saw you. And Jasen's right. You can hardly stay on the thing. No offense, Sweetie, but you don't really want to risk it while a murderous Horseman is chasing you and trying to cut off your head."

Corey straightened his shoulders, looking away towards the bridge again. "Well… I still have a few hours to practice. It's a straight shot down the road here. I wouldn't even have to steer it hardly."

I looked at the girls uncomfortably, then took a deep breath. "I hate to say it, but he's right. The motorcycle probably has a better chance of beating the horseman to that bridge."

Emily and Elayne looked incredulous. Corey looked at me with a thankful grin.

"Go get your bike, Corey" I said. "Let's see what you can do."

Chapter Fifteen

All Hallows Eve

 t got dark earlier than usual under the shade of the huge trees. Still we practiced. Corey drove back and forth between the elm tree and the bridge probably a hundred times that day. With each pass, he got a little better and by the time the big moon started weaving through the overhead branches, I was starting to think that maybe our plan had a shot at working.

The girls had gone to buy some salt. Lots of salt. They came back with two big sackfulls and we attached them like saddlebags to the sides of Corey's motorcycle.

We were standing together on the "safe" side of the bridge, near the old church, when I handed Corey the small silver vial to collect the magic in. Corey put it in the pocket of his jacket and looked up at me. I could tell that he was starting to get nervous.

I put my hand on his shoulder. "You'll do great." I said. "Simple plan. If he shows up, grab a handful of salt and toss it on him. Hold the vial up to his sword to get some of the fire, then take off on your motorcycle and get across the bridge, just like you've been practicing all day. Emily, Elayne, and I will be waiting on the other side of the bridge when you get there."

Corey nodded. "And what if he throws his head at me like he did in the story?"

I gave him a reassuring smile. "Then just duck."

"Alright. Good advice." Corey nodded seriously. "What time is it?" he asked.

"It's almost ten." I said. "You should probably get going."

Corey straightened his shoulders bravely. "Wish me luck."

I looked at him for a second, then I did something that I almost never did: I reached forward and gave him a hug.

Corey looked flabbergasted. "Gee, bro. Why don't you act like you'll never see me again? That will make me feel so much better..."

I laughed and moved away as he gunned the engine on his motorcycle and drove a few yards to where the girls were standing on the slope of the hill by the stream. In the shadowy darkness, I saw them each lean forward and hug him. Emily gave him a kiss.

Moments later, he gunned the engine again and took off across the bridge. We watched him disappear into the darkness, his single dim headlight getting further and further away. Finally, it became nothing but a barely-seen speck in the darkness as he reached the spot by the distant elm tree and turned around to face us again.

Seconds later, Corey's voice broke through the static from the Walkie-Talkie in my hand.

"Yo-yo-yo. Come in Big Brother this is DJ CoreyMaster in da house. Do you read?"

I picked up the radio and pressed the button. "Loud and clear." I answered.

I heard Emily sigh nervously in the darkness close by.

"He will be safe." Elayne said to her softly, although her own voice sounded uncertain.

We sat down together in the darkness beside the quiet stream and we watched the tiny speck of Corey's headlight… and we waited.

Midnight came and went. Most of our time was spent in tense silence, waiting anxiously for something to happen. Sometimes one of the girls would whisper something, and from time to time Corey would call out something crazy on the radio to break the tension (*"Clean up on isle five!"* or *"That was one small <burp> for man… one giant <BURP> for Mankind!"*)

For the most part, though, we all just sat nervously watching that distant light. When the air was still, we could faintly hear the stutter of the motorcycle engine, but then that sound would get lost again in the rustle of the cold wind through the overhead trees.

Sometime close to one o'clock, I started to get frustrated with the waiting.

"He's not coming. " I said finally. "Halloween is over. It's past midnight. He's not coming."

"All Hallows Eve lasts until the sun comes up." Elayne corrected. "And the witching hour for spirits is not midnight as so many of your stories say, It's four hours before dawn."

"We can't keep this up all night." Emily said worriedly. "Corey has got to be terrified out there by himself. We need to give him a break or something."

"You know that we cannot go past the bridge." Elayne said. "On foot, we would have no chance against the Horseman."

"But he's…" Emily began, then she let out a startled gasp and jumped to her feet.

"What?" I asked, jumping up beside her "What's wrong?"

"His light!" Emily said in a trembling voice. "The motorcycle light just went out!"

I strained in the darkness to see the distant light that we had been watching for hours. She was right. It was gone. My heart started pounding fearfully, and I snatched up the radio. "Corey." I said frantically. "Corey! Are you there?"

There was long, terrified moment when there was nothing but darkness and the sound of static from the radio. Then, Corey's voice broke through again. "It's alright!" Corey said. "I'm here. I'm alive."

At the sound of his voice, the terror in my chest loosened a little. I heard Emily and Elayne breathe again in the darkness.

"Out of gas." Corey's voice continued ruefully through the static. "I had filled it up before, but I didn't expect to be waiting this long."

"Hang on." I said into the radio. "We've got the gas can here. I'll bring it to you."

Walking down the shadowy lane in the darkness was unnerving, and I started to understand how Ichabod Crane may have felt in Washington Irving's story, coming home from a party late at night alone down this long, eerie stretch of road. The leafy vines hanging from overhead had looked so beautiful in the daytime, but now they seemed like tentacles reaching down from the ominous treetops.

When I reached Corey, he was talking on the radio with Emily. "Yes I'm sure I'm alright." he was telling her. "Hey! Here's Jasen now. He just got here. I gotta go."

Corey slipped the radio into his back pocket and turned towards me. "Man, Emily is really freaking out." he said.

I smiled in the darkness. "She's been like that for the last three hours now."

Corey was still straddling his silent motorcycle. In the darkness, I could see him unscrewing the cap from the gas tank. When he had it off, I lifted the can and the gurgling sound of gas pouring into the tank filled the silence before the wind picked up again.

"I think she really likes me." Corey said after a moment.

I laughed. "Yeah. She always has."

Corey shook his head and his voice got serious. "No, I mean... I think..." Corey hesitated.

"You think what?" I asked.

Corey bit his lip. "I think that she loves me."

Although I shouldn't have been surprised, I found that I was. "Really?" I asked. I heard the sound of the pouring gas tapering off and I pulled the can up, spilling a little across the top of the tank. I looked at Corey. "Has she said so? Has she told you that she loves you?"

Corey shook his head and took the cap in his hand, twisting it back on. "No, but I can tell."

I paused for a moment in the darkness, trying to read his face. "How do you feel about that?" I asked him.

Corey was quiet for a long moment, then he said quietly. "I think I may love her, too."

The sound of the wind rustling the trees overhead picked up again as I stood in the darkness and considered my little brother's startling confession.

"It just scares me, you know?" he said.

"Why?" I asked.

"Well, you and Elayne. You two were in love once. Now look at you. You can barely talk to each other without getting angry."

The wind sent a shower of fall leaves spiraling to the ground around us in the darkness. One of them landed on my shoulder and I plucked it off.

"I still love her." I said to Corey. "That hasn't changed."

Even without seeing his face, I could feel Corey's shock. I took a deep breath and shook my head. "It's just gotten so..."

Corey shifted in his seat and a static pop crackled from the radio.

I froze at the noise, holding my breath. "Um... Corey." I said carefully. "Were you sitting on the radio?"

Corey lifted the radio in the darkness. "Yeah, but it's alright I just..." his voice trailed off. "Oh no." he said with dawning horror. "You don't think that the girls could just hear what we were talking about, do you?"

I felt a dread in my stomach as I realized that they probably had. I was about to say so to Corey when I saw the red eyes appear suddenly in the darkness right behind him.

The shadows under the huge elm tree seemed to swim together for a moment, then shimmer into the form of a huge horse and rider. They stepped up silently behind Corey as the wind tossed a shower of leaves down around us again.

"What should we do?" Corey was asking me. "Should I call them up and tell them that it was just a joke?" he slapped his hand over his mouth suddenly. "Oh, man! Did I say that I loved Emily? Did she hear me say that?"

The hairs on the back of my neck were tingling as I watched the huge rider approach in the darkness. "Corey!" I whispered urgently.

Corey was pulling at his hair now. "Argh! This is going to make things so freaking awkward! How could I have not known the stupid radio was on! And what about you... what you said about Elayne. That's pretty..."

"Corey!" I hissed. "Behind you!"

I could see the terrifying horse clearly now. It had glowing red slits where eyes should have been. In the red glow, I saw its steamed breath puffing from its flaring nostrils. The rider on its back stood straight and silent. He must have been at least seven feet tall. His hands were hidden beneath a long cape, but even as he approached I could see only the stump of a neck where a head should have been.

Corey, finally sensing my warning, turned around and found himself face to face with the monstrous steed. With a sudden jolt of terror, he let out a terrified scream and jumped away, getting tangled up in the motorcycle and tumbling to the ground.

When Corey screamed, it was like a signal for the silent horseman. He threw open his cape and withdrew a sword as his black horse reared up on its hind legs and let out a bone-chilling wail. The sword burst into flames and lit up the terrifying apparition in a shimmering red glow.

"You'd better duck." I heard a voice say, and I recognized it instantly as Charlie's voice, seeming to come from somewhere close to my left ear.

Even as the horse's front hooves came down, the rider was swinging his sword towards me. In my paralyzed terror, I almost didn't move in time. When I threw myself to the ground at the last minute, I felt the red-hot flames of the sword sear the back of my neck, missing me by an inch.

I rolled on the ground as the demon steed jumped forward, trying to crush me beneath its hooves. I banged my shoulder hard against Corey's fallen bike. My hands clutched the bag of salt without thinking… and when I pulled, I could hear a rip as it ripped free. I tossed it upwards as the horse came down and a plume of salty powder burst from the bag. I screamed and I braced myself for the horse's hooves to come crashing down on my skull.

When the crushing blow didn't come, I looked up.

The huge horse was there, his heavy hooves hovering six inches above the top of my head.

The terrifying black horseman sat unmoving on its back, his flaming sword still raised high above his head.

Someone grabbed my shoulders and I screamed again, my heart about to burst through my chest. It was Corey. He dragged me quickly out from underneath the massive horse.

"You did it!" Corey shouted, out of breath. "Awesome shot, bro. Now we've got to get some of the fire from his sword before he can break free."

Seconds. I heard Elayne's voice in my head. *We have seconds.*

"Give me the vial." I said to Corey as I pulled myself up again.

Corey instantly slapped the cold silver vial into my hands. The red eyes of the horse glared at me and steam puffed from its nostrils furiously.

"It's still breathing!" Corey said in wonder, waving his hand in front of one of the horse's glowing red eyes. "They can't move, but I think that they can still see us and hear us."

"Yes." I said, looking at the fiery eyes of the black horse. "And they are mad."

Corey looked up at the flaming sword, burning high above the Horseman's head in his outstretched hand. "How are you even going to reach that?" Corey gasped.

I swallowed hard, feeling the hot breath of the horse on my face as I neared. "I'm going to climb up there." I said.

Corey looked shocked. "But it's a ghost! You can't climb up on a ghost!"

I thought differently, though. When I had thrown the salt, I had seen the change. The smoky, shadowy rider had gotten more solid. I gritted my teeth and approached the side of the huge horse. Reaching out in the darkness, I felt the cold, bristly fur on its side.

"Get the motorcycle started." I said, looking up at the flaming sword high overhead. "Be ready to run."

Corey didn't argue. He jumped on the motorcycle and started getting his helmet on frantically as I reached forward and pushed the Horseman's heavy leather boot out of the stirrup in front of me. With the seconds ticking away in my mind, I pulled myself up. Even standing in the stirrup, the dark rider towered above me. I started to step up onto the saddle, eyeing the flaming sword and praying that the Horseman wouldn't spring to life suddenly and cut off my head.

When I pulled my foot up onto the front of the saddle, I found something was already there. When I looked down, I was horrified at what I saw in the flickering red light of the flames. A face was looking at me, bearded and furious. Long, stringy hair framed dead-pale skin. Black teeth grimaced from the bristly beard. It was a man's head, and it was glaring at me with murderous rage from where it sat on the front of the saddle.

I let out a startled scream and almost fell, but grabbed out and caught the back of the rider's long cloak and steadied myself.

The sound of my startled scream was drowned out by the growl of the motorcycle engine trying to start below. Corey was trying to kick start the bike, but it sputtered and grew silent again.

I looked up and saw the flaming sword gripped in the rider's gloved hand just a few more feet above me. I stepped up on his massive leg and pulled myself up. I was now eye-level with the stump of his severed neck. Although it was right next to my face, I forced myself not to look and instead concentrated on the fiery sword.

Below me, I heard Corey try again to start the motorcycle. It sputtered some more, then died again.

Clutching the rider's coarse cape, I pulled the silver vial to my mouth and grabbed the cork in my teeth, pulling it out with a "pop!" The heat from the sword was bearing down on me, but I reached up anyway with a trembling hand and touched the open mouth of the vial against the flaming blade.

The wind kicked up and the tree branches above us clashed as the trees shook. The cold silver vial in my hand flashed a bright orange, and I knew that I had gotten the magic we needed. I pulled it back down and pushed the cork in.

I heard the motorcycle below suddenly kick to life and when I looked down, I saw the head lying on the saddle suddenly twist upwards and glare at me. Before I could scream, a gloved leather hand shot across the headless rider's chest and grabbed my throat. I fell back, startled, but the hand held me in a cold iron grip.

I heard a chilling scream, and I couldn't tell if it was coming from Corey or the head on the saddle below me. I looked up to see the fiery sword start to swing down.

In the same instant, the hand holding my throat dissolved and I was falling right through it. I hit the ground hard and the giant horse was above me again, kicking up its legs furiously.

This time it was Corey screaming as he gunned the motorcycle engine and the back wheel sprayed leaves behind it. "Get on!" Corey was yelling. "We've got to make it across the bridge!"

The steed came down on me then. I thought I was dead. The huge iron horseshoes passed right through my head and pounded onto the ground by my feet. The horse was a phantom again. The salt had worn off.

I had barely enough time to breathe, though, before the flaming sword was coming at my head. I threw myself to the side and the sword missed my neck by inches.

As the monstrous animal reared up once more, I jumped on the motorcycle seat behind Corey. He gunned the engine and we sprang forward. I scrambled to hold on as we started moving fast through the darkness.

I had watched Corey ride this stretch a hundred times while he practiced, but it had never seemed so bumpy. I was thrown up and knocked high out of my seat with every bump we hit. I could barely hold on, but Corey gunned the engine and suddenly we were going even faster.

The bridge was fast approaching, and I began to think that we may actually make it back across it alive. I could see the shadowy figures of the girls on the other side, waving and screaming at us. Suddenly, though, the hot breath of the demon's steed was bellowing beside us and I realized with horror we weren't going to outrun him after all.

"Corey! Look out!" I yelled as I caught the flicker of the flaming sword coming at us from the right. Without thinking, I pulled Corey hard to the left and sent us off balance. The flaming sword sliced through Corey's hair and orange embers danced where it had cut some off.

The motorcycle flew out of control, veering wildly to the left. Corey struggled with the steering and then jerked to the right, narrowly missing a tree.

There was a sudden, terrifying drop as we fell off of the side of the dirt road and then we were tearing through the dark woods. Branches and bushes clawed at us as we sped through the darkness… away from the road and away from the safety of the bridge.

I turned to look behind us as another huge bump nearly threw me off the motorcycle. I saw the Horseman there, crashing through the darkness and catching up again. His burning sword was setting fire to trees and limbs as he passed, leaving a trail of flames behind him.

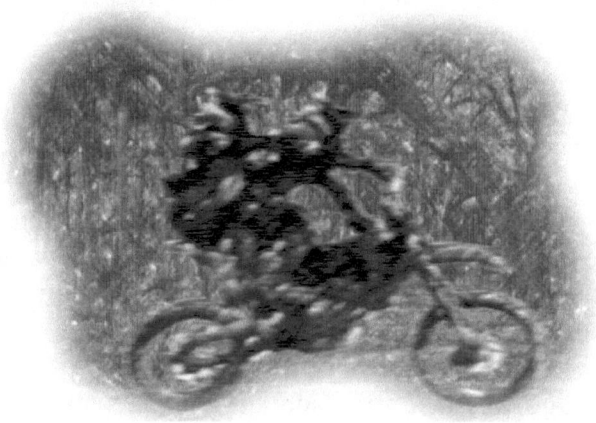

My mind raced. There was no way we would be able to turn around now to get back to the bridge… and if we stopped, we were dead. Even if we could make it to an open road, I knew that the Horseman would be faster and could catch us. We would never be able to outrun him and there was no place to hide.

Corey jerked to the left and just missed smashing into another tree. We were racing blindly through the dark woods and it was only a matter of time before we hit something.

"Get to the lake!" I yelled to Corey.

He half-turned towards me, straining to hear me over the roar of the engine and the fiery mayhem that was at our heels.

"The lake!" I shouted. "We've got to make it to Lake Sorrow!"

Chapter Sixteen

Terra Bog

 knew that the lake was coming up fast, but in the darkness with the murderous Horseman right behind us, it was impossible to see anything or even slow down. While Corey dodged trees and rocks in our frantic flight through the woods, the ghostly horse and rider behind us jumped right through them, passing through tree trunks like a shadow and catching up fast.

Within minutes, he had covered the space between us and was within striking distance again and no amount of maneuvering could shake him off.

"Tell your brother to stop in five seconds." Charlie's bland voice said calmly in my ear.

The Horseman was raising his sword for the final deadly blow.

I hesitated only an instant, then yelled "Corey! Stop the bike!"

Corey, frantically trying to steer as we flew blindly through the darkness, twisted his head and saw the Horseman beside us. "What? Are you crazy?"

"Better do it now." Charlie said again boredly.

"Now, Corey!" I yelled. "Stop now!"

Corey threw us to the side just as the flaming sword came down and we fell, skidding and bouncing roughly across the leafy ground. Corey flew away from me and the bike skidded in another direction. Then, we were out of the trees and I saw the starry sky overhead.

The Horseman, taken aback by our unexpected stop, had ridden past and disappeared suddenly over a drop-off. When I finally came skidding to a stop, I saw why: We were at the edge of Lake Sorrow. We had come just inches from going over the bank and into the muddy lakebed.

We saw the Horseman ride out across the lake, then pull at his horse and turn it around to face us again. The ghostly rider and his steed did not sink down into the blackish mud as we would have. He glided across the lakebed as easily as he had passed through the trees in our pursuit.

The motorcycle was still running nearby. Its front wheel was hanging over the edge of the embankment. As I got up, I saw the Horseman spur his horse forward and he started towards us again.

"Corey!" I shouted into the darkness... but he was already there, running towards the fallen motorcycle and pulling it up.

I climbed on behind him and looked out across the empty lakebed, trying to figure out what side of the lake we were on. "Do you still have the clover around your neck?" I asked frantically. "Can you see where the portal is?"

Corey gunned the engine. "I see it." he said loudly.

That was all I needed to say. He knew what I was thinking and he took off, speeding along the edge of the lake before the Horseman could reach us. Seeing that we were moving again, the demon steed turned and started running along the lakebed parallel to us. The horseman raised his flaming sword high and I saw now that he was holding his terrible bearded head high in his other hand.

I saw a big, twisted tree looming on the bank ahead and although I couldn't see the menagerie of fairies around it, I remembered that the portal was about twenty feet out in the lakebed from there.

The Horseman was keeping up with us and moving closer with each passing moment. My heart started to pound in panic. *How would we get out there? We'll never get past the Horseman. There was no way to…*

But then Corey sped up and I realized what he was planning to do.

I didn't even have time to react. I just lowered my head and held on tight as Corey pulled back on his handlebars suddenly and raced up and over the edge of the lakebed. We were off the ground and flying through the air for a few horrifying seconds. There was a terrible sound like metal tearing and the bike jolted in midair, then we were falling and I braced myself for the crash into the muddy ground.

Instead, we kept falling. There was a dizzying, weightless sensation. It felt like we were falling for a long time in the darkness. I screamed and I heard Corey scream, too.

Then, I was splashing into water.

I was disoriented and turned-around. I didn't know which way to swim for air and my chest was burning.

When I finally broke the surface, I gasped for breath. Slimy, wet grass and vines matted my arms and face. It was dark, but the moonlight lit everything around us with a shimmering glow.

We were in a swamp. Corey was gasping for breath beside me. There was a terrible crashing sound to our left and Corey's motorcycle fell out of the sky and smashed into a huge, jagged rock that jutted out of the water nearby. Even before the motorcycle toppled over into the black water, I saw that the back wheel had been sliced in half and the severed edges of the spokes still glowed a hot orange. The Horseman had taken one last furious swing at us with his flaming sword before we had passed through the portal. Although Corey's motorcycle was sputtering its last breath, Corey and I were thankfully, unbelievably, still whole and alive.

The water wasn't deep, but the muddy bottom sucked at our shoes as we struggled through the marsh. Will-o-wisps floated silently through the air around us, and sometimes something would skitter or splash through the water close by. I was terrified that at any moment, something under the water would sink its teeth into my leg and drag me under, but thankfully Corey and I had only gone a little way in the dark swamp before we came across the overgrown hut.

It was built on a small dry hump of land and was completely covered with a tangle of weeds and vines. Even by the dim glow of the nearby will-o-wisps, I could tell that it had been empty for a long, long time.

I pushed on the door and its rotten wood crumbled in my hands. Inside, things looked even more overgrown than on the outside. Tiny creatures slithered and scattered in all directions at the sound of our footsteps on the bare dirt floor.

There was almost no furniture, but things here were dry and there was a crooked old fireplace against one wall. Looking at the rotting pieces of the fallen door, I had an idea. I began to gather the pieces and stack them in the fireplace.

Corey, standing there covered in moss and vines, soaking wet and shivering cold, looked at me doubtfully. "That will never burn, bro. You know that it's way too damp and rotten."

I reached into my pocket and produced the tiny silver vial. "True for ordinary fire." I said. "But we have a little hard-earned magic fire here."

As I popped open the cork and leaned into the fireplace, Corey shuddered, rubbing his arms across his chest. "Won't that waste it?"

As soon as I tilted the vial over the rotten wood in the fireplace, a big fire burst to life, lighting up the whole room and making it instantly warmer.

"It's the 'flame that forever burns'... remember? It never goes out." I said. "Once we're through with it, we just put it back in the vial."

Corey looked impressed. "Good thinking."

We hung our clothes up in front of the fireplace to dry out and we found several huge burlap sacks in a crumbling cabinet. We tore holes in the sacks for our head and arms and threw them on as oversized (and very itchy) shirts.

Neither of us spoke about what had happened or where we were. We may have been in shock, or we may have just been exhausted. I only know that we were thankful to be alive and we both seemed to know instinctively that wherever we were, it would be morning before we could hope to accomplish anything else.

Lying on the floor in front of the fire, I found sleep coming quickly and easily. Right before I nodded off, though, Corey spoke in the darkness. We had been chased, bruised, nearly killed, and now stranded in another world... but Corey asked the one thing that I now realized worried him more than any of that:

"Hey Jasen." he whispered in the shadows of the flickering fire.

"What?" I mumbled sleepily.

Corey hesitated. "Do you really think that Emily overheard me on the radio when I said that I loved her?"

Despite the horrors of the last few hours, a smile curved my lips as I drifted off to sleep.

"--- orey!"

Crackle. Hiss...

"--- orey! ---asen!"

I heard voices that sounded warbly and thin. Like a bad connection on a cell phone. They echoed loudly in the air of the empty hut.

I blinked awake to sunshine streaming in through a huge hole in the roof above my head. There was a moment of strange disorientation as I tried to figure out where exactly I was.

I sat up and I realized that I was wearing only the old burlap sack we had found last night. In the daylight, I saw that it was black with mold and I realized for the first time how badly it smelled.

I pulled myself to my feet and looked around the hut in the daylight. It had seemed much cozier last night in our exhaustion. In the light, I saw that it wasn't much more than four crumbling walls and a collapsing thatched roof. Corey lay on the hard dirt beside me. He was curled up tightly into a ball with his arm over his face to shield it from the sunlight pouring in from overhead. The fire in the fireplace still burned bright and hot.

"—asen! --orey! –you there?"

Static cracked and popped again... and this time I could tell that it came from where our clothes were hanging beside the fireplace.

What in the world?

I stepped carefully over to the clothes and followed the hissing sound to Corey's jacket. There, in the inside pocket, was the Walkie-Talkie we had used last night. When I pulled it out, swamp water dripped from the bottom of it and it crackled loudly, letting out an electric whine that jolted Corey awake.

"I don't want to go to school, Grandpa!" he shouted, blinking into the sunlight.

"—orey! –ome in!"

Corey turned to me and saw the radio in my hands. His eyes grew wide beneath his wild tangle of messed blonde hair. "Is that…"

I nodded, a huge smile breaking out on my face. I lifted the radio up and pressed the button. "This is the Brothers Stillwell calling. Welcome back to Wonderland, girls."

We pulled on our dry clothes and did the best we could to pick the dried grass and moss from our hair and faces. I uncorked the silver vial in my pocket and held it up to the fire in the fireplace. It sucked up the burning flame like a vacuum and the vial burped up a few tiny orange sparks before I corked it again. The splintered remains of the wooden door that I had put in the fireplace remained, untouched. They had not burned at all.

We had barely enough time to run outside the hut before we heard the girls splashing through the swampy water and up onto the grassy knoll. They were muddy and soaked, their hair tangled with vines and wet grass. They each carried a big backpack, but the second Emily hit the dry land, she threw the backpack down and rushed into Corey's arms.

I had just enough time to see Emily kissing him passionately before I was caught up in a massive hug from Elayne. She embraced me tightly, and when she finally let go, I could see tears sparkling in her eyes.

"You're okay." she said, smiling even as tears rolled down her face and over the black mole on her cheek.

I looked back at her, taking her rough hands in mine. "I'm okay." I said quietly.

"I thought I had lost you."

I smiled, looking at her gently. "You didn't lose me."

She reached out and touched my face lightly, then nodded and sniffled again. "Good." she said.

She watched me a moment longer, her eyes searching mine. She looked just about to say something else, then we heard Corey say to Emily "How in the world did you know where we were?"

Emily was clutching Corey's hands in hers. "Oh, it wasn't hard to follow the trail of fire and destruction you guys left for us." she said. "We had no trouble figuring out that you had made a run for Lake Sorrow. Once we saw that you had both made it safely through the portal, we went and got some supplies and followed you through as soon as it was light enough to see."

"What happened with the Horseman?" Elayne asked. "Did you get the fire?"

I nodded and dug the corked vial out of my pocket. "Sure did. Now we're ready to take the fight to Sidhera! I can't believe we were able to finish so quickly."

Elayne turned and started digging through her backpack. "Don't get too excited. We're not finished yet."

She rummaged around in her backpack and finally pulled out the piece of wood that Dryan had given us. Corey and Emily came closer and we all gathered around as Elayne held it up to the sunlight.

The message in the wood grain had disappeared and now the face of the wood had rings once more.

"The clue is gone!" Corey said.

"That's because we got the fire like it told us to." I said. "But we still don't know how to use it to get Elayne back in her own body."

"Ask it." Emily prompted.

Elayne looked at the piece of wood in her hand, and cleared her throat. "We want to know how to use the magic fire we have collected to return me to my body."

We all waited for a long moment, watching the grain of the wood. A moment later, it began to spin again and words formed across its surface.

You need the North Star...
below the city that can only be found in dreams .

We all looked at the words in disbelief. I read them over again just to be sure I was seeing them right.

"Are you kidding me?" Corey sputtered. "That's not an answer! You asked how we can use the fire to stop Sidhera. It's sending us on another scavenger hunt!"

"Maybe it's a mistake." I said. "Try asking again."

Elayne asked the question again, making sure to say each word carefully. We waited expectantly, but the words did not change.

Corey threw up his hands. "The woodchip has gone bonkers! The North Star? That's insane. First of all, unless some aliens come down in their spaceship... we're going to have a hard time getting up to it. Secondly, unless Jasen brought one heck of a big vial, I don't think we're going to be able to carry a freaking STAR back with us even if we could get to it!"

Emily shook her head. "But it's weird. It doesn't say that the North Star is in the sky. It says that it is below a city. What kind of star is below a city?"

"The city that can only be found in dreams." Elayne recited. She looked thoughtful. "That sounds so familiar."

I looked at her. "Do you know it?"

Elayne put her hand to her forehead. "Yes...and no. I mean, I've heard it... I just can't remember where."

We gave her a moment to see if anything came to her, but she just shook her head again. "I'm sorry, I can't remember."

"That's alright." I sighed. "We need to take some time to figure out where we are, anyway. We assume that we're back in your world, but we have no idea where."

Elayne looked around. "Yes, I was wondering about that myself. There are many swamps in our world, but there's really no way of telling..."

Elayne's eyes rested for the first time on the crumbling hut where Corey and I had spent the night. As she looked at it, slow realization washed over her face and her eyes grew wide. She inhaled sharply.

I looked at the hut, then back at her. "You recognize it?"

Elayne turned and looked at the swamp around her, then back at the hut. She shook her head in amazed wonder. "Of all the places..." She stepped closer to the little hut with silent awe. "But of course it would have been close to the portal..." she said quietly. "And the one that came out by Lake Sorrow. It makes sense, really."

I looked at her confusion. "What is it?" I asked.

Elayne gestured to the dense swamp around us as if she couldn't believe that we didn't already know. "This is Terra Bog." she said incredulously, then she pointed to the dilapidated hut. "And this..." she said. "Was the most feared place in my kingdom when I was growing up. I've never been here, but I've seen pictures of this very hut. It was described to me vividly as a child and it haunted my dreams for years."

I looked at the ramshackle hut. It was creepy enough with the swamp and the whole middle-of-nowhere vibe, but I didn't get why it would terrify her so much.

"This place," Elayne continued, "is where Sidhera lived before I was born. This is Sidhera's lair."

A cold chill ran through me and I took a few involuntary steps away from the crumbling hut. I noticed that Corey and Emily had done the same.

Elayne stepped closer, though, looking at it with wonder. "I often dreamed of coming here when I was younger." Elayne said. "Confronting Sidhera... demanding that she lift the curse from me before..." she trailed off thoughtfully.

A moment later, she cleared her throat. "She wasn't here, of course. My father sent a legion of soldiers here to find her, but she had already abandoned the hut by then. She went into hiding soon after I was born."

Corey looked at the crumbling hut. "Really?" he asked. "But I thought that she was supposed to be a fairy queen. Why would she live *here*?"

I scratched my hair thoughtfully. "You know, he's right. Sidhera seems awfully full of herself to settle with this run-down old place. She's pretty arrogant, right? I mean, the whole reason she cursed you was because your parents snubbed her. That's a pretty big ego."

Elayne looked at the old hut thoughtfully. "You know, that's true. Now that we know Sidhera, I realize that this little hut in the middle of the swamp isn't like her at all."

"Maybe this is her vacation home." Corey said.

I looked down at the dry hump of land in the middle of the vast swamp. "Or maybe that hut isn't her home at all." I said carefully.

Elayne turned and looked at me. "What do you mean?"

"She's an Earth fairy, right?" I said. "Doesn't it seem more likely that she would want to be… in the earth?"

"In the earth?" Emily asked. "You mean… underground?"

Elayne nodded. "Yes, that does make sense." She looked again at the tiny hut. "So this hut wouldn't be her home at all, it would be…"

"The entrance?" I asked.

Corey jumped in quickly at this point. "Hey! If you guys think that I'm stepping foot in Sidhera's underground lair, you are crazy-nuts."

I considered. "No, you're right. There's no reason right now to risk something like that. She probably has all sorts of traps set on the place to protect it."

Corey seemed to relax. "Now you're talking some sense!"

I looked at the hut thoughtfully. "Still, though. That's a good thing to know for the future."

Corey grunted. "Right. If you're ever feeling suicidal, you know just the place to come visit."

Chapter Seventeen

Kissing Emily

 mily shuddered, looking at the crumbling hut with new fear. "I agree with Corey. Let's get away from here."

I held up my hands. "Where? We don't know where we are going yet."

"Well, let's figure it out quick before some of Sidhera's mud monsters decide we're loitering too long on her doorstep." Corey said uneasily.

I thought for a moment, running my fingers through my tangled hair. "Terra Bog, right? That means that we're almost on the other side of the world from the Castle of Lions. We're near the Panarian Ocean, right?"

Elayne, Corey, and Emily all looked at me in surprise.

"What's wrong?" I asked.

"I thought you said you didn't know anything about Elayne's world, bro."

"When did I say that?"

"When you told her that you didn't want to be king. You said that you can't be king because you hardly know anything about her worl--- OW! Emily! You're digging your nails into my hand!"

Emily, with her hand clutched tightly around Corey's, turned to him and whispered loudly "Don't talk about that! Can't you see that they are starting to get along again. Don't mess it up!"

I glanced at Elayne uncertainly and she cast her eyes downwards, but said nothing.

"Well..." I said uncomfortably. "I mean, I have read some of the books Elayne gave me. I know *some* stuff."

Everyone was silent. Corey was rubbing his sore hand.

I cleared my throat. "Alright. So if I remember right, the ocean is to the east of Terra Bog, right?"

Elayne nodded. "Yes. About ten leagues."

"A league is three miles!" Corey piped up. "I remember that one."

Emily patted him on the back. "Very good, Corey. We'll give you a lollipop later."

Corey looked down at the backpack lying nearby. "Seriously? You have lollipops?"

"Isn't there a town there?" I asked Elayne.

Elayne, looking at me with an odd smile playing across her face, nodded again. "There is. The seaside town of Lisette's Cove."

"We're staying in this world?" Corey asked suddenly.

I shrugged. "'A city found only in dreams' sounds like something from Elayne's world—not ours. She even says that she remembers something about it."

Corey sighed and looked at the swamp that stretched endlessly around us. "Fine." he said. "Lisette's Cove. Sounds good. Maybe they will have a nice hot shower there and an all-you-can-eat seafood buffet."

I looked at the marsh stretching all around us and thought about the thirty-mile trek ahead of us. I turned to Elayne. "I don't suppose you girls happened to pack up a boat in one of those backpacks, did you?"

Terra Bog was deep in places, but for the most part we could wade through. Sometimes, we would even get lucky and come across stretches of dry land, but these were rare and far between.

The air smelled like rotten eggs and the mud quickly covered every inch of our bodies... even our faces and hair. By midday, we looked like four mud monsters stalking through the shady swamp. The creatures of the swamp left us alone for the most part. We saw plenty of creepy things, mostly half-glimpsed through the trees or diving under the surface of the water just before we passed. I vaguely remembered that one of Elayne's magical gifts was a kinship with animals, and it seemed that this extended to even the snakes, alligators, and whatever else may be lurking just below the murky surface.

The going was slow, and it was nearing sunset when we finally reached a hill that rose up out of the swamp and continued into the shade of a large forest. The water gave way to dry, leaf-covered earth and I knew that we had finally made it out of the swamp. By the time the sun was setting, we had built a fire with the flame from the vial and we changed into the dry clothes that the girls had brought us. We ate peanut butter sandwiches in the firelight as the moon rose high overhead.

When it started to get late, Elayne found some odd bushes with bright purple leaves and pulled off a few handfuls. She scattered the leaves in a wide circle around our campsite and told us that these would keep the "unfriendly" fairies of the forest away from us while we slept.

I was going to ask her what kind of "unfriendly" fairies she meant exactly... but then I decided that I really would rather not know. I lay down beside the fire on a bed of crisp leaves. Corey and Emily were already sleeping nearby and Elayne (who never slept anymore after her 1300 years of enchanted slumber) sat prodding the fire gently and watching the coals.

Pretending to sleep, I lay there and watched her for a moment with my eyes cracked open. Her big, pudgy body squatted uncomfortably by the fire and her hair was a muddy mess, with a string of wet grass clinging to her face near the black mole on her cheek. Despite this, though, her brown eyes, set in her pale face beneath wiry black eyebrows, still seemed to shine as they reflected the dancing flames. I found that despite her appearances, I still felt a flutter of nervous joy when I looked at those eyes. It was Elayne... and no matter what she looked like, I realized that I loved her more than ever.

Sometime later, still watching those shining eyes, I fell asleep.

I awoke to shouting.

I was confused and disoriented. I wasn't lying down anymore. As I awoke, I realized that I was kneeling. Somebody yelled and a moment later, a pair of hands shoved me roughly back and I fell hard to the ground.

"Corey! Stop!" it was Elayne's voice.

"Are you crazy?" Corey was yelling. "I can't believe you! How could you do something like that?"

When I finally woke all the way up, I saw that it was still nighttime. I had fallen on my back just inches from the

campfire and as my eyes focused in the orange firelight, I saw
that Corey was up on his feet and shouting angrily. In fact, he
seemed to be shouting at me, red-faced and furious. Emily sat
on the ground beside him. She was looking at me, too. Her
face was shocked and white and she held her hand up over her
mouth.

Elayne came rushing to me and put her hands on my
shoulders. She squinted into my eyes as if looking for
something there.

"What's going on?" I mumbled, still half asleep.

Elayne pushed her face closer, staring at my eyes like a
doctor looking at a sick patient. I pulled my face away from
her and sat up. "What happened?"

Corey looked ready to lunge at me. He was shaking with
rage. "You're disgusting!" he was screaming. "I can't believe
you would even think she was interested in you!"

I turned to look around, just to make sure Corey was
actually talking to me and not someone else nearby.

"Who?" I asked.

"Settle down." Elayne said gently, trying to calm Corey.
"One of the forest fairies may have put a spell on him."

I was confused. "Are you talking about *me*?" I looked at
Emily, sitting in the pile of leaves where she had fallen asleep.
She was still watching me with fearful, stricken eyes. "What
happened?" I asked.

"Don't play dumb!" Corey yelled. "You kissed my girl,
that's what happened! I can't believe you, bro! You wait until
I fall asleep and then make your move!"

I was dumbstruck. "What? What the heck are you talking
about? I kissed *Emily*?"

Elayne took me by the arm and led me over to a rock to sit
me down. "Here," she said. "Sit here and be still. Give me a
minute." She strained to look into my eyes again.

I glanced again fearfully at Corey and Emily. Corey was
pacing back and forth, kicking at the leaves on the ground.
Emily was still watching me warily. "I didn't!" I said quickly.

"Really! I don't know what you're talking about. I don't remember anything!"

Elayne lifted my eyelids back with her thumbs, then furrowed her forehead in confusion. "You're not under a spell." she said at last. "I don't see any traces of fairy magic that would have made you act like that."

"I knew it!" Corey roared. "This is… this hurts, bro. I can't believe you would do this to me!"

"WHAT?" I shouted at last. "WHAT EXACTLY DID I DO?"

Emily was the one that finally spoke. "You really don't remember?"

I shook my head. "Really. I really don't."

"Liar!" Corey yelled. "I saw you, man! I saw you kissing her!"

Elayne held her hand up again. "Corey, be calm for a moment." She was still watching me carefully. "What's the last thing you remember?"

I shrugged frantically. "I don't know! I mean, I was lying there by the fire and I fell asleep, I guess."

Elayne furrowed her eyebrows. "You fell asleep?"

"He wasn't asleep!" Corey said angrily. "You saw him! He was awake and walking and talking."

I felt like a splash of cold water was thrown on me. "I was?" I asked.

Elayne, still watching me closely, nodded. "Yes. You sat up just a few minutes after you had laid your head down. You got up, stretched like you were just waking up, and looked at me and said 'Hey there, Mole-Face.'"

My eyes got wide. "What? I did not!"

Elayne continued. "Then you looked around and saw Emily sleeping. You walked over to her and shook her awake. Then you started talking to her. You said…something."

My heart was pounding furiously now. I didn't remember doing any of this. I looked at Emily. "What? What did I say?"

Emily's face grew bright red. "You know what you said."

I shook my head. "No. I really don't."

Emily glanced at Corey uncomfortably, then back at me. Her face was burning with embarrassment. "You said that I was beautiful. You said that you loved the way the firelight danced in my eyes. You asked me why I was with Corey." She glanced again at Corey. "You said that he was a loser and that I should be with you instead. Then, you kissed me on the lips." Emily looked down quickly, too mortified to even look at me. Corey stood beside her, trembling with silent rage and looking at me with an incredulous expression.

I was stunned. "I don't... remember." I said slowly. "I don't remember any of that."

"Oh, come off it!" Corey snapped. "Elayne just said that you aren't under any kind of spell. Are you going to try to tell us that you were just sleepwalking?"

Then, it clicked.

Sleepwalking.

My stomach dropped at Corey's words and I suddenly understood. "Charlie." I whispered.

Elayne looked at me. "Charlie? Who's that?"

"Come on," Charlie's voice chided suddenly in my ear. "You're not really going to tell them about me, are you? I was having fun watching this little drama unfold here. Go kiss the pretty one again. I want to see your brother's face when you do it right in front of him."

I pointed into the air beside my left ear. "THAT's Charlie." I said.

Everyone turned to look at the empty spot where I was pointing.

"Where?" Elayne asked.

"You didn't just hear him?" I asked.

"No she didn't" Charlie said.

"No, I didn't." Elayne said.

I turned to Corey. "How about with your four-leaf-clover there? Didn't you just hear him?"

"Nope." Charlie murmured.

Corey just looked at me as if I had gone crazy.

I ran my hand through my hair frantically, desperate to make them believe me. "The car!" I said at last, snapping my fingers. "The car didn't roll down the driveway like I said. I woke up in the morning and found it smashed into the birdbath in the front yard."

Corey shrugged. "So?"

"It was Charlie!" I said. "He does something while I'm sleeping. I think he gets into my body and takes over. Remember the day before that when I woke up and my bed was full of food? That was Charlie."

Now Corey really did look at me like I was losing my mind.

"They think that you've gone nutzo." Charlie laughed in my head.

"I'm not crazy!" I snapped, and then I saw that Emily and Corey were *both* looking at me like I was crazy now.

Elayne put her hand gently on mine. "When did this start happening?" she asked carefully.

"It's from the Kasner's." I said. "He's like a ghost or something. He sometimes tells me things before they happen."

"Prove it!" Corey said. "Tell me the next word that I'm going to say!"

There was a moment of silence as they all watched me expectantly.

"Well?" I asked Charlie out loud.

There was silence.

I clenched my teeth. "He is choosing not to cooperate right now."

"Tangerines!" Corey yelled wildly. "The word I was going to say was tangerines!"

"I love tangerines." Charlie said wistfully in my ear.

Elayne looked thoughtful. "I do remember something at that house." she said. "Something trying to get into my head."

"Yes!" I said. "Charlie told me that he couldn't get inside of you because there was so much magic inside of you."

Elayne considered this. She stood up and walked to the edge of our campsite and picked up one of the purple leaves she had scattered in a ring there. When she returned, she knelt down in front of me and held it up.

"Chew on this." she said.

Emily and Corey were watching me closely.

"What's that?" Charlie asked curiously in my head. "What is she doing?"

Without saying another word, I snatched up the leaf and threw it into my mouth. The moment I started to chew, I heard Charlie begin to scream.

"Stop!" he bellowed. His wails shot through my head and I instinctively threw my hands up over my ears. It didn't help. His screams pounded through my mind.

Unable to take it anymore, I spit out the half-chewed leaf and Charlie grew instantly silent again.

My head still hurt, though, and I could feel a headache coming on. "That witch!" Charlie screamed in my head. "That big, fat, ugly, mole-faced trollop!"

Elayne looked at me carefully. "What happened?"

I held my forehead in my hands. "He didn't like that." I said.

"I suspected he might not." Elayne said worriedly.

Finally, Emily spoke up. "I believe him." she said at last.

Corey turned to her, surprised.

"That really wasn't Jasen a few minutes ago," she said. "He would never act like that or say the things he said."

Corey thought about this a long moment with his arms crossed tightly in front of his chest. Finally, he took a long breath. "You're right." he said. He looked back up at me. "Sorry Bro. I guess—I guess I believe you, too."

I felt my stomach relax with relief, even as my head continued to pound.

Corey jabbed his finger into the empty air. "If I ever see this Charlie fella, though... he'd better watch out!"

Chapter Eighteen

Lisette's Cove

 one of us could sleep after that. Even though Elayne promised to keep an eye on me, I was too shaken up to try to lie back down again. Things were still awkward around the camp, but I had the feeling that the worst of it had passed. Corey said he was sorry he had pushed me and Emily gave me a hug, even joking that I wasn't a bad kisser (a joke which Corey did NOT find at all funny). We eventually settled into a quiet circle around the campfire while we waited for dawn.

Elayne was still watching me with some concern, as if trying to figure something out.

"It's a coach-catcher." she said at last. When we looked at her in confusion, she waved her hand absently, trying to come up with the right phrase. "A 'hitchhiker' you call them in your world. Someone who jumps aboard for a ride."

She was talking about Charlie, who had remained sullenly silent since his last angry outburst.

"You actually have a ghost inside you?" Corey asked uncomfortably.

"He's not really inside me, I don't think." I said. "Sometimes, I can catch a shadow out of the corner of my eye and I think that it may be him. He stays close by and he waits, I think, until I'm asleep before hopping inside."

Elayne looked worried. "He's getting stronger." she said. "I remember that first afternoon in the library, he took over and you were mumbling and moving your hands. Just a couple of nights later, he was able to make you drive your car. Now this with Emily…"

"What are you saying?" I asked.

"The stronger he gets, the more control he is going to have over you. Tonight, you had barely closed your eyes before he jumped in. Eventually, he may be able to jump in while you are wide awake."

Corey looked shocked. "What about those purple leaves? Chew on a handful of those until he takes off for good."

I shook my head, which still throbbed with a headache. "I don't think it will be that easy." I said. "The leaves hurt him, but he hurt me right back. I don't think he's going to go away without a fight."

Emily jumped up as if she had an idea and ran to the backpacks. There, she pulled out the magic piece of wood. Holding it in her hands, she spoke clearly. "We want to find a way to keep Charlie out of Jasen's head." she said.

We all watched her expectantly as she looked down at the face of the wood.

A moment later, she looked disappointed. "Nothing." she said. "It still just has the message about the North Star."

"It's alright." I said. "We'll just have to take some precautions. Tie me up when I go to sleep or something. Right now, we have to concentrate on helping Elayne."

Elayne watched me across the fire. "We're going to have to do something about this soon, though, Jasen. I have a feeling that Charlie is more dangerous than you think."

I considered this, but remained silent. Charlie had already saved me a few times when the Horseman was after us. His ability to see what was about to happen had kept my head from getting lobbed off. Still, though, after what Elayne said, I began to think that maybe Charlie was interested in keeping me alive only long enough to take over altogether.

... and what would happen to me then? Would I become the shadow that he saw out of the corner of his eye? Just a voice in his head?

As I watched the firelight, I decided that it was something I would have to think about.

After a quick breakfast of some bread and beef jerky, we packed up and started walking east again.

Sometime after lunch, we crested a big hill and we saw the ocean for the first time. It was an incredible sight, stretching from horizon to horizon with the sunlight glittering off rolling waves like diamonds. We all stood on the hilltop for a long time, watching with silent awe. In that short moment, our quest was forgotten and we were overwhelmed by this natural wonder.

A town lay below us, nested in the rocks and waves. Its collection of tin roofs sparkled in the afternoon sun and we saw the tall swaying masts of big wooden ships docked against long weathered piers.

I looked at Elayne. "Lisette's Cove?" I asked her.

She nodded silently, still watching the ocean. She seemed to be looking at the distant horizon across the water as if trying to remember something.

After a moment, she shook her head, unable to grasp the threads of whatever thought she had been chasing. She took a deep breath, then led the way as we started walking towards the town below.

After days of hiking through the swamp and wilderness, it was wonderful to see buildings again.

The town looked like it had been thrown together at random over the years from broken pieces of old ships and scraps of glass and metal. The houses and shops were made of dark, weathered wood and many of them were leaning to one side a bit. The streets were crowded with men, women, and children who all hurried about in their daily routine. The air smelled like fish, and in fact several men called to us as we passed, holding up dead fish and trying to get us to buy some.

If we looked strange in our muddy blue jeans and tee-shirts, nobody seemed to pay much attention. We walked through the town, huddled together and looking around in amazement.

"We need to find a motel or something." I said.

"An inn." Elayne smiled. "Here it would be called an inn."

"Oh, right. Sorry."

"They usually have signs that are easy to spot by travelers." Elayne said, craning her head to look around. "It shouldn't be too..." Elayne trailed off. A moment later, without saying another word, she started to walk across the crowded central square.

"What?" I asked. "Did you see one?"

We all rushed to keep up with Elayne as she wove through the busy crowd. When she finally stopped, we were under the eaves of a tall, crooked building with a swinging wooden sign over its door. *The Singing Mermaid* the sign read. The clatter of dishes drifted out to us from inside, along with the smell of frying fish, making my stomach rumble.

"Now you're talking!" Corey said, rubbing his hands together. "I like the way you think, Elayne. First we eat!"

But Elayne remained silent. She was staring at a big wooden carving that sat outside the door. It was a statue of a mermaid, her eyes turned upward and her mouth open as if she was singing. Faded paint was peeling off of it in places and the base of the statue was chained to the building (so nobody would be tempted to steal it, I guessed).

"She's hot." Corey said, and Emily instantly responded by smacking him on the shoulder.

Elayne was staring at the statue thoughtfully. "I think I know what it means," she said.

"You know what *what* means?" I asked.

Elayne tore her eyes from the mermaid statue and looked at us. "The second clue. The city that can only be found in dreams. It's Atlantis. King Neptune's city at the bottom of the sea."

Corey and Emily both looked as shocked as I was.

"I don't get it." Corey said at last. "What does a city of dreams have to do with a city at the bottom of the ocean?"

Elayne held her hand up to her forehead. "I knew that it was from a story I heard when I was little. I just didn't remember until I saw the statue here. The city of Atlantis, at the bottom of the ocean, is not on any map. Supposedly, the only way to find it is while you are sleeping. The legend says that it enters the dreams of sleeping sailors as they pass over it."

"That's a crazy story." Corey said.

"I've heard crazier." I said.

"And what about the North Star?" Emily asked. "The clue said it is *under* a city at the bottom of the ocean? Does that make any sense?"

"No." Elayne admitted. "It does not make sense... but I think that Atlantis is where we need to go."

"Alright." I said. "So we need to get in a boat, sail out there and… sleep. Right?"

Elayne nodded. "Right. We'll know we're in the right place if the dream comes… but…" she bit her lip worriedly. "I can't."

I paused. "You're afraid of boats?"

She shook her head. "No! I can't sleep, remember?"

"I'll volunteer!" Corey said quickly. "You need a sleeper… I'm your man."

I couldn't help but smile. "Thanks, Corey. We can always count on you to volunteer for the tough jobs."

Emily laughed. "Right. Now, about a boat…"

Luckily, in the town of Lisette's Cove, boats were easy to find.

We quickly found a captain with a ship and a small crew that were willing to take us out into the middle of the ocean… as long as we could pay them. That part ended up being a bit of a problem.

I had my wallet with me, but the captain took one look at the soggy twenty-dollar bill I handed him and just laughed. Apparently, paper money was not very popular here (especially when it had a picture of a president that he had never heard of). We considered telling him that Elayne was royalty and could pay him a sack full of gold later… but we knew that he would have laughed that off, too.

What finally did it was the radios. We showed him the Walkie-Talkies and when he looked interested in them, we showed him how they worked. They still sounded warbly and hissed and popped with static since they had gotten wet, but he was amazed nonetheless by the pair of "Magic Talking Boxes". He agreed to take us out and even bought us lunch in *The Singing Mermaid* in exchange.

By sunset, we were standing beneath the towering masts of the sailing ship as the three-man crew set to work raising the sails. The salty air blew across our faces as the boat rocked and swayed in the tide. By the time it was dark, the clear night sky glistened with stars and Lisette's Cove was only a huddle of distant lights on the horizon.

Chapter Nineteen

Sea Monsters

 had never been on a boat.

The closest I had come was a rented paddle boat in the surf at the Jersey Shore when I was ten... but this was so much different.

The massive wooden boat was never still. It rocked endlessly, climbing and falling over the rolling waves that slid beneath us and splashed against the sides. It was hard to walk, and for the first day I had to clutch ropes and railings with each wobbly step I took.

Elayne, of course, adjusted immediately. Despite her frumpy body, she walked with the grace of a princess across the swaying deck. Even Corey and Emily had the hang of it within a few hours. I felt really foolish, but I just couldn't steady myself.

Once the land was out of sight, I realized how hard this was going to be. The ocean was huge. We had only one other clue that Elayne could remember: legends told that Atlantis was somewhere along the path of the North Trade Currents. When the captain asked where we wanted to go, we told him to just find the current and let it take the ship where it would.

He looked hesitant at first, but finally shrugged. We had the ship for three days. If we wanted to waste it going nowhere, that was fine with him. He got paid either way.

We had two tiny cabins below deck. One for Corey and I and one for the girls. They were each smaller than the walk-in closet in my bedroom back home. Two swaying cots and a bucket was all the furniture we had. I won't go into details about what the bucket was for, but it isn't hard to figure out.

Corey stuck to his word about sleeping. As soon as we were out to sea, he lay down and we didn't see him again for ten hours. Emily and I forced ourselves to stay awake for the next shift, and by the time Corey emerged from the cabin around lunchtime the next day, Emily gladly took her turn and headed off to sleep.

"Any dreams?" I asked Corey as I handed him an apple.

Corey nodded, squinting in the sunlight. "Yeah. Loads. I dreamed I was in a Dairy Queen drinking a milkshake the size of a barrel. As I was drinking, this crazy three-eyed bunny popped up and..."

I cut him off. "Any dreams about an underwater city?" I asked.

Corey shook his head. "Uh-uh. But speaking of water, remind me to empty our bucket later on."

We passed the hours mostly in silence. Even Charlie hadn't spoken since the incident with Emily. I had not slept in two days and I was exhausted, but I was still terrified about what Charlie would do when I fell asleep next. I also thought constantly about what Elayne had said: *"He's getting stronger."*

One of the crewmen loaned us an old, tattered deck of playing cards to help pass the time more quickly. Elayne was trying to teach us how to play a game she knew called "Falling in the Garden". She had just dealt the cards when Corey suddenly gasped.

"It's your mom!" he said. "The queen of hearts here on this card is a picture of your mom!"

Elayne nodded. "That's right. She's queen. What did you expect? You will find my father's picture on the king's cards and my picture on the princess cards."

I raised my eyebrow. "Princess cards?"

Elayne nodded. "They are like the 'jacks' in the decks from your world."

Corey dug a princess card out of the deck and looked at it. It was indeed a picture of Elayne. It was a painting of her posing in a rose-colored dress, her long blonde hair spilling over her shoulders and her blue eyes shining.

Corey grinned, handing it over to me to look at. Just then, one of the crewmen passing by happened to look down at the card in my hand. "Aye! She's a pretty peach, innshe?"

I glanced at Elayne and saw that she was smiling. "Beautiful." I said, looking at Elayne instead of the card. "I think that she's the most beautiful girl I've ever seen."

I looked right into Elayne's face with the black mole on the cheek. "In fact," I said. "I think she would be beautiful no matter what she looked like."

Elayne's smile faltered as she looked at me and realized what I was saying. Her eyes sparkled for an instant and in that moment I knew that she loved me.

"Aye." the crewman went on, not seeing any of this. He was still looking at the faded picture of Elayne on the card. "Shame 'bout her and that boy."

I turned then. "What boy?"

The crewman laughed. "As if you don't know! That boy they say came here from another world. Jasen somethin'. He was hailed as a hero last year, but now as I hear it he was in league with the foul Sidhera the whole time!"

Corey's eyes got wide.

The crewman nodded, apparently happy to be the first to tell us the latest gossip. "Aye! They say that Sidhera attacked the princess... in her own castle! By luck, the princess was unharmed and Sidhera was captured. The next day, though, seeing that his dark mistress had failed, the traitor Jasen attacked the princess again and tried to finish the job. He was captured, too."

I was shocked. "Traitor Jasen?"

The crewman nodded. "Aye! But the worst part of it is... his foul brother helped them both escape! Through a portal into another world. Luckily, the fair princess found a way to seal that gate..."

Corey was sputtering, red faced. "'Foul brother'? Seriously? I can't believe..."

"Corey..." I warned.

The crewman snapped his fingers. "Aye! That's right! The brother's name was Corey!"

I glared at Corey and he looked furious, but kept his mouth shut.

Elayne cleared her throat carefully and looked at the crewman. "What other news hear you from the castle these days?"

The crewman shrugged. "The princess will be crowned queen in five days' time."

Elayne glanced at me uncomfortably.

The crewman smiled brightly. "And she'll be looking for a new man now that there's a death sentence on the traitor Jasen!" He ran his hand through his scraggly beard. "I'm single myself. I was thinkin' about maybe goin' an payin' the princess a visit to see if me an' her hit it off."

Corey looked like he was choking down a startled laugh.

Just then, there was a commotion on the other end of the deck. Some of the crewmen were shouting and pointing over the railing. As the three of us stood up to go see what was going on, the crewman talking with us dug something out of his pockets. Without a word, he pushed a handful of cotton into each of our hands.

Corey looked at the wadded cotton in his hand. "Hey, what the heck are we supposed to do with…"

But even as Corey was talking, we watched as the crewman frantically stuffed a wad of the cotton into each of his ears and gestured for us to quickly do the same.

I was confused. "What's going on?"

Then, I heard the sound. A high, eerie, warbly sound that went right to my spine and caused a shiver that turned my chest cold.

Elayne grabbed the cotton and jabbed it into her ears, then snatched the bunch from my hand and started pushing it into my ears before I could say anything else.

That sound was in my brain… echoing through my whole body. It almost started to sound like a singing. A supernatural, trembling song that spun my head around and made me dizzy.

Elayne pushed the cotton in my ears and my head cleared suddenly. The sound was still there, but distant and muffled now. I blinked, stunned at the way the song had coursed through me.

Corey still held his cotton in his hand. When I looked at him, I saw that his face had gone blank and his mouth hung open. He was staring at the side of the ship.

The crewman nearby seemed to know what was about to happen, and he grabbed Corey's arm roughly just as Corey lunged forward as if he wanted to dive over the railing.

As the crewman held him tight, Corey struggled desperately, trying to get free. His eyes were blank and hypnotized.

I was still confused about what exactly was happening, but I saw Elayne snatch up the cotton and point to Corey's ears. As the crewman held him, Elayne and I stuffed his ears with the cotton. Instantly, he blinked and stopped struggling.

He looked around as if just waking up. "What happened?" he asked, although I could barely hear his voice through the cotton.

The crewman led us to the side of the ship and pointed down at the water.

The water's surface churned into frothy foam where the ship cut through the waves. There, splashing in the foam and swimming alongside the ship, were several huge fish. I caught the glimpse of two large, black-scaled tails as they splashed below the water.

Then, when they surfaced again, I was stunned to see that they weren't fish after all. They were... something else.

They had long, greenish-black hair that looked like seaweed. They had faces and arms which were covered in scales. Their eyes were an oily black and their ears were like scalloped fins on each side of their heads. Two slits for a nose were just above a mouth that opened to reveal rows and rows of sharpened teeth. As we looked down at them, they held their arms up to us, their mouths open and singing that warbly, chilling song. Their black eyes stared at us and they seemed to be begging... pleading... *Come to us. Come closer. Come to us...*

Looking into those terrible eyes, I was horrified. I shuddered and tore my gaze away as they dove back down below the waves.

"What are they?" I asked Elayne. "Are those mermaids?"

Elayne shook her head quickly. I could tell that she, too, had been disturbed by the sight. "Sirens." she said with a shudder. She looked back down at the churning water. "And they're hungry."

That *really* creeped me out. I looked down at the water just in time to see the two come up again, followed by a third. They sang their high, desperate song, reaching for us, calling for us. Trying to hypnotize us. One of them seemed to lock her black eyes on me and I saw her smile hungrily and beckon to me with her scaly webbed hands.

The crewman spat with disgust. Then, adjusting the cotton in his ears, he turned around and went back to his work with the rest of the crew.

The chilling, warbling song continued for hours... and we all did our best to ignore it with the cotton stuffed in our ears. We couldn't talk to each other without yelling, so we soon gave up and just played cards on the wooden deck in silence.

When Charlie's voice spoke up, it was loud and clear... despite the cotton stuffing.

"So..." he said. "The ugly one is a princess in disguise. Interesting story. Man, I sure hopped aboard the right train when you came along."

I looked up at Corey and Emily, but they continued to play cards. They hadn't heard him, of course.

I decided to ignore him.

"I've been thinking about what your ugly girlfriend said earlier." he continued, "About me growing stronger."

I shifted uncomfortably on the wooden deck. The wailing cry of the sirens filled the air.

"It's an interesting idea." Charlie continued. "Having a body again. I think I really might like that."

With these words, to my horror, my left had started to rise on its own. A moment later, my arm was high above my head and waving in the air.

Corey and Elayne looked at me uncertainly. "What's up, bro?" Corey asked in a muffled voice.

"Oh, dear." Charlie said suddenly. "The pretty one is about to get eaten alive. That's a shame. She was a good kisser."

With these strange words, my hand dropped and I was able to move it on my own again.

Elayne and Corey were watching me   questioningly. My heart was pounding.

He did it. I thought fearfully. *I wasn't even asleep and he was able to move my hand. How much longer before he takes over completely?*

It had been an awful feeling to not have control over my own arm. I rubbed my knuckles absently and moved my fingers to reassure myself that they were mine again.

And what the heck was he saying? "The pretty one is about to get eaten alive." What in the world did that...

But then I knew and my heart jumped. The song of the sirens seemed to grow suddenly more excited and desperate. I turned just in time to see the hatch that led below swing open and Emily step out into the sunlight. Her eyes instantly lost focus and glazed over. She took two unsteady steps forward, then started running at full speed towards the side railing.

I leapt up and ran, struggling to keep my balance on the rolling ship. Without pausing, Emily got to the railing and took a giant leap to dive over it. I was there at the last instant, tackling her from the side and throwing her back down to the deck roughly.

She was screaming. Fighting, clawing, desperate to get up. She grabbed hold of the railing and started to pull herself out of my grip, struggling to jump into the waves and join the singing sirens below.

She punched me--- hard, and I fell back, stars filling my vision. I heard Charlie chuckling in my ears and Emily was up on the railing again, climbing over. Then, Corey reached her at the same time as two other crewmen. They were able to pull her back, but she was still kicking and screaming. Corey moved in front of her, trying to calm her down while pushing his hands over her ears to block out the sirens' song.

Emily's eyes were still locked on the railing, though, the song filling her head. When she saw Corey in front of her, she brought her leg up and kicked him in the chest. At that moment, the ship swayed to the side and it was enough to throw Corey off balance. He stumbled back against the railing and in horrible, slow-motion terror, I watched as he flipped backwards and tumbled over the side.

I screamed, jumping up and running to the railing. I saw Corey splash into the foamy water beside the ship and the sirens that had been swimming there were instantly upon him. He was yelling and flailing his arms, trying to swim, but then scaly, webbed hands were grabbing him and pulling him down. The singing stopped and one of the sirens looked up at us with those oily black eyes and smiled a greedy smile through rows of razor teeth. As Corey was pulled under, it turned and flipped its black tail at us, then was gone.

I threw myself forward to dive in after him, but suddenly there were hands on my shoulders holding me back. One of the crewmen was holding me tightly and Elayne was there beside me, her face stricken and white. I screamed, fighting to break free, but they held me tight.

There was no sign of Corey or the sirens anymore in the water below.

I threw back my head and wailed. *"I can save him! Let me go!!!"*

"You can't" the crewman said roughly as he held me. "Your friend is gone. There is nothing you can do to save him now."

Tears started streaming from Elayne's eyes and she sobbed.

Now that the sirens' song had stopped, Emily was waking up from her trance and the men holding her loosened their grip. She blinked in the sunlight and looked around, confused. "What's happening?" she mumbled. "What's going on?"

My mind was screaming. The sailor still held my shoulders tightly and the siren song had now been replaced now by my anguished cry.

Corey!

My brother.

Corey was gone, and the world was crashing down around me.

Chapter Twenty

Water

 veryone was silent. Even though the cotton had fallen from my ears in my struggle, there was still only the sound of my gasping sobs and the waves slapping against the wooden sides of the swaying ship.

I felt too weak to stand. My body was limp and cold.

Tears were pouring from Elayne's face as she clutched my hand and moved at the same time towards Emily to console her.

The crew watched the ocean waves solemnly, their faces sad and shocked. Even the wind seemed to have stopped. The sails hung loose and flat. The ship had stopped moving through the water and now just rocked on the waves.

My head was pounding with disbelief. As the seconds turned to minutes, it became more real. Corey was gone and he wasn't coming back. It may have been ten minutes later, it may have been an hour... but eventually I just collapsed, laying on the wooden deck and crying. I had lost my parents when I was young. That had been devastating. Now, Corey was gone and my chest burned with an aching sadness.

As my head spun and I squeezed my eyes tightly to block out the last terrible image I had of Corey being pulled under by those monstrous creatures... I began to realize that something else was happening.

The crewmen were yelling again. Boots thundered across the deck, making it tremble against my cheek. Someone was shouting orders.

The sirens are back. I thought. *They fed and now they want more...*

When I looked up, I saw one of the crewmen tossing a rope overboard. Elayne and Emily had jumped up and were looking over the railing. They were shouting, too, and then the men were pulling the rope back in, straining as if there were something heavy at the end of it.

Whatever it was, it didn't matter to me. Nothing mattered. Corey was gone. Corey was...

...climbing over the railing and being helped back onto the ship.

I blinked in confusion, seeing Corey's soaking mop of blonde hair dripping down over his eyes. He was whole and alive.

The crewmen were still quiet as they lifted him up, staring at him in disbelief. Emily ran forward to embrace Corey, but before she could get to him, Corey bent over and coughed up a huge splash of water onto the deck... then, some more. Almost a minute later, he was still spitting out seawater and the wooden deck was covered.

The captain, standing nearby, was clutching his hat in his hands as he watched Corey fearfully. The other crewmen around us stared wide-eyed and terrified.

"He drowned!" one of them muttered to another. "He was under water for more than ten minutes! Nobody can survive that! Look at all of the water that he took in! The boy should be dead."

The other crewman must've agreed, because he looked pale and scared and took several steps back.

Elayne and Emily, tears still streaming from their faces, watched Corey as he finished coughing up water. Finally, Corey seemed to realize that everyone was staring at him silently and he looked up at all of the shocked faces.

He flashed a grin as he pushed the wet hair from his eyes.

"What's the matter?" he asked. "Did I miss something?"

The crew all kept a fearful distance from us after that. The captain eventually got them all working again, adjusting the sails and getting us back into the current... but they cast wild looks at us as they passed and muttered superstitiously, looking at Corey as if he were a walking ghost.

Later, when our emotions had settled and we were able to find a quiet corner of the deck to huddle, Corey told us what had happened.

"I really thought I was dead." Corey said solemnly. "It was crazy. As soon as I hit the water, they were all over me. They pushed me down fast. I don't know how far we went down, but it got so dark that I couldn't see the sunlight from the top of the water anymore. I was kicking and fighting them and I held my breath for as long as I could and then..."

Emily leaned forward, her eyes bleary and wide. "Then what?"

Corey looked at us hesitantly. "And then... I couldn't hold my breath any longer. The sirens were all over me. I took a breath and water came pouring into my mouth and lungs."

Elayne's eyes were shocked.

I shook my head. "But... how?"

Corey looked a bit scared himself just telling the story. "I don't know," he said. "It felt really weird, but I took another breath and I realized suddenly that I wasn't drowning. I could... breathe."

Elayne looked shocked. "You could breathe water?"

Corey nodded. "Yeah. And when that happened, the sirens all got all still for a moment, and then they let go of me suddenly and swam off into the darkness... like they were afraid of me or something."

I took a deep breath, unable to even imagine what it would feel like to breathe water.

"But humans cannot do that." Elayne said.

Corey cast her a sideways glance. "No kidding. Like I said, I thought for sure I was a dead man. When I realized I was alone in the dark down there and I was still alive, it took me a minute before I came to my senses and started to try to swim for the surface again."

I was completely bewildered. I had no idea how Corey could have done what he just described.

I rubbed my hands across my face and in that moment, I felt the cold metal of my ring brush my cheek. I froze, then pulled my hands away and flipped them over to look at the ring.

"Bridgette's ring." I said suddenly.

Corey looked down at his own hand where he wore the ring that Bridgette had given him.

"The ring of a water prince." Elayne whispered.

I looked down at the ring on my hand, sparkling blue in the sunlight. "So it *is* magic." I said. "Bridgette's a water fairy. We're now her grandsons. Does this mean I can breathe underwater, too?"

Elayne nodded. "Most likely. That would also explain why the sirens left you alone in such a hurry, Corey. If they realized they had attacked a fairy prince, they no doubt feared for their lives."

Corey was looking thoughtfully at the ring on his hand, too. Emily took his other hand in hers. "I'm just thankful that you're alive. I never want to feel like that again."

"Me neither." I agreed.

Corey grinned and looked embarrassed. "Aww, you bunch of sissies. Crying for no reason…" But I could tell that he was secretly pleased.

Just then, Elayne jumped as if she had just remembered something. "We're moving again!" she said.

We looked up and saw that the sails were once more filled with wind and we were moving through the water.

I nodded. "Yep. We sure are."

Elayne held out her hands. "Well? Shouldn't one of you be sleeping?"

After the stress of the last hour and the days without sleep, I found that my exhaustion far outweighed my fear of what Charlie may do in my sleeping body.

Corey, Elayne and Emily all squeezed into our tiny cabin and helped to tie me down with some rope that the crew had given us. Emily and Elayne used their years of experience tying up horses and were able to secure me tightly but comfortably to the cot. It was a strange feeling at first, but I soon realized that I was too tired to care.

Just before I drifted off to sleep in the swaying bed, I saw Elayne smiling beside me. "Sleep well." she said. "I'll be right here when you wake up."

"If I say anything in my sleep..." I said tiredly.

"I know." Elayne smiled. "Don't worry. I will have no trouble at all knowing the difference between you and Charlie."

Even as she was speaking, I was already slipping off to sleep.

My dreams were troubled, random flashes of images and nightmares.

The image of Corey being pulled under by the sirens played over and over again, and mixed in between were others: Being chased by the Headless Horseman through the dark woods; facing the dragon Grendesh in his lair beneath Brightwest Mountain; Elayne dying in my arms on the rooftop of the school; facing Sidhera for the first time.

They were terrible flashes that churned through my mind like the frothy ocean water that the sirens had called from. It was like that for hours. Restless, frightening dreams that just played over and over again.

Then, there was water.

Cool, blue water that washed over me and pushed the bad dreams from my mind. There was silence finally, and a wide-open darkness that stretched all around me.

I realized that I could swim, and I began to move through the water with a steady grace that made my body feel strong and new. It was calming and beautiful. I felt more relaxed and safe than I had felt for as long as I could remember.

Then I realized that the darkness in front of me was glowing a little brighter... a lighter blue. As I moved through the water, the light grew stronger, and now I heard a singing. Not the desperate, wailing cry of the siren... but a beautiful chorus that stirred my heart.

Shapes emerged in front of me and I began to see other colors now. A rainbow of colors. Red, pink, yellow, and more.

There were towers. Not golden, straight towers... but rocky towers made of coral and decorated with a thousand colors. Fish swam in and out of a whole system of tunnels and arches. And there were other things, too... shadows of something coming closer. Not frightening, but beautiful.

I felt elated. I was home. I had found where I belonged at last.

I opened my mouth to breathe and a rush of air came pouring in. I opened my eyes and the dream dissolved instantly, replaced by the darkened wooden beams of the cabin ceiling above me.

The night sky was visible through the tiny open window in the corner and the small candle on the bedside table flickered in the salty breeze that blew in.

My heart was aching at the loss of the beautiful dream. I felt so disappointed to have to leave that place.

When I turned my head towards the candlelight, I saw Elayne there reading a book. She looked up at me and smiled, her yellowish, crooked teeth reflected in the light. "Well, hello there sleepy-head," she said. "Any dreams?"

I couldn't help but smile back at her. "Tell the captain that we have arrived at our destination."

Chapter Twenty-One

The City Found Only in Dreams

 aybe we could share the rings somehow." Corey was saying as we stood on deck. He slid Bridgette's ring halfway off his finger and took Emily's hand and tried to slide her finger into it along with his.

Emily winced and pulled her hand back. "Ow! That's sweet, Corey, but it just isn't going to work. You and Jasen are the only ones that will be able to go down there."

We stood on the deck of the rocking ship beneath a cloudy night sky. The waves were definitely much bigger here and the ship was swaying more than ever.

Elayne stepped closer to me and took my hands. "It's fine. Emily and I will stay here with the ship until you two get back. Find the North Star. It is supposed to be somewhere beneath the city--- whatever that means."

Corey snorted. "Right. Maybe we should bring some shovels."

Elayne's face turned serious. "You know that the captain will most likely turn the ship around by midday tomorrow. We will try to stall them for as long as we can, but I have a feeling they are going to want to leave with or without you."

I nodded firmly. "I understand. We'll be back in time."

Elayne continued to watch me in the darkness as the ship around us rocked steadily on the waves. The wooden masts creaked and groaned from high above.

"Be careful." Elayne said quietly, and she leaned forward and kissed me.

I was startled at first. Less than a week ago we were barely speaking to one another. Things were so mixed up and confused.

I smiled at her. "We'll be alright." I said reassuringly.

I waited for Emily and Corey to finish and a moment later Corey and I were sitting on the railing and looking down at the black, churning water below us. The salty breeze picked up and whipped our hair in our faces.

I looked at Corey. "You ready?"

Corey nodded, bracing himself. "Ready, bro."

Without stopping to hesitate any longer, I threw myself off the side of the ship and into the water.

It was so much colder than I expected.

Immediately after I hit the water and went under, I heard Corey splash somewhere close by. The cold water was like an electric shock making my muscles rigid. Instinctively, I swam upwards and broke the surface, taking a breath of air. The waves, which looked smaller up on the ship, seemed huge from down in the water. One of them surged over my head and I was under water again instantly.

I tried to make myself open my mouth and take a breath of the cold, salty water, but I couldn't do it. It was like my throat was frozen with fear.

You can do it. I tried to convince myself. *You can breathe water. Go ahead. Inhale. Take a deep breath...*

But I just couldn't make myself do it. My chest was burning for air now. I started kicking for the surface again to get another breath. Something grabbed my ankle, though, and pulled me back down.

In terror, I screamed and the air in my lungs flew out in a flurry of bubbles that scrambled for the surface. When I looked down, I saw Corey there. He was holding onto my ankle.

I kicked, trying to get away. My lungs were empty now. I needed to get up top to get a breath of air. I scrambled, frantically, my chest burning and my head ready to explode.

When I couldn't hold it any longer, my lungs heaved and inhaled. I felt cold water rushing down my throat and into my chest. I was panicking, but then I realized that I was okay.

I took another shaky breath, feeling the water flowing in and out as I breathed. It was a strange, alien feeling.

I slowly felt my panic subsiding and I started to relax. Corey's grip on my ankle loosened and when I looked down, I could just make out his face in the murky shadows, grinning up at me like a watery ghost as his hair swayed in the current.

I swam down until his face was level with mine. He inhaled and made a funny face, as if he was struggling with something in his throat. Finally, he held his hand up to his neck and started moving his mouth. I could hear his voice, strange and distorted.

"Down?" he asked in his watery voice.

I nodded.

It was too dark to see anything below our feet. If there was something there, it may have been miles down.

I took off my shirt and tied one sleeve firmly around my belt. I motioned for Corey to do the same and a moment later, we were tied together.

Without another word, we turned and started swimming down into the darkness.

Corey and I saw nothing as we swam. We moved through the cold darkness blindly. After awhile I wasn't even sure if I was swimming downward anymore. It felt like we were floating in an emptiness that went on forever. It was a scary feeling and more than once I had to force myself to stay calm. I felt very alone in the darkness. The only way I knew that Corey was beside me was that I would feel the tug of the shirt that was tied between us.

Eventually, my eyes started to adjust and I could make out shifting shadows in the water. Currents that carried bits of seaweed and algae. Still, the world was mostly black around us as we swam on.

Time was strange as we moved through the emptiness. It felt like we were swimming forever before we first started to notice that the water around us was getting lighter. For a moment, I thought perhaps that we had gotten turned around and what we were seeing was the rising sun above the surface of the water. Soon, though, I saw the colors... the bright rainbow of coral colors that I remembered from my dream.

Towering, twisting mountains of coral were connected in complex patters that looked like beautiful underwater spires. We began to see fish again... strange, colorful, fish that looked so unusual I thought that they must be fairies living here among the city of coral.

Then, we saw the shapes and silhouettes of other things moving among the spires. At first, my heart jumped because I thought that they were sirens. They swam with huge fish tails and had arms and heads with hair. Then, I caught a glimpse of one passing through an archway that glowed with a soft pink light and I could see that they were really...

The shirt tied around my arm was pulling frantically all of the sudden. I looked up at Corey just in time to see some shadows coming at us quickly from the right. Before I could react, there were more to our left and in front of us.

The silhouettes emerged from the shadows and we could see them clearly now. They were people. Or... almost people, anyway. There were men and women... some younger and some older. Some of the men had beards, but most looked not much older than Corey or I. The men were shirtless with pale skin and bulky muscles. The women wore tops of shells or woven seaweed. At their waist, every one of them had scales starting right below their belly-buttons, and instead of legs they each had massive, scaly tails that propelled them with surprising speed through the water.

As they surrounded us, they held out what looked like pitchforks and pointed the sharp ends menacingly at us. Corey and I froze, my heart pounding in sudden fear.

One of them swam forward from among the group of fierce-looking warriors.

She was a girl who looked no more than sixteen. Although she, too, was dressed as a warrior, she was clearly different from the rest. Her face was beautiful, with big, blue eyes that watched us with an icy gaze. Instead of shells or woven seaweed, she wore golden armor across her chest and covering her head was a gold helmet with a fin along the top crest. As she moved forward, she looked at us with an air of authority.

"Halt!" she said in a watery voice that trembled in the current around us. Her lips were the color of bright orange coral and her teeth were a bright white. "What manner of creatures are you?"

I looked at Corey, then fearfully at the sharpened weapons that they were pointing at us. "What manner... er... I guess we're... humans? Is that what you're asking?"

That elicited a mixed reaction from the stern-looking group around us. Some of them gasped… others sneered doubtfully.

The girl in the armor obviously looked like she thought we were lying. "If you are humans then you would be drowned and dead." She thrust her three-pointed spear forward and poked me in the arm. I yelped and rubbed it painfully. "You are flesh-and-blood, not ghosts," the girl continued, narrowing her eyes at us suspiciously. "Are you fairies? Shape-shifters? Show us your true form! I command you!"

Corey looked at me and I thought desperately about how we could explain. "We're not fairies." I said."We've come here to find the North Star."

That certainly caused a stir in the group. Some of them began to yell angrily and the girl raised her spear to my throat.

Instantly, I held up my hands. "Whoa!" I yelled desperately. "Wait!"

Suddenly, there was a startled gasp from several members of the group, and many of them backed away from Corey and I, glancing at the girl in the armor uncertainly. Confused by this sudden reaction, I looked at the girl and saw that she was staring, stunned, at the ring on my hand.

"Where did you get that ring?" she asked quietly.

I hesitated. "The fairy queen Bridgette gave one each to me and my brother." I said. "She is married to our grandfather."

This time there was silence. The others lowered their weapons in astonishment and the girl looked from me to Corey with an expression of growing amazement.

Without another word, she lowered her spear and pulled off her golden helmet. Long, beautiful, bright red hair flowed out into the water around her. She handed the spear and the helmet to a silent man beside her, then, without warning, she lunged forward and embraced me tightly. I was so wound up that I almost let out a startled scream, but choked it back at the last second. She held me for a long moment, her red hair swirling around us, then kissed me on the cheek with her cold lips. A moment later, she embraced a terrified Corey and did the same.

"Hello, my brothers!" she said warmly. "Welcome to Atlantis!"

It took a few minutes for Corey and I to recover from the shock of almost being killed by the group of fish-people, and in that time, the girl explained that her name was Rhiannon. She was a mermaid and the queen of Atlantis.

Most of the others that had surrounded us had now been dismissed. Only two of the mermen remained. They stood on either side of Rhiannon as guards, keeping a protective stance and staring straight ahead with stony expressions.

Rhiannon had lost the intimidating tone in her voice and now took our hands warmly and led us towards the city, smiling and talking the whole way.

"I cannot believe Mother did not tell me of your impending visit!" she said excitedly. "We could have prepared a feast! There is so much we need to talk about! Oh, how is she?"

I was so busy trying to take in the amazing sight of the city and creatures around us that I had lost track of what she was saying. "How is who?" I asked.

"Mother." Rhiannon prompted.

Corey cast me a confused look.

"Er…" I said carefully. "I don't know. We just got here, remember? We haven't met your mother."

Rhiannon stopped swimming and blinked at me. "Bridgette." she said.

I was confused. "You mean that Bridgette is… your mother?"

She nodded. "Yes. That makes you my brothers."

"What?" Corey asked, shocked. "When you said 'welcome my brothers' I thought that was just a fancy mermaid way of saying hi."

Rhiannon laughed. "No. I mean that you are actually my brothers. I am your sister."

Corey and I exchanged startled looks in silence.

Sister? I thought.

It was a shocking thing to hear. We had a sister... and she was... a mermaid. This was turning out to be a day full of surprises.

I looked around at the fantastic coral city again. "So this... this is Bridgette's kingdom?"

Rhiannon smiled. "Well, she was already the fairy queen of the Sylphs when my father met her... but when they married she became the queen of Atlantis as well."

Corey choked. "Say what? Bridgette is already married?"

Rhiannon's smile faltered. "She was married to my father, but he died long ago. He was not an immortal fairy like Bridgette."

"Oh." I said carefully. "I'm sorry to hear that. Our real parents died, too. How old were you when it happened?"

Rhiannon seemed to consider this. "It was about half a century ago... so I guess I was about two-hundred and twenty."

If Corey had not been floating in water, I think that he may have fallen over in shock. "What!?"

Rhiannon looked at him and she furrowed her brow uncertainly. "What is wrong?"

"We just thought you looked... younger." I said wryly.

Rhiannon looked surprised for a moment, and then laughed, her red hair swirling in the current around her.

A strange orange-and-black striped fish swam by us. It had two normal eyes, and a third eye perched up high on a stalk that extended from its forehead.

Corey cleared his throat just then and when I looked at him, he tapped his arm where a watch would be if he wore one. *We gotta hurry, bro.*

I nodded and turned back to Rhiannon. "Right... well, listen, can you tell us about the North Star?"

Rhiannon looked at us seriously. "What brings you to it?" she asked.

I took a deep, watery breath and thought for a moment. "Well..." I said. "It's a long story..."

Although our time was short, I had decided that we should tell Rhiannon everything. It was strange to learn that we had a sister... and I found that I already felt an odd trusting affection for her. It took almost thirty minutes to tell her our story from the beginning... from that first fateful day last October when Corey and I had found Elayne sleeping an enchanted sleep deep in the woods near Jacob's Rest.

I ended with our encounter with the sirens and finally my dream and our swim down to Atlantis.

We were in a huge underwater cavern now. It glistened brightly with the glow of a thousand sparkling crystals embedded in the coral ceiling high overhead. Rhiannon had settled down into a huge sponge chair. When I finally finished telling our story, she was quiet for a long time.

"So it was you that finally broke Bridgette and Dryan's spell over the world." she said thoughtfully. "For my whole life, the ocean was still and unmoving and the non-magical creatures floated like driftwood in the water. Then, a year ago, the world came back to life."

I nodded. "Right. When we broke the spell on Elayne, the spell on this world was broken, too."

Rhiannon's big blue eyes watched us with awe. "Amazing." she murmured.

At that moment, Corey was admiring a cluster of red and black striped coral that grew from the wall. He had reached out to touch it when Rhiannon turned her attention to him. "Corey, my brother. Please do not touch that."

Corey pulled his hand back and looked at Rhiannon. "What? Oh! Sorry. I wasn't going to break it."

Rhiannon shook her head. "You would not have broken it. You would have been dead instantly at the slightest touch of it. It is deadly poison."

Corey gaped at the cluster of coral and swam back from it carefully. "Oh... well. Alright then. Nice thing to just have sitting out for anyone to brush up against there."

"My father gave it to me." she said. "He told me that it was both beautiful and dangerous... like me."

"That's so... sweet." Corey said, still eyeing the coral uncomfortably.

"So what's this North Star?" I prompted, feeling the pressure to speed things up a bit. I was worried that our captain would set sail for land without us.

Rhiannon looked at us thoughtfully. "The North Star is a legendary jewel." she said. "It shines more beautifully than any other gem in the world."

"And it's here in Atlantis?" I asked.

Rhiannon bit her lip. "Well... not exactly. It is hidden among the collected treasures of the fairy Niella... and guarded closely by her in her lair."

I sighed a watery sigh. "Silly question... but fairies who guard their treasures in a lair... they're not usually too friendly, are they?"

Rhiannon shook her head. "No. Niella is a fearsome creature. The entrance to her lair is marked by the scattered bones of the unfortunate creatures that have come too near."

"Typical." Corey rolled his eyes.

"Where is the lair, exactly?" I asked.

"In the caverns deep beneath the city." Rhiannon answered.

I looked at Corey. "That matches the clue we have." I said. "Sounds like we're in the right place."

Corey looked at me in surprise. "Um... hello? Were you not listening to our dear sister? 'The entrance is littered with the bones of those unfortunate enough to get too close'. Doesn't that send up a red flag, bro?"

I considered this for a moment. "We're just going to have to come up with a way to sneak in. Take the North Star somehow without her knowing."

"Right!" Corey snorted sarcastically. "That *always* works out."

Rhiannon shook her head. "You cannot take the North Star."

I waved my hands. "I know, I know. Stealing is bad. We don't have much time, though, and I don't see that we have any other choice."

Rhiannon interrupted. "No... you do not understand. The North Star is an enchanted jewel. It cannot be stolen. Only the rightful owner can pass it to another. If someone tries to take it, then it will melt into seawater and disappear forever."

I looked at Rhiannon uncertainly. "You mean that this Niella has to decide to give us the jewel on her own?"

Rhiannon nodded. "Yes, my brother."

I looked uncertainly at Corey. "This is going to be a little more complicated than we thought..."

Corey shrugged. "Always is, bro. It always is..."

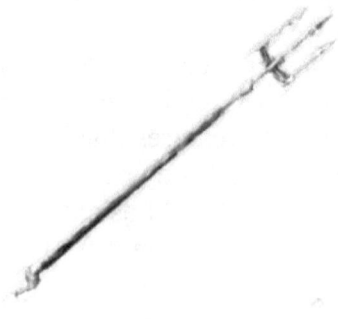

Chapter Twenty-Two

To The Lair

 e felt the pressure of the hours moving by quickly. We knew that we had to be back at the surface by midday... and we suspected that it may be almost dawn already. If we had even another day, we may have been able to come up with some clever, foolproof plan for getting the jewel. As it was, though, we could think of nothing and I finally had to just tell Rhiannon that Corey and I had to go and see Niella before our time ran out.

She looked at us uncertainly. "But I only just discovered that I have brothers!" she said. "I would be sad for you to be killed so soon!"

"Gee," Corey said, "You're right. That *would* be a bummer..."

Rhiannon lifted her helmet and spear from a nearby nook in the coral wall. "I'll come with you!" she said. "We'll bring the army of Atlantis into the foul Niella's lair! She'll have no choice but to obey or be destroyed!"

I held up my hands, surprised and flattered by her fierce and loyal determination. "That won't be necessary." I said.

Corey gave me a look. "Hey! Shut up, bro. If Sis wants to bring the cavalry, then let's not argue with her. She would be really sad if we were killed so soon, remember? We haven't even gotten a chance to catch up on seven hundred years of missed birthdays!"

I shook my head. "No. We need to get Niella to give us the North Star freely. If we go barging in on her with an army, there's no way she's going to cooperate."

Rhiannon looked deflated. "You are right, brother." she said. Then, she looked up at me with renewed determination. "But I will accompany you, nonetheless."

"You're the queen." I said. "You can't risk your life to help us."

Rhiannon straightened her slim shoulders. "You are correct. I *am* queen. And as such, there is no one that tells me what I *cannot* do."

She watched me for a moment with that same icy-blue defiant gaze that she wore when we first saw her.

Corey finally laughed. "You know, bro... this is the way Elayne is going to be when she gets to be queen, too. You think she's stubborn now? Ha! I have a feeling that you haven't seen *anything* yet."

I decided to just give it up. "Fine." I said. "Lead the way."

Rhiannon led us through her underwater palace until we came to a room with nothing else but a huge boulder against one wall. She ordered her two fierce-looking guards to roll it aside and when they did, we saw that it had been blocking the entrance to a dark tunnel.

She made her guards stay at the entrance as the three of us swam into the hole.

There were no glowing crystals embedded into the rocks here to light the way. The tunnel turned sharply downward and became a black hole that seemed to go down forever.

"Aren't we already like a mile down in the ocean?" Corey muttered as he looked at the hole. "How far does this thing go down?"

Rhiannon looked at him seriously. "Far." she said simply. Then she spun her spear in a small circle and it began to give off a faint blue light. Not very much, but enough to see a little way ahead. "Ready?" she asked.

Corey looked at me doubtfully. "Not really, but..."

"We're ready." I said. "Lead the way."

Rhiannon nodded, and with that, she gave a kick of her huge tailfin and shot forward into the tunnel. Corey and I had barely started paddling and we watched in shock as the blue light from her spear sped off out of sight.

Feeling a sudden panic in the blackness of the tunnel, I tried to swim in the direction the light disappeared, but soon got turned around and ended up hitting the jagged rock wall of the tunnel and scraping my arm painfully.

A few seconds later, we saw a light coming back as Rhiannon swam to us, stopping just in front of us. "What's the matter?" she asked. "Are you not coming?"

"You have got to be kidding me!" Corey grumbled.

I smiled at Rhiannon. "Sorry. We just can't swim quite as fast as you." I said.

"This is only like the third time I've been swimming in my whole life." Corey complained. "And now I'm at the bottom of the freaking ocean. I can barely dogpaddle."

Rhiannon looked baffled. Not being able to swim was probably a strange idea to her.

"Would you be able to go slower?" I asked her. "So we could keep up, maybe?"

Rhiannon looked surprised. "Oh! Of course. I just thought that you were in a hurry to return."

"We are." I said. Then I hesitated. "Wait a minute... how far exactly is Niella's lair?"

Rhiannon seemed to consider. "Well, swimming at your speed, it will take about three days to get there... assuming we did not stop to sleep or eat."

I gagged. "Seriously?"

She nodded. "Yes. The tunnels beneath Atlantis are an endless labyrinth. I will take you the shortest path, but it is still a great distance... some of it against a strong current."

Corey looked panicked. "Um, bro... we don't have that long."

I inhaled the seawater deeply. "How long would it take *you* to swim there?" I asked Rhiannon.

"I could swim there in less than two hours." she said, then her blue eyes brightened. "And I could carry you!"

I looked doubtfully at her slender arms.

Corey must have been thinking the same thing. "Maybe we could get your pumped-up guards out there to carry us instead."

Rhiannon's face darkened. "Are you saying that I am too weak to carry you? I am the warrior queen of Atlantis!"

I smiled. "Alright, alright. No need to get all riled up again. Fine. You carry us."

Rhiannon looked at my smile suspiciously, and then finally smiled too, looking a bit embarrassed.

She handed me her spear and then held out her hands to Corey and I. I took one hand and Corey took the other. Her hand was very smooth and delicate, but her grip was cold and firm.

"Are you ready?" she asked as her grip tightened.

Corey didn't answer, but I nodded.

Then, without another word, Rhiannon turned into the blackness, whipped her massive scaly fin once, and we shot forward with terrifying speed.

It was a dizzying ride.

Rhiannon's tail flashed behind us and propelled us forward at breakneck speed. The cavern branched off in all directions and sometimes we would shoot to the left or right... or sometimes we would suddenly rocket up into a tunnel above us, then just as quickly make a sudden dive into a downward tunnel. It made my stomach lurch with every sudden, unexpected turn.

This seemed to go on forever. Sometimes I would close my eyes, but that never really helped. It was like riding some twisted underwater roller-coaster for two hours straight.

My arm began hurting after just a few minutes, and after the first hour, it felt as if my shoulder was going to tear right off. Still, Rhiannon's grip on my hand never loosened and she never slowed. She seemed to know instinctively where to go, and there was never any pause or hesitation.

We never could have done this without her. I thought to myself, then I couldn't help but laugh when I remembered her stubborn determination to accompany us. Was Elayne really that stubborn?

Yes. I decided. *She is.*

And so am I about some things. Maybe too stubborn...

When we finally began to slow, the ache in my arm was almost unbearable. We emerged into a massive underground cavern... and Rhiannon released our hands. I tried to lower my arm, but found that I couldn't. The muscle was too cramped. I started massaging it and I saw Corey wincing and doing the same to his arm.

Rhiannon was breathing hard as she flipped her tail and spun around to face us. She lifted her helmet off of her long red hair and pulled it back up again before setting her helmet back in place. The golden armor on her chest heaved up and down with every labored breath, but her face was cool and determined. When I handed her back her spear, she looked around the darkness and pointed ahead. "The entrance to Niella's lair is on the far side of this cavern." she said. "Before you continue, you should decide how best to proceed."

Corey, who had finally gotten his arm to move a little, was still trying to move it painfully. "Right, bro. What's the plan, here?"

"I'm going in." I said, trying my best to sound confident even though I had absolutely no idea what I was going to do. "I'm going to go in to talk with her."

Rhiannon looked stunned. "I mean no offense, but that is not much of a plan, my brother."

I shrugged. "It's all I've got."

"So what exactly is Niella?" Corey asked. "Is she like a sea monster or something?"

Rhiannon shook her head slowly, looking frightened for the first time. "Niella is a fairy, so of course she can choose the form she wishes to appear in… but the few who have survived an encounter with her tell tales of a creature far more terrifying and monstrous than anything they had ever encountered."

Corey looked at me, his face whiter than usual in the pale glow of Rhiannon's spear. "Hear that, bro?" he squeaked. "Terrifying? Monstrous? You sure you want to go through with this?"

"Corey, the only way to get the North Star is to get Niella to give it to us. I've faced monsters before. It can't be worse than facing Grendesh."

At the mention of Grendesh, Corey's eyes grew doubly wide. "Oh sure… right. The difference is that we had a plan going into that."

"I have a plan." I bluffed, squaring off my shoulders and rubbing the last of the cramps out of my sore arm. "Just stay here and I'll take care of everything."

"We're going with you." Rhiannon said.

"No." I said flatly. When Rhiannon's eyes sparked, I waved my hands "And don't go giving me your 'I'm-the-queen-and-nobody-tells-me no' speech. It's not because I think you're weak, either, because obviously you are the only one that would have any real chance in a fight with a sea monster. I want to go in alone because I want Niella to know that we mean her no harm. If I'm going to get her to give me the North Star on her own, she needs to be able to trust me."

"But what's to stop her from biting your head off the moment you step inside?" Corey asked.

I shrugged. "Trust goes both ways."

Corey crossed his arms. "That's a dumb plan."

"Well that's the plan and that's what we're doing." I said. "End of discussion."

When I looked at Rhiannon again, I saw her blue eyes shining as she watched me. "Well said, Brother." she said with admiration. "Spoken like a true leader. You will make a great king someday."

That really startled me. "What? Who said anything about□"

But before I could say anything else, she moved forward and hugged me tightly. "I will miss you my stubborn, newfound brother."

"Miss me? Why?"

"She means that she'll miss you when Niella chews your head off with her two-thousand razor-sharp teeth." Corey said.

Rhiannon turned to Corey and shook her head seriously. "No. Actually she may chew his legs off first and laugh cruelly as he swims in circles, dying slowly in front of her."

Corey nodded thoughtfully. "Right. Right. That's probably more her style."

I rolled my eyes. "Thanks for the boost of confidence, you two. I'm not changing my mind, though. Wait here."

Corey and Rhiannon looked at me with matching expressions of pity and remorse, waving goodbye to me dramatically.

With a heavy sigh, I turned and started moving through the darkness in the direction of the lair.

Chapter Twenty-Three

The Terrible and Fearsome Niella

s I moved across the huge cavern, I began to see that there was a faint light ahead in the darkness. Swimming closer, I saw that it was a single green crystal, pulsing weakly, embedded in the rock above a cave and throwing out a dim, sickly light. It threw shadows across the sandy floor of the cavern, which I now saw was scattered with little shards of rocks and shells.

Then, there was a skull lying amid the shells, followed soon after by other bones, scattered and crushed and half-buried in the sand. The trail led right up to the cave entrance, which gaped huge and black in the water ahead.

There was a current moving here, stirring the sand and bones closest to the cave entrance. In, then out. In, then out. A steady rhythm, which I quickly recognized as the pattern of something huge breathing slow, deliberate breaths.

Then, I saw the eyes... perched high on each side of the cavern entrance. It was then that I realized... this wasn't a cave at all. It was the gaping, open mouth of something huge and hungry... a giant sea monster waiting for me to swim right into its open mouth.

I jerked backwards and my heart pounded. *I was too close! I would never be able to outrun it!*

In my electric fear, I blinked my eyes and the illusion was gone. I saw that the "eyes" above the cavern mouth were actually two massive gemstones set in just the right place to make the illusion complete. Even as my heart began to slow down a bit, I marveled at the illusion. The swaying current and the eerie green light made it almost perfect.

"Creepy." I heard Charlie's voice agree in my mind. It was the first time he had spoken since I had gone underwater.

"Great." I muttered sarcastically. "So glad you're here. I was beginning to think that you had stayed up on the boat with the girls."

Charlie chuckled... a laugh that was more chilling than humorous. "Not a chance, partner. Where you go, I go."

"Lucky me." I said, then I moved forward and into the mouth of the cave.

The sickly green light from the outside cast shadows that moved over the walls and ceiling. There was light coming from somewhere far back in the cavern, too, shimmering and multicolored. *Maybe the treasure she's guarding.* I thought.

My heart was pounding, and I braced myself for something huge and monstrous to come swimming out of the shadows at me... but so far, all was quiet. The cavern seemed empty, all the way back to the shimmering light in the far back.

"Hello?" I called. "Niella?"

I paused just inside the cave entrance and waited. A moment later, I called again. "Niella! I need to talk with you!"

"Pooh!" a huge voice echoed, high and screechy through the cavern. "Why bother announcing yourself? You see the way to my treasure is clear. Go. Try to get to it. I will not stop you. I *promisssssss.*"

I glanced nervously towards the shimmering light at the back of the cavern. There was no way to tell where the voice was coming from.

"I'm not here to steal your treasure." I said loudly.

"But of course you are!" The high-pitched voice echoed. "Why else would you come? Let me guessssss… you are a mermaid and want to trade your voice for a pair of legs so you can woo a handsome prince…"

I hesitated uncertainly. "Er… no. I just want to talk."

The voice interrupted me. "Nonsense! Try for the treasure. Go on!"

I didn't move. This was not at all what I had expected.

"No." I said firmly.

There was a long pause, and then the huge voice echoed again. "Pooh!" it said. "You're no fun! I really wanted to see the look on your face when you tried to sneak back out with it and I ate you alive."

That made my heart jump nervously. Charlie was laughing in my head. "Ah… I like her already…"

"I get it." I said shakily. "You promised not to stop me from getting to the treasure, but you didn't promise that I would make it out alive."

"Perceptive." The eerie voice echoed. "You have obviously dealt with fairies before."

"Yes." I said carefully. "In fact, I am the grandson of Bridgette, the queen of the Sylphs." I held up my ring into the darkness.

"Ungh!" the voice scowled. "I hate Bridgette. That little purple pest is far too self-righteous for her own good."

"Oh" I said, lowering my hand slowly. *Well,* I thought, *there goes my best chance of getting any favors out of her. I'd better think of something else… fast.*

"What have you come here for, boy?" the voice asked.

A shiver ran up my spine when she called me *boy* like that. For a moment, she sounded just like Sidhera... and I realized that I needed to be very, very careful about whatever I decided to do next.

I knew that time was short, and so, for lack of a better plan, I just decided to tell the truth.

"I need the North Star." I said.

The sudden cackle of laughter that rang through the dark cavern was a chilling sound. It went on for a long time, then finally the voice spoke again. "Very humorous, boy. You have made me laugh, which is something I have not done in three hundred years. You had better leave now while you are ahead. I may even let you make it out alive."

"No." I said. "I will not leave until you have given it to me."

"THEN YOU WILL NOT LEAVE AT ALL!" The high cackling voice roared back at me.

I floated nervously in place, still trying to find the source of the monstrous voice. My mind was screaming for me to run... but I knew that there was no turning back now. If I tried to run, she would kill me for sure. I had to just keep bluffing my way through.

"How can I persuade you to give me the North Star?" I asked.

The voice hesitated. "Why settle for just that jewel?" she said slyly. "I have greater treasures than that one in my possession..."

I shook my head. "I want only the North Star. Nothing more."

"Why?" the voice spat instantly.

Again, I decided to tell the truth. "I am trying to undo a spell cast by Sidhera." I said.

The voice grew silent for a long moment, as if considering this.

Finally, the voice whispered in the watery darkness. "If there is anyone I despise more than Bridgette, it is that proud and spiteful witch Sidhera."

I took a deep breath. "Then you will help me? Give me the North Star?"

The voice cackled with laughter again, but this time it was more thoughtful. "I did not say that, boy. I am not foolish enough to dole out my treasure to anyone that floats into my lair with a good story. I will need something in return. Something even more valuable."

I hesitated for a long moment, my stomach clenching nervously. I had nothing with me that I could trade. I considered the ring that Bridgette had given me. "What about my ring?" I asked, and even as I said it, I conjured up the horrible image of removing the ring here, miles under the ocean, and dying a painful and terrible death as its magic left me.

"Pooh! I want nothing to do with such a trinket."

I held my hands up. "I have nothing." I said.

"Then you will leave with nothing." The voice said sourly. "Be gone! Go before I change my mind and decide to eat you after all."

I remained still, floating in place uncertainly. What could I...

Then I remembered the vial in my pocket.

I struggled to reach into the pocket of my wet jeans, and after a long moment, I was able to dig out the small silver vial.

Niella's voice spoke up again in the darkness, reluctantly curious. "What's that?"

I hesitated.

A flame that forever burns should still burn underwater, right?

I hoped I was right.

Carefully, I uncorked the tiny vial and a bright orange flame leapt out of the top, instantly lighting up the whole cavern.

The effect on Niella was immediate. "Ooooo…" she cooed softly. "Now that is something I have not seen for a long, long time."

I could already feel the fire warming up the cold water in the cave. Its flickering orange light licked the uneven walls.

"Come closer." I said, sensing an opportunity. "See for yourself."

There was a pause, and then I felt something moving up above me. Something was swimming out of a hole hidden in the shadows right above my head.

She could have killed me and I never would have seen her coming. I thought with a chill.

Then, as she swam from the shadows and into the light, I got my first good look at the Terrible and Fearsome Niella.

She was about the size of a large goldfish.

She had red, mottled scales and… it was true that she had rows of sharp teeth in her mouth, but… they were so tiny! She may have been able to bite off the tip of my finger, but even that may have been too much for her to chew.

She was transfixed by the dancing flame and swam towards it as if hypnotized.

"Amazing." she cooed, looking into the orange light. "And the warmth! It has been centuries since I have felt such warmth!"

I let her stare at it in awe for a moment longer, and then I pushed the cork back into the silver vial and the dancing flame disappeared once more.

The tiny Niella-fish swirled around to face me and the cavern once again filled with her booming voice. "Bring it back!" she snarled.

I considered my situation.

Was this what I needed the fire for? I thought. *Had Dryan's piece of wood known all along that I needed the fire to trade for the North Star?*

Finally, I decided that it was the only option that I had at the moment. "Fine." I told Niella. "I'll trade you. The magic flame for the North Star."

Niella was nothing more than a tiny silhouette floating in the shadows in front of me now, but I could sense that she was considering her own options.

"Fine." she said at last. "Leave the fire. Go and take the North Star."

I hesitated. "No. Bring the North Star to me." I said.

There was a long moment of silence. I began to worry that Niella would transform suddenly into a great white shark in the shadows and devour me. Instead, I saw a faint blue glow moving towards me from the treasure room. From out of the shadows, a sparkling blue crystal, about the size of a softball, fell onto the sandy floor in front of me.

"Take it." Niella said again. "Leave the fire and go."

I started to reach down to pick up the gem and hesitated just before my fingers touched it.

It has to be given by its rightful owner or it will melt to seawater. I thought.

I straightened up again. "Give it to me."

Niella snarled. "You really do want to be eaten, boy, don't you? What makes you think I won't just kill you and take your fire?"

I swallowed nervously. I had not considered this.

"Because the laws of magic forbid it." I bluffed.

Niella hissed. "And what know you of the laws of magic?"

Nothing, really. I thought.

"Bridgette is my grandmother, remember?" I said.

Niella seemed to consider this, then swam down and lifted the jewel in her teeth. She moved towards me and spat it in my hand.

"There," she said. "Our transaction is complete. The fire is mine."

I held the jewel and the vial and thought for a moment. "One more thing." I said.

Niella's voice grew to a raging screech again. "Our transaction is done, boy! Leave the fire and go!"

I held up the vial. "Only if you promise that I will be able to leave unharmed and alive."

Niella grew quiet. When she spoke again, her voice was a hiss in the darkness. "You've been tricked by fairies before, I see."

"Yes I have." I conceded.

"Fine. Go unharmed… and never return to disturb Niella."

That was all I needed to hear. I uncorked the vial and the fire leapt out of it and lit up the cave once more. Even as I was turning to go, I saw Niella move towards it again, wide-eyed and enchanted.

I pocketed the vial, clutched the jewel tightly and swam out of the cave. Once safely outside, I unclenched tense muscles and breathed a big, watery sigh of relief.

Corey and Rhiannon emerged from the nearby shadows. Rhiannon's spear was still glowing a soft blue.

"You guys just couldn't stay put, could you?" I said.

"Hey! We let you do your thing." Corey said. "We were just waiting outside in case you needed… backup."

Rhiannon looked at me with wonder. "You were very brave, Jasen. Was she a huge and monstrous beast as the legends say?"

I thought about the guppy-sized Niella I had met inside the cave.

"She was pretty hideous." I agreed.

Rhiannon looked at me in amazement. "You truly do have the brave heart of a king." she said. "Elayne is a very lucky girl to have you."

"Lucky to have her heart broken by you." Charlie chided in my head.

"Shut up." I murmured.

"What?" Rhiannon asked.

"Nothing." I said, holding out the blue gem in my hand. "This is it, right?"

Rhiannon looked at the gem and nodded. "Yes. That is the North Star."

"Good." I said. "Let's start back. We're already late."

Chapter Twenty-Four

Beached

 orey and I switched sides on the ride back through the caves. We thought that would help spare our aching arms… but instead both arms were sore by the end of the ride.

Still, I couldn't help but feel a sense of elation. We had gotten the North Star as we had set out to do… and hopefully it was the key to undoing Sidhera's spell somehow. By the time we made it back to the Coral Palace, we knew that our time with our newfound sister was coming to an end.

"I can come with you!" Rhiannon offered. "Join you on your quest!"

I smiled thankfully. "You've already been a huge help." I said. "I'm thinking that the rest of our journey from here will be over land, though."

Rhiannon looked disappointed. "Well, now that you have found Atlantis, you should always be able to make your way back here." she said. "And you will be welcomed any time."

"Thanks." I said. "I hope that all of this will be over soon and we will be able to come back and visit without the pressure of the whole 'saving the world' thing hanging over our heads."

Corey snorted. "Yeah, right. It's never quite as glamorous as it sounds..."

Rhiannon hugged each of us again tightly. "I look forward to that day, my brothers. When you return, you can meet the rest of the family, too."

Corey and I paused, looking at each other. "Rest of the family?" I asked. "I thought your father had died?"

Rhiannon nodded. "Yes, but we have sixteen other sisters."

Corey and I both fell into coughing fits, gasping and choking seawater.

Since we were running late, Rhiannon offered to escort us back up to the surface. Even before we got there, though, I knew something was wrong. The currents were much stronger, pulling at us so hard that even Rhiannon had to work to stay on a straight course.

At one point, Charlie mused calmly in my head. "Incoming from above..."

I looked up into the black water and couldn't see anything as Rhiannon sped upwards. "Rhiannon!" I shouted through the churning water. "Something is coming."

Rhiannon didn't slow, but did turn to look at me questioningly as she swam "What are you talking about, brother? I don't see any..."

But then she must have sensed it, too. She looked up to see a huge shadow coming at us fast from above. She gave a fierce whip of her tail and we shot off to the side… just in time to miss being crushed.

At first my mind could not understand what I was seeing. It was still so dark, and whatever had just narrowly missed us was huge… easily as big as a building. I looked down just in time to catch a glimpse of it speeding towards the bottom of the ocean like some impossibly huge creature falling to its death.

My heart raced as I looked at Corey and blinked in surprise. "Was that…?"

Corey looked horrified. "I think that was our ship!" Corey said.

A moment later, another huge piece soared by like a spear rocketing towards the bottom. I recognized it as the splintered mast of our ship. The tattered sails flapped in the current as it disappeared down below.

"Rhiannon!" I shouted. "We need to get to the surface… now!"

Rhiannon set her jaw with fierce conviction and turned towards the surface again. We rocketed upwards with such stunning speed that my whole body shook with the force of the water pounding against me. Without slowing down, we broke the surface and we rocketed high into the air.

Thunder exploded in the sky above us and lightning stabbed down at the water from every side. The wind was howling, throwing rain in all directions. The waves were mountainous swells that crashed down upon themselves with tremendous force.

Rhiannon held on tight to Corey and I, and it took me a moment to understand what was happening. The world had turned to chaos here on the surface. As I choked and coughed up the seawater in my lungs, I caught a glimpse of several dark shapes moving in the water.

When the lightning seared the sky again, I saw a wave-tossed boat. It looked like the small rowboat that had been tied alongside our big ship. There were several people in it, struggling to hold on and… something else. It looked like they were fighting against an onslaught of dark shapes that swarmed in the churning water around them.

"Over there!" I shouted above the roar of the wind. I choked and spat up some more seawater. "Sirens!" I managed to shout before gagging again.

Rhiannon rocketed under water again, pulling Corey and I with her. I got turned around in the churning dark current, but when we broke the surface again, we were beside the boat and in the midst of the attacking group of sirens.

They had the captain by the shoulders and the other people in the boat—including a rain-soaked Emily and Elayne—were struggling to hold on and keep the captain from being pulled under.

Our sudden appearance in their midst caused everyone in the struggle—people and sirens alike—to cry out in surprise. The two sirens that had been pulling on the captain let go suddenly, dropping his face into the water. Rhiannon used the surprise to her advantage and with amazing speed she whipped around in a circle and took out two more with her massive tail… hitting them so hard that they were knocked out of the water and splashed back down thirty feet away.

A siren nearby opened its mouth with a furious hiss and reached for Rhiannon's back with its scaly hands. I jumped up without thinking and grabbed its arm to stop it. The sharp, jagged scales cut into my palm as I held it, and a moment later, Rhiannon pulled off her golden helmet and brought it around hard and fast across the siren's face. The terrible scaly monster went limp in my hands and I let go just as it sunk back below the water.

Elayne and Emily were helping Corey into the boat and a huge wave appeared from nowhere and tossed everyone sideways suddenly. The crewmen inside threw themselves against the far side of the boat to keep it from tipping over. Emily was thrown forward and almost fell out, but the captain reached out and caught her just before she fell into the water.

The sirens were gone, but the boat was not going to last much longer in these waves. The girls had pulled Corey up onto the small boat and they were shouting for me, but just then another wave threw me under again. I struggled against the strong currents to get back to the surface, and when I finally made it, lightning flashed again and I saw that I was far from the small boat and it was moving away fast without me.

A hand grabbed me from behind, and I almost screamed, ready to fight off another attacking siren. Above the noise of the rain and wind, though, I heard a voice close to my ear. "Do not worry, brother. I have you."

I was propelled under the waves again and a moment later I was thrown up out of the water and landed hard right in the boat… between a startled and soaking group of the crewmen, the girls, and Corey.

Even before I could pull myself up, the small boat lurched again and we braced ourselves to be thrown sideways by a wave. Instead, we began moving forward… through the water and against the waves. When I looked out, I saw Rhiannon's slender hands gripping the sides of the boat as her massive tail kicked up the water behind us and kept us moving.

The crew stared in stunned silence as the mermaid steered our boat through the fury of the terrible storm. Lightning forked through the dark clouds above and all we could do was hold on for our lives.

The predawn sky was red as we waded out into the surf.

The small boat, which Rhiannon had steered to safety, had been pulled up high on the sand and away from the water. The crewmen slept, exhausted, on the powdered sand close by while the captain was shaking a nearby tree to make some fruit fall from its high branches.

Emily, Elayne, Corey, and I waded out into the calm morning waves to where Rhiannon had pulled herself up into the shallow water. With the top half of her body out of the water, she looked almost human. Her golden armor reflected the light from the red sky and her long, red hair spilled out in waves over her slender shoulders. Although her face looked weary, she smiled at us brightly as we approached.

She looked at Elayne, whose brown tattered clothes clung to her heavy body, and she bowed to her. "It has been an honor to meet you, princess Elayne. The tales my brother Jasen has told me of your beauty and grace are true."

"How can you even say that with a straight face?" Corey said. "Seriously... look at that mole. She's disgusting."

Elayne ignored him and bowed deeply to Rhiannon "And it is an honor to meet you, queen of Atlantis. I hope thy merpeople are well."

Corey rolled his eyes. "Alright. All of this is *way* too formal. Stop with all of the bowing and... did you just say 'thy' Elayne? Don't ever let me hear you say that again!"

We all laughed and Corey put his arm on Rhiannon's shoulder. "Anyway, you are a Stillwell boy now, Rhiannon. It's going to be awesome having a tough sister! Jasen has always been a little too wimpy for my taste."

Rhiannon looked happily surprised. "Thank you! I am happy to be called a Stillwell boy! And you, my brothers, are now daughters of Atlantis!"

Corey furrowed his eyebrows. "Gee... thanks. We probably should keep that just between us, though."

We laughed again and we all hugged Rhiannon and thanked her for her help. As she caught me in a fierce hug (that may have bruised some of my ribs against her armor), I said to her quietly. "Thank you for everything. It is good to have family."

Rhiannon pulled away from me and smiled at me with her blue-green eyes sparkling. "It *is* good to have family, my brother." she said. Then, the salty air gusted and whipped her long red hair around her face. She pulled the stray hair away from her eyes and looked at me again. "You will come see us soon?" she asked.

I nodded. "If all goes well and we're all still alive in a week... then we will visit soon."

Rhiannon clasped my shoulder reassuringly and nodded, then she pulled her hair up and tucked it once more under her golden helmet. With a smile, she turned and dove back under the frothy waves.

Some time later, we joined the captain up on the beach and he offered us some of the red fruit that he had collected from the nearby trees.

"We are truly sorry about your ship, captain." Elayne was saying as she took a bite.

The captain waved dismissively, his beard juicy from his mouthful of fruit. "If it be God's will, I cannot argue."

Elayne hesitated. I saw her touch the black mole on her face uncertainly. "Captain, I am... distantly related to the royal family. When next we are in the vicinity of the castle, I will be sure to mention the bravery of you and your men to the princess. I'm sure that she will be more than happy to reward you... perhaps even buy you a new ship."

The captain smiled a crooked smile at Elayne. He looked touched. "It's nice of ye to say, miss... but if you are related to the royal family, then I am a flying humpback whale."

Elayne looked startled by this.

The captain laughed. "Still, it's been a grand adventure. I think that my boys and I are going to head up the coast a bit and see where the salty wind leads us."

He took another bite of the fruit and seeds trickled down his bushy chin. "Where is your group off to, then?"

I glanced at the others. "We're... not sure yet."

The captain smiled. "Well, if ye be headin the same direction, we'd be glad of your company."

We thanked him and moved up the beach a little and settled beneath some palm trees. The morning sun was starting to warm up the air and our clothes were almost dry. The gusting wind picked up loose sand and threw it against our legs and arms, making them sting.

As we sat down, Emily pulled out a leather drawstring bag that she had kept in her pocket and had tied to her belt for extra safety. She untied it and pulled it open to reveal Dryan's wood piece. As she held it up, we could see that the spidery writing across the grain was gone once more.

We all looked at Elayne expectantly and she took a deep breath.

"We want to stop Sidhera's plan and return me to my own body." she said loudly and clearly.

Almost instantly, the grain on the wood started swirling and a moment later, a new message appeared across the surface. I could see already that this one was longer than the two we had seen before.

Emily held it closer so she could read it to us.

The Spear of Zeus pries a soul asunder
And replaces it before the thunder.
Seek this in the Airy Tower.
Used but once, it will lose its power.

After Emily had re-read it silently to herself, she passed it around for each of us to look at.

"It sounds like this could be the clue we've been waiting for." Elayne said as she read the message again. "It talks about prying a soul and replacing it… like pulling Sidhera out of my body and putting me back in."

I nodded. "I think you're right."

She shook her head. "But I am not sure what the Spear of Zeus is…"

"Lightning." Corey said instantly.

We all turned to look at him as he took another one of the fruits the captain had collected and bit into it. He paused, juice dripping down his chin, and saw us all staring at him. "What? I'm smart! Don't look so surprised! I loved Mythology. That was like the one thing I ever paid attention to in Mrs. Crouch's class."

Emily looked at Corey proudly. "He's right, I think. Zeus used to throw lightning bolts like spears."

"That would make sense." I said. "The next line talks about thunder... so it really could be lightning."

Elayne tapped the wood piece. "This is the part here that worries me." she said. "It says that once we use it, its power is gone."

I considered this. "That means that we've only got one chance with it and we had better not blow it." I said. "I still have the silver vial that we kept the fire in before. That should hold the lightning, too... I hope."

Corey took another huge, sloppy bite of the fruit. "But where is it?" he asked with his mouth full. "What is the 'Airy Tower'?"

Elayne thought about this. "I heard a legend once about a castle that rode atop the clouds. That could be where we may find an 'airy tower'." she said.

Corey nearly choked on the bite he was chewing. "Say huh?"

I looked again at the message. "That would also fit in with the whole thunder and lightning theme." I said. "Something up in the clouds."

Corey looked at us like we were crazy. "I think I'd rather go back to the bottom of the ocean."

Emily looked worried. "How are we going to do this? I mean, a castle in the clouds... that's going to be..."

"Pretty hard to reach?" Corey finished for her. "Hey... maybe we can get started right now. Collect some driftwood right here on the beach and start building a really tall ladder. Do any of you have a hammer?"

I rolled my eyes. "Don't start, Corey."

"Well… come on now, bro. Someone has to be the honest voice of hopelessness here. We've only got three days until Sidhera is crowned evil ruler of everyone, we're on the *other side of the world*, so it's not like we could make it anyway, even if we started running really fast right now. Oh, but wait! Before we can even do that, we need to climb up into the clouds and snag us a bolt of lightning… and that's assuming that Dryan's poetic little wood chip over there is even telling us the truth… which I'm starting to seriously doubt because every time we follow one of these clues we almost get ourselves killed!"

We all looked at Corey for a moment in silence. Elayne's face looked crestfallen, as if the terrible hopeless truth was finally crashing down on her. Emily stared silently at a spot on the ground in front of her.

I just sighed. "Did you get that all out of your system, Corey?" I asked. "Do you feel better now?"

Corey shrugged. "A little. I think that this fruit is making me gassy, though."

I pulled the North Star out from where I had hidden it tied up in my shirt. "Fine." I said. "Because I just saw something and it made me realize how we're supposed to use this jewel to solve all of those problems."

Elayne looked up at me. "What? What did you see?"

I pointed over her shoulder to the jagged line of mountains that crested the horizon. The rising sun was just then throwing its light across one large, snowcapped peak above them all.

Elayne looked at the peak with widening eyes. "Brightwest Mountain." she said in a hushed whisper.

Corey doubled over suddenly into a violent coughing fit and Emily's face paled to a terrified white. "You're not talking about Grendesh, are you?" she said with a weak, trembling voice. "You can't possibly be talking about Grendesh…"

I held up the sparkling blue gem in my hand. "Well… we know that he has a soft spot for big, shiny gems. Maybe it will be enough to let us hitch a ride."

Chapter Twenty-Five

Return to Brightwest Mountain

orey screamed.

Fruit juice still dripped down his face, and he *kept* screaming... totally out of control. He ended up waking the sleeping crewmen a little way down the beach, and they jumped up as if they expected to be attacked.

Even when we got Corey to stop screaming, he spun on me and started yelling.

"Are you nuts? *Grendesh?* That dragon is going to kill us! It's a miracle he hasn't hunted us down and killed us already... and you want to just walk right up to him and offer to make it that much easier?"

The crazy thing was that the rational part of my mind completely agreed with Corey. *What the heck was I thinking? Grendesh is a terrible monster that will kill us before I could blink.* However, the moment I had seen Brightwest Mountain, I had known, without a doubt, that this was where we had to go. Grendesh had haunted my nightmares for a year, but I was determined to stop Sidhera and I knew that this was the way that we had to do it.

"I'll show him the jewel and offer to give it to him if he helps us." I said, trying hard to make my voice sound decisive.

Corey screamed again and pulled at his hair. "Are you hearing yourself? You have gone completely bonkers, bro. You're going to try to *talk* with a fire-breathing, man-eating dragon? Dragons don't talk, remember? During out last visit, he just did a lot of roaring and crushing and burning."

"Actually," Elayne interrupted uncertainly. "Grendesh is very intelligent. If we could get him to listen to us, then Jasen's plan may work."

"But if we can't get him to listen?" Emily prompted.

Corey threw up his hands. "There will be more roaring, crushing, and burning, of course!"

"This is the right thing to do, Corey." I said firmly. "It terrifies me maybe more than anyone... but I'm sure that it's the next step."

Corey let out a loud, frustrated sigh and pushed his palms over his eyes for a long time, trying to make himself calm down. Finally, taking a long, deep breath, he looked up at me. "Alright... just tell me this... are you going to go in with a real plan this time or are you just going to try to wing it like before?"

I shook my head. "I'm not stupid enough to try to wing it with Grendesh. I've got an idea... I just need help working out the details. It will still take us a day or two to get there."

Corey held up his hands. "Fine, bro. But just for the record... I think that this is a bad, bad idea."

Corey continued to voice his misgivings for the rest of the day and into the evening. No one else spoke much as we walked. Each of us watched the huge mountain looming closer and kept our own dark thoughts to ourselves. Despite their fears, though, they followed me... and that scared me worse than anything else.

By the middle of the next day, we had stepped into the shadow of the mountain and the ground had turned rocky and barren. Giant boulders were strewn about and sometimes we would come across the crumbling bones of some long-dead animal. The sheer rock walls of the massive mountain rose high above us, eventually disappearing into the clouds above.

By the time we setup camp that night, we were all tense and terrified. We knew that in the morning, we would most likely face Grendesh.

"What is your plan?" Elayne asked me as she stirred the campfire. Emily and Corey sat huddled together across the fire from us. We had slept on the ground last night since we had nothing else with us. Although we had managed to gather a few handfuls of grass tonight, the rocky ground here was going to be brutal to sleep on.

"Right." Corey said. "You say that you're going to offer a deal to Grendesh, but last time he was all 'kill-first-and-ask-questions-later'. He's going to attack you the moment he sees you."

"It's true." Elayne agreed. "Dragons have an excellent memory. Some have been known to hold bitter grudges for thousands of years."

"And we all made Grendesh pretty mad last time we came here." Emily added. "You can bet he hasn't forgotten that."

I looked into the campfire thoughtfully. "I know." I said. "I fully expect him to try to kill me."

Corey's eyes bugged. "Well then don't go looking for a fight! Come on, now. It's not too late. We'll figure out another way to find this cloud castle and get back to Sidhera."

I shook my head. "No. I'm going in to face Grendesh."

Emily looked worried. "But we haven't got anything. Last time we at least had a magic potion from Bridgette to keep us from getting Bar-B-Qued. This time, we don't even have a blanket to sleep on! How do you expect to survive with no protection?"

I looked at them carefully. "I have Charlie." I said.

They were quiet for a long moment. Elayne looked like she *definitely* did not like this idea. "Charlie can't be trusted to protect us." Elayne said.

It was then that Charlie, after two days of silence, finally spoke up again. "Awww.. now that just hurts my feelings."

"I agree, Elayne." I said. "He can't be trusted to protect all of you. That's why I'm going in to face Grendesh alone."

Corey, Elayne, and Emily all opened their mouths at once, ready to argue. I silenced them with a hand in the air. "No," I said. "I think that this will work. I don't trust Charlie either… but he's kept me alive this far. He can help keep me out of Grendesh's reach long enough for me to try to make the deal, at least."

Elayne looked really worried now. "Jasen, you cannot trust him."

"I don't." I said. "But he'll keep me alive… won't you Charlie?"

I heard Charlie make a sound like a clicking of his tongue. "You betcha pardner." he said with a mock cowboy accent. "I'm just hitchin' a ride here. If you die, I'll be stranded without a horse. That's no place for a cowboy to be!"

"What did he say?" Corey asked.

"He said 'yes'." I said wryly.

Elayne looked at me doubtfully, but said nothing. Corey and Emily turned their attention back to the fire and grew silent.

After a while, I laid down on the jagged, rocky ground to try to get some sleep before dawn. As always, I asked Elayne and Emily to tie up my arms and legs.

In my mind, I heard Charlie scoff. "So you trust me to save your life, but not enough to leave yourself untied for the night…"

I closed my eyes and ignored him, doing my best to calm the uncertainty and fear that spun like a hurricane in my chest.

Chapter Twenty-Six

The Bargain

lay awake until I finally saw the dark sky above start to lighten and the small sliver of a moon drop below the horizon.

I turned and saw Elayne still there, awake as always, watching the fire and lost in her own thoughts. I lifted my head and saw Emily and Corey asleep beneath the overhang of a nearby boulder.

I pulled myself up and Elayne lifted her head to look at me.

"Elayne," I said. "I need to go before Emily and Corey wake up."

Elayne, unsurprised, moved towards me and loosened the knots that tied my arms and legs. Her face looked worried, but she said nothing.

I could have told her *Don't worry, I'll be fine...* or something else to ease her nerves... but the truth was that I wasn't feeling so sure about this plan myself anymore. Thinking back on it, I wondered what strange conviction had come over me to make me so sure that this was what we should do. Whatever it had been, I didn't feel it now.

Despite my fears, I forced myself to stand up and Elayne stood in front of me. I could see that she wanted to say something, but she just looked at me for a moment, then kissed me. "Good luck, Jasen." she whispered in her hoarse raspy voice.

I took a deep breath, checked to make sure that I still had the North Star tucked away in my shirt, then turned towards the base of the mountain and started walking.

Even though I could feel Elayne watching me as I left, I forced myself not to look back. I was afraid that if I looked into her eyes again that I would never be able to make myself go.

"Alright, Charlie." I murmured as I walked through the morning shadows at the base of the mountain. "It's time for you to earn your keep, here. If you are so fond of riding along with me, then you had better keep me alive through this."

There was a long silence.

"Charlie?" I said aloud.

Still, no answer.

I paused next to a big boulder and my heart started pounding. "CHARLIE?" I yelled... and my voice echoed through the rocks around me.

I heard a low, quiet chuckle in my ear. "Gotcha." he said. "Woo! You should have seen your face. Priceless."

I gritted my teeth as I struggled to calm my wild heartbeat. "Ha. You're a real laugh riot. It's not going to help either of us if I die of a heart-attack before we even get there."

"Aw." Charlie said. "Lighten up, Big J. We're going to have some fun... starting in about thirty seconds now, actually."

I rolled my eyes and kept moving through the rocky landscape. "What are you talking about? Grendesh's cave isn't even close yet. It's way on the other side of the..." I froze, "Wait... what do you mean, exactly? What's going to happen in thirty seconds?"

"Twenty." Charlie corrected.

My heart leapt into my throat and I started looking around frantically. "If this is another joke, it's not very..."

"Ten." Charlie said calmly. Then: "Oh, boy. This may be a little harder than I thought. Alright. You had better pay good attention if you want to stay alive."

My muscles were fiery with tension now. I tried to swallow, but my mouth was completely dry. "What's going..." I began to ask, but then Charlie barked "Dive to the left... NOW!"

I moved without thinking. The boulder that I had been leaning against suddenly exploded into a shower of dust and pebbles. A giant, black clawed foot now stood in its place, grinding the remains under its heel.

I looked up just in time to see the long, snakelike neck of Grendesh uncoiling above me. Huge leathery wings, each wider than a house, gave a final sweeping gust before folding back behind the dragon's shimmering black body.

"YOU!" a voice bellowed, shaking the rocky mountainside.

I looked up to see golden eyes glaring at me from three stories high and I had just enough time to think in shock: *It talked! Grendesh just spoke!*

"Jump backwards, then to the left *fast*." Charlie said with a tense voice.

I stumbled backwards just as Grendesh reached out and took a swipe at me with his terrible claws, then I dove to the left and narrowly missed being skewered by the needles that grew from the end of his whip like tail that had appeared without warning from the side.

Grendesh had obviously expected that last move to kill me, because now he paused for just an instant, narrowing his evil-looking golden eyes at me suspiciously. "What magic is this?" he growled in a low rumble that shook the ground beneath my feet.

I took the opportunity to start talking fast. "Wait!" I yelled. "I want to talk with you! I have an offer to…"

"Run forward." Charlie warned.

In that second, Grendesh picked up a boulder as big as a car and threw it at me. I had just enough time to dive forward as it shattered into the ground where I had been standing. Pieces of it pounded into my back as I fell forward and hit the ground hard. Grendesh raised his serpentine head and howled a deafening roar. I could feel the ground shake with his growing rage.

"He's mad now." Charlie commented dryly. "Oops! Roll left."

I threw myself hard to the left as the deadly needled tail smashed down.

"Left again. Now right. Get to your feet. Back two steps and be ready to fall to the ground again."

Charlie's orders came at me fast and furious then. The world around me exploded into chaos as Grendesh pounded and roared and smashed everything around me, just barely missing every time. I couldn't even see him anymore through the smoke and debris that had been kicked up, but still I threw myself each time the instant a direction was called.

"Go right, then… watch it! Watch it!"

As I threw myself to the right, I stumbled and an attack from Grendesh's tail sliced the air next to me. There was a searing pain in my left arm and blood began to flow.

"Get back… no! Boulder. Boulder! BOULDER!" Charlie yelled.

I blindly threw myself behind a nearby boulder just as a jet of fire exploded around me. For several frantic seconds, I cowered behind the huge rock as the flames scorched the entire area.

When the firestorm stopped, the ground all around me was smoldering and charred black. It looked like a bomb had just gone off.

"Alright." Charlie said. "Get ready to move. He's... wait. What are you doing?"

I stepped out from behind the boulder and stood there in front of the monstrous dragon. I lifted my head up and shouted at the top of my lungs "STOP!!!!"

My voice echoed against the rocky mountainside and in the silence that followed, I could hear the burned rocks around me crackling as they cooled. I braced myself for more orders from Charlie, but they didn't come.

Grendesh paused for a moment, looking down on me with slitted eyes like a huge snake eyeing a tiny mouse.

For a moment, I was too stunned at the sudden silence to even speak. My ears were still ringing from the last deafening attack.

"I have an offer for you." I said quickly, my voice hoarse and cracked. When I spoke, I ended up coughing on the acrid smoke that still lingered in the air.

Grendesh narrowed his eyes at me evilly. "You are the human that crept into my lair while I slept!" his voice was terrible and thundering-- a gravelly hiss that shook my bones. "You stole my treasure and then harnessed me like a farm animal to ride! The only thing you can offer me is your death."

"It was Sidhera that sent us!" I yelled. "You should seek your revenge on her!"

Grendesh scoffed, a huge sound that caused a small landslide further down the mountain. "Oh I have made that meddlesome fairy pay. She sorely regretted ever involving me in her scheming."

I hesitated for a moment, wondering what he meant by that, but I said nothing. Instead, I quickly reached into my shirt. "I have come to offer you a trade." I said.

I pulled out the North Star and held it high in the sunshine for Grendesh to see. The sparkling blue crystal caught the morning light and I saw Grendesh's golden eyes lock on it immediately. I knew in that moment that I had him.

Grendesh snorted and black smoke billowed from his giant nostrils. His tail whipped around behind him in slow, steady spirals.

"Why would I care for such a worthless bauble?" Grendesh scowled through sharpened teeth. "My treasure collection holds a hundred such jewels."

This time, I smiled. Even in my terror, I could tell that he was bluffing. "There is no other jewel like this one in the world." I said. "I will give it to you… if you help me."

Grendesh's eyes stayed locked on the blue crystal. "I have a better idea, human. I think that I will kill you and then take the jewel for myself."

Grendesh inhaled as if he was about to launch a torrent of deadly fire right then and end our conversation, but I held my ground.

"I don't think you want to do that." I said.

Grendesh paused again, narrowing his liquid gold eyes at me.

"This is the North Star." I said. "If you try to take it from me, it will melt into seawater and be lost forever. It can only be yours if I give it to you freely."

Grendesh's eyes locked again on the blue jewel in my hand and he seemed to consider his options.

Finally, he lowered his huge head towards me and brought his glistening teeth right to my face. "Although I will most likely kill you, I will hear your offer before you die." he said with a grating whisper that still shook the ground at my feet.

I coughed as I inhaled a mouthful of his sulfurous breath.

When I could breathe again, I did my best to keep my voice steady and face the dragon, trying hard not to think about those deadly teeth within arm's reach.

"We need transportation." I said.

The dragon reared his head back and let out a booming wail. "Transportation? I will not be harnessed like a domesticated pet and I will not be ridden by filthy humans!"

He shifted his huge legs again as if he was about to attack.

"It will take only minutes for a mighty dragon like you!" I said, trying to think quickly. "We need to go to the castle in the clouds, and then the Palace of Lions. If it will help persuade you, you should know that this is all for the purpose of thwarting the fairy Sidhera."

Grendesh pawed at the ground and snorted a great black cloud of smoke, but he did not attack.

He was watching the gem again.

"I will kill your friends." he said. "They are close. I can smell them. Give me the jewel, or I will kill them all."

My chest clenched fearfully, but I tried not to show it on my face. I prepared myself to jump if Charlie barked a sudden warning.

"No." I said firmly. "The only way you're going to get your claws on this jewel is to make a deal. Kill them. Kill me. You will never get the jewel then."

Grendesh's eyes flared with sudden rage. I could tell that he was furious and trying still to think of a way he *could* kill me and still keep the jewel.

"Uh-oh." Charlie said suddenly in my mind.

I clenched.

"This is very, very bad." Charlie said. "He's going to kill you in twenty-two seconds."

My mind flooded with panic. My hand clutched the jewel tightly.

"I can't get you out of this one." Charlie said frantically in my mind. "It's too much. You'll never make it. I need to…

you've got to let me do it for you. I'll be faster. I'll move your body and keep you alive."

Grendesh was glaring at me, his teeth opening slowly. I could tell he was about to do something.

"Seven seconds." Charlie warned. I could feel a soft pushing at the back of my brain. A nudging, as if someone were trying to push me out. "You will die if you don't listen to me NOW."

I was panicked. Grendesh was unfolding his wings. When he struck, it would be lightning-fast.

"NOW, JASEN!" Charlie screamed suddenly. "IF YOU WANT TO LIVE, LET ME DO THIS NOW!"

At the last instant, I gave in to the pushing sensation in my mind and let whatever it was come rushing in. I was thrown out, feeling like I was sliding through the slippery air and being spun around. It was a crazy moment of disorientation, and then I was standing there, face-to-face with my own body.

I saw my eyes widen for an instant of surprise, then my chest heaved with a deep, slow breath. My lips curled into a satisfied smile. "Well, thank you, Jasen. It's about time."

I felt like I was floating above the rocky ground. I tried to move my arm, but found that I didn't have an arm to move.

Because I'm not in my body. I thought with sudden horror. *Charlie is...*

The attack that Charlie had been warning about never came. Instead, I saw Grendesh lean his huge head down again to face me (Charlie).

"We have a deal." Grendesh said with a menacing growl. "Rejoin your friends and I will find you at midday." He then looked at Charlie suspiciously. "If you break your word, you should know that I will kill you and all of your friends... and still be satisfied with my fortune."

I saw my face smile calmly at Grendesh, then Charlie pocketed the North Star and gave the huge dragon a wink. "Good doing business with you, big fella. See you then."

Chapter Twenty-Seven

Flight

 was trapped in a nightmare.

I watched helplessly as my body strolled back to camp. Charlie used my lips to whistle a happy tune and I was pulled along beside him like a bobbing balloon on a short string. I was tied to him somehow, and all I could do was float there helplessly and watch.

"Enjoying the ride there, Big J?" Charlie asked.

"Charlie. Get out of my body." I demanded.

Charlie pursed his (my) lips as if he were thinking about it. Then, he shook his head. "Nah. I don't wanna."

I pulled myself closer to my body and tried to push myself in. I could feel an odd force, like a magnet, propelling me back.

"Sorry, Big J. You ain't getting back in here."

I felt furious and struggled again to push myself in. I tried to pull my arms up to grab hold of him, but I couldn't feel any arms to move.

"You've got to sleep sometime." I said coldly. "When you sleep, I'll take over again."

Charlie just shook his head. "I really don't think so. I know all the tricks. Those doors are locked, now."

"I'm getting back in." I said. "And when I do I'm going to kill you."

"Already dead." Charlie laughed.

"Get out of my body!" I yelled in frustration, trying frantically to think of a way out of this. "You're not going to fool anyone." I said. "They're going to know right away what has happened."

Charlie just laughed again. "Oh, I think that I could fool your idiot friends easily. Not that it matters, though. I've decided to set out and see the world on my own. Your little play group can go their own way without me."

I felt fear buzzing in my brain as I realized what he was saying. If he took off on his own, then I really would be stuck like this forever... and I would not be able to help stop Sidhera.

I struggled to pull at Charlie as he moved my body through the boulders. He was walking the opposite direction of the camp, where the others were waiting for me.

At that moment, though, Elayne, Corey, and Emily came running around the corner behind us. They were all holding rocks and sticks and looked ready to fight. When they saw me, their eyes got wide with relief and they looked around for Grendesh.

"We heard you!" Emily shouted. "We heard the awful noise. We didn't know what was going on."

Charlie reacted quickly. As he turned around, I watched his grin disappear and he put on a serious expression, trying hard to imitate me. "It was Grendesh." Charlie said.

Corey looked stunned. "You saw him?"

Charlie nodded solemnly. "You were right—he wasn't happy to see me at first. Thank goodness Charlie was around. He really saved me this time." He turned and looked into the air, raising his voice. "Didn't you Charlie?"

"CHARLIE, GET OUT OF MY BODY!" I screamed.

Charlie nodded and turned back to the group. "Yep. He did good."

Elayne moved to my body and looked at my arm where Grendesh's tail had cut it open. "You're hurt!" she said worriedly.

Charlie looked at the cut with surprise. "Oh! Right. That. It was totally my fault. Charlie told me to move but I'm such an *idiot* that I didn't move fast enough. I guess I should have listened better."

"Elayne!" I shouted desperately. "Can you hear me?" She was right next to me, but she didn't even flinch when I shouted. She was busy tending to the cut on my arm.

Corey, brandishing a long, heavy stick, looked at Charlie closely. "What happened?" he asked. "Did Grendesh agree to help us?"

Charlie sighed heavily, a perfect imitation of me. "It was not easy, but yes. He agreed to carry us to the cloud castle and then to Elayne's palace."

Corey looked stunned. "Seriously? He did?"

Charlie nodded. "Yep. The big guy wanted that shiny rock pretty badly."

Emily looked up at the sky cautiously. "Did he promise not to kill us afterwards?" she asked.

"Hold still!" Elayne was telling Charlie as she tied a tourniquet around the cut on his arm.

"Corey!" I yelled frantically. "Corey! Can you hear me? You've got to see that this isn't me! Help me!"

But even as I watched Charlie's calm, perfect imitation, I realized that they *did* think he was me. He had them fooled. Completely.

When Elayne had finished bandaging my arm, she smiled at Charlie and kissed him quickly on the cheek. "There." she said. "You'll live. You were lucky that it wasn't worse. I told you that Charlie couldn't be trusted to keep you unharmed."

Charlie nodded thoughtfully at Elayne. "I'm starting to think that you're right. Charlie shouldn't be trusted at all. I can feel him... always floating there close by. We really do need to work on a way to get rid of him for good."

Still, I struggled. Helpless and frantic. For a while I just screamed. I had no throat to get sore... so I could keep screaming for a long, long time. Nobody heard me, though... and Charlie's face remained calm and unflinching the entire time.

I pulled away... trying to see how far I could get. Every time I got more than twenty feet from my body, something would pull me back, like a rubber band around my waist.

Moving was like swimming through water. I tried several more times to push myself forcefully back into my body, but I was pushed back every time.

Corey, Emily, Elayne and Charlie moved around, talking and planning their next moves. The sun was climbing higher into the air and Grendesh would be returning soon. Charlie still had not had a chance to get away from the group, but I could see him watching for the opportunity. I knew that as soon as they were distracted, he would slip away.

I buried my panic and fear long enough to force myself to start thinking of a plan. It was in that silent moment of thought that I first started to realize something.

There was some new part of my mind that was playing a thousand different images every second... a blinding blur of light and sound. When I forced myself to concentrate on these strange flashes, one image came into focus: Corey tripping over a rock that was sticking up from the ground.

This was an odd thing to visualize, I thought. Then, just as I was trying to figure out what it could mean, I heard Corey cry out and looked up just in time to see him tripping and falling.

At first, I thought that I may have caused him to do it... but then I realized what had actually happened: I had seen into the future. Now that Charlie and I had switched places, I could see into the future as he had been able to before.

So instead of screaming and pushing helplessly to get free, I began to concentrate on those thousand flickering images in my mind. I think I was seeing all of the things that *could* happen... but then when I concentrated and focused, I could see the one thing that was going to happen. It made me dizzy at first, but after a while, I started to understand how it worked.

As I floated silently nearby, the four of them began talking.

"So, tell us about this castle in the sky." Corey was saying to Elayne.

They had settled down among a group of boulders at the base of the mountain. The sun was high in the sky and it was almost midday.

"Well..." Elayne said. "It moves... obviously. Like all clouds, it goes where the wind takes it, so it is hard to find. That's probably where Grendesh has gone now. My guess is that he has gone to find the castle first before he takes us there."

At the mention of Grendesh, Corey and Emily looked up at the sky nervously.

Elayne thought for a moment. "There are many tales told of this castle. One that I believe crossed over to your world is the tale of a boy who reached the castle by climbing a beanstalk."

Corey looked at Elayne wide-eyed. "You mean the story of Jack and the Beanstalk?"

Elayne popped her hands together. "Yes! That is the one."

Corey glanced at Emily, then back at Elayne nervously. "Um… Elayne. In that story, there was a huge, man-eating giant living in the castle in the clouds. Fee-fi-fo-fum and all that…"

Elayne nodded seriously. "Yes. He was supposed to be a terrible brute. But don't worry, as you may remember from the story, the giant fell to his death and the castle has been empty ever since."

"You sure about that?" Emily asked.

Elayne shrugged. "I guess we'll see. Right, Jasen?"

Charlie looked up at them from where he had been lost in thought. He smiled. "Yep. I guess we will."

Just then, Emily looked up and gasped. We all turned to see the massive shadow of Grendesh approaching. His huge wings pushed the air so hard as he landed that it knocked everyone back several steps.

Once on the ground, he wasted no time. He lowered his towering snakelike neck and turned his narrow golden eyes on Charlie. "Stand together two and two." he growled with smoky breath.

Charlie looked at the dragon uncertainly. "Why should we…"

"DO IT!" Grendesh roared… and Elayne moved quickly to stand beside Charlie and Corey and Emily moved together.

Elayne held up a rope that she had woven from grass. "We can use this as a harness to---"

"I will wear no harness." Grendesh thundered, then he gave his wings a mighty flap and his two massive claws shot forward. Corey and Emily were scooped up in one and Elayne and Charlie were scooped up in another.

I heard Corey, Elayne, and Emily all start screaming as Grendesh shot up into the sky. The invisible rubber-band around my waist yanked me up with them and a moment later we were flying with blinding speed through the air.

It was a strange sensation for me, since I could not feel the wind. I watched it all like I was watching a movie. The world became a blur of colors as Grendesh moved miles within a heartbeat.

When he began to slow less than a minute later, I had no doubt that we were hundreds of miles away from Brightwest Mountain. Grendesh approached a giant white cloud that floated alone in an empty blue sky. There was a forest of trees below and I could no longer see the ocean or the mountains on any horizon.

When we came up over the edge of the cloud, I was astonished to see the biggest castle I had ever seen. In fact, as we approached it, it seemed to grow even bigger. It was like a strange optical illusion. When Grendesh finally alighted on the open wooden drawbridge, I realized that the castle was almost as big as a mountain and it felt like we had shrunk to the size of mice. The gaping open hole that led inside was a hundred times bigger than the entrance to Elayne's castle.

Grendesh dropped everyone roughly to the wooden ground and I saw him wipe his claws against the wood as if trying to wipe off the feel of the people he had been carrying. His claws left huge, splintery gashes in the drawbridge.

"I'll be back tomorrow at midday." Grendesh growled again. Then, just as everyone was getting unsteadily to their feet, he leapt into the air and took off again.

Corey, looking windblown and dizzy from the terrifying ride, stumbled to his feet first and watched Grendesh disappear over the edge of the cloud. The others were holding their heads and also trying to get their bearings. I saw with some satisfaction that Charlie leaned over and threw up.

"He left us!" Corey shouted frantically, looking around.

"It's alright." Elayne said, still holding her head to try to get it to stop spinning. "It will take time to find what we need, anyway."

Emily looked pale and sick. "Ungh! Was it that bad for you last time, Jasen?" she asked, looking at Charlie.

Charlie, wiping the vomit from his chin and looking dazed, could only grunt in response.

Chapter Twenty-Eight

Castle in the Sky

 wo things became quickly apparent as we entered the huge castle. First, we realized immediately that a giant had indeed lived there… and second, we could see that it had been empty for a long, long time.

Towering furniture was overturned and falling apart in nearly every room. The cobblestone floor was cold and uneven… and we had to be careful to jump over cracks that gaped like dark trenches in the stone. Everything was covered in a thick layer of dust. The glass windows were brown with ages of dirt and grime and acres of cobwebs covered every corner from the floor all the way up to the high, shadowy rafters.

One of the first rooms we came across was a kitchen. Massive cabinets with doors the size of billboards stood open and empty. At one point, we came across a fork, twice as big as I was, lying on the dusty floor. There was a giant wooden table surrounded by four splintered chairs. The table was draped with cobwebs and the top was far too high for any of us to see what was up there.

Other rooms were much the same, all looking abandoned and undisturbed for hundreds of years. There was one room with a great stone fireplace and a cushioned chair that was tattered and torn. In the same room, sitting on a shelf that was low to the floor, was a giant glass bowl... easily as big as a house. Although the glass was smudged and dusty, we could still see clearly inside. The bottom of the huge bowl was filled with about a foot of fine white sand. Partially buried in the sand were clusters of faded colored rocks, twisted and bent into exotic shapes.

"What is this thing?" Charlie asked.

"Is that... coral?" Corey pointed.

Emily took a few steps back and looked at the enormous bowl. "It's a fishbowl." she said with wonder.

Corey blinked, looking at the bowl again with the dry sand and coral at the bottom. "But where is the water? Where are the fish?"

"The water is long gone." Elayne said. "Probably hundreds of years ago." Then, as her eyes scanned the glass bowl, she let out a horrified gasp. "No! Oh... no!"

Startled, the others followed her stare until they saw the pile of white bones scattered in the sand near the far side of the bowl.

Emily's eyes grew wide. "Is that..."

"A mermaid." Corey said darkly. "There was a mermaid in this bowl."

Emily looked like she was about to cry. "But who would do such a thing?"

"A mean, nasty giant." Charlie said. "Just like in the story. I'm less worried about those old bones than all of these giant cobwebs I'm seeing everywhere. All of those webs didn't just make themselves. The giant may be long gone… but that doesn't mean the castle is empty."

The others looked around in surprise as if just seeing all of the cobwebs for the first time.

"Giant spiders?" Corey croaked.

Elayne looked around the huge room. "Jasen's right. We need to keep moving. If we can find some stairs, they should lead up to the tower."

Taking one last uncomfortable look at the old bones in the glass bowl, the group turned and continued their search.

The stairs were just off the main hallway. The huge, uneven stone floor met with what looked like a giant stone wall that was about twenty feet high. When you looked up from there, you could see that it wasn't a huge wall after all, but instead a single stone stair. In fact, it was the first of many, many stairs that spiraled up endlessly into the darkness above.

The group gaped in stunned silence at the towering first stair.

"We're going to need a ladder just to climb one stair." Corey said.

Emily tilted her head upwards, trying to see how far into the darkness the stairway went. "But even if we found a ladder, this is going to be slow going. We may need to tell Grendesh to come back next week instead of tomorrow."

"We could get some pixie dust and fly up there." Charlie commented dryly.

I saw Elayne look at him for a moment and furrow her eyebrows, but before she could say anything, Corey spoke up again. "Hey, what's that?"

Corey was pointing to a tall, thin window near the stairs. Its glass was smudged and dirty like all of the others, but there was something else as well. Something green and leafy grew outside and covered the window, almost blocking out all of the sun.

"What is that?" Emily asked curiously. "Looks like some kind of ivy or something growing outside."

Elayne looked at the window thoughtfully. "Let's go outside and take a closer look." she said.

Outside the castle, the group walked back onto the massive drawbridge.

From there, they could see the nearby tower which stretched high into the deep blue sky above. Covering the tower, and spiraling around it, was a tangle of curling, knotted green vines. They were so thick in places that they completely covered the stone... and they reached all the way to the top.

"You know what that is, don't you?" Corey smiled.

Emily and Elayne shook their heads.

Corey laughed. "It's a beanstalk! Look. It's growing wild everywhere... and take a look at those footholds. There's our way up the tower."

I looked at the twisted web of vines and realized that Corey was right. They would be easy to climb. I smiled to myself, proud of my little brother's ingenuity.

I saw Charlie look at the immense tower fearfully and lick his lips. I realized that he was thinking of some way to get out of it without raising suspicion. He knew, though, that there was no way to slip away from the group at the moment. We were all trapped on the cloud together until Grendesh came back tomorrow.

"Ready for a climb, bro?" Corey asked Charlie with a grin. "Just like the oak tree in Grandpa's backyard, right?"

Charlie smiled weakly. "Right."

As the group was nearing the top of the tower, I saw Elayne fall to her death.

The group had been carefully picking their way through the tangled, twisted knots of vines, moving steadily upwards. The wind got much stronger as they moved higher and, judging by the way everyone shivered and shook, it must have gotten much colder. I couldn't feel any of this, of course, but I could see their pale faces and their breath fogging in the air in front of them.

Elayne especially, in her overweight and uneven body, was struggling with the climb. In her own body, she would have had no trouble with it. Now, though, her short arms and clumsy feet made the climb much more difficult for her.

Then, about an hour into the climb, an image flashed through my mind... clear and sudden. I saw Elayne pulling herself up, a handful of vines in her grip as she lifted her foot to the next step. The vines in her hand snapped and suddenly she was falling backwards. She never screamed, but I saw her face, terrified and pale, as she tumbled back and fell... dropping quietly out of sight far below.

"Charlie." I said quickly. "Elayne is about to fall! Warn her that the vines in her hand are going to break."

I looked at Charlie in my body as he struggled to climb the vines. His cheeks were reddened from the cold and he was breathing hard. When I yelled to him about Elayne, I saw him hesitate for a moment. Then, without saying a word, he smiled quietly to himself and continued his climb.

"Charlie!" I yelled. "She is going to die! You've got to warn her!"

Still, Charlie ignored me, pulling himself up the vine with that dark smile playing on his chapped lips.

I looked frantically at Elayne and saw her start to reach for a thin bundle of vines to pull herself up with. I knew that this was it. She was about to fall.

"Charlie." I warned in a desperate and menacing voice. "You need me. It could be you that falls next and… I won't warn you about it."

I saw Charlie pause, listening.

"If you don't warn Elayne," I said with cold determination. "I don't care if you're in my body or not… I will let you fall to your death."

Charlie licked his lips and looked up. The tower still loomed high above and there were still lots of twisted vines to climb before he got there safely.

Elayne grabbed the handful of vines and started to pull herself up and Charlie finally called out a terse warning. "Elayne!" he said. "Find something stronger to hold on to. Those vines you have your hand on now aren't going to hold you."

The others all froze and looked at Elayne. She watched Charlie for a moment, then carefully released the bunch of vines in her hand and reached for a stronger handhold a little further up. "Thank you, Jasen." she said.

Charlie just nodded at her. I could almost sense his disappointment.

As they began to climb again, I watched him moving in my body, climbing alongside the others. I couldn't read his thoughts, but I knew one thing for certain now: He wouldn't hesitate to kill any of us if he had the chance.

At the top of the tower, everyone worked together to pry an opening in the thick layer of vines and a moment later they revealed the dirty glass of a window beneath. Once they had a big enough opening, Corey gave the glass a hard kick.

I almost expected his foot to bounce back, the glass being almost a half a foot thick. Instead, though, the brittle glass shattered with a spectacular crashing sound and the entire thirty-foot window crashed inwards, revealing a circular, dark room inside.

They stepped into the window and onto a table that sat beneath the ledge. Like the rest of the castle, the furniture in this room was massive. There were huge shelves that circled the walls and they were full of crumbling books draped with spider webs. One giant book lay open on the table near the window and the group walked over its faded pages, leaving dusty footprints across it. The writing was faint and unreadable, in a language that I couldn't understand.

There were other windows in the room, but they were dirty and covered with vines as well. The only light coming in was from the fading sunlight that streamed through the broken window behind us. That was why it was so easy to see the odd flickering white light on the high shelf in the corner.

We couldn't see exactly what the light was coming from... even when I floated as high as my leash would allow, I still could not see over the edge of that high shelf. The light was a flickering electric blue, though. It flashed and created pulsing patterns and shadows across the nearby walls.

"It's up there." Elayne said, watching the light and breathing hard from the two-hour climb.

Although the shelf seemed impossibly high, the cobwebs that draped the shelves created a crisscross of netting that seemed to lead right up to it. Corey reached out and touched one of the webs cautiously, then pulled his hands back quickly and rubbed his palms together.

"Is it sticky?" Emily asked.

Corey shook his head. "No it's dry. Kind of feels like rope."

"Probably an old web." Elayne said, looking around the room. "Whatever made them is probably long gone."

Corey looked at her doubtfully. "I don't know. Maybe it's just waiting in the shadows for someone to be stupid enough to start crawling over its webs."

Emily reached out and grabbed the web, giving it a big shake. They all looked up and saw that the motion had caused all of the webs around them to sway and jiggle. They watched to see if a monster spider would come running out of the shadows to devour its prey… but nothing came.

Elayne looked outside through the huge shattered window we had come in through. "The sun is going down." she said. "If we want to do this, we should do it before it gets too dark to see."

Straightening her shoulders, she took a deep breath and reached out to take hold of the web. A moment later, she started climbing, making her way quickly up the face of the towering bookshelf.

Corey looked at Emily and Charlie.

"After you." Charlie gestured.

They began to climb up after her. With the four of them on the web, things really shook and bounced, but the web held strong. I concentrated hard and tried to watch for any danger ahead, but the four of them made it to the top shelf quickly and without incident.

What lay on the top shelf was something like a giant crystal ball… about ten feet around. Inside, brilliant blue electricity arced and danced. It reminded me of those glass balls we saw in the mall sometimes. With those, you could press your fingers to the surface and the dancing electric arcs would reach out to lick your fingertips.

The electricity inside *this* massive ball was much bigger and brighter, though. When it flashed, I saw the others covering their eyes from the brilliant blue light.

Elayne watched the dancing blue electricity intently. Without taking her eyes from it, she held out her hand to Charlie.

"Hand me the silver vial." she said.

Charlie looked at her blankly for a moment.

"In your pocket." I said. "The silver vial in your pocket."

Charlie suddenly understood and reached into the pocket of his (my) jeans to pull out the corked silver vial that we had used to carry the fire in earlier. He handed the vial to Elayne and she took it, pulling the cork loose.

Everyone watched the blinding blue lightning inside the glass ball as if mesmerized by the patterns it created. As Elayne lifted the vial up to the ball, I said a silent prayer. The instant the open vial touched the glass, the lightning inside flared up and then shot through the glass and into the vial. Elayne pushed the cork into place and in the sudden darkness, I could see that the vial was now glowing with a soft blue light.

I heard Corey, Emily, and Charlie all exhale a tense breath. Elayne held the vial up and looked at it thoughtfully.

The broken window now showed a darkening purple twilight sky outside.

"We did it!" Emily said breathlessly. "I can't believe we actually did it."

Even Corey was grinning as he looked at the glowing vial. "All right! Now, we just take this sucker to Sidhera and we get Elayne back to her old blonde and beautiful self, right?"

Elayne didn't answer. She was watching the vial in her hands quietly.

Just then, I saw it.

I saw it in one of those sudden flashes and I knew what was about to happen. For a moment, I was too stunned to even say anything.

"No." Elayne said quietly. "We can't take this to Sidhera. There's been a change of plans."

The others watched her face in that soft blue glow and glanced at each other in confusion.

"What are you talking about?" Emily asked. "This is the last piece, right? The clue said that we can use this to tear Sidhera out of your body and put you back in."

Elayne took a deep breath and looked up at Emily. "That was the clue, yes." she said, "But something else has come up unexpectedly." She looked at Corey and Emily as if just making up her mind about something.

Corey shook his head. "What are you talking about, Elayne? Are you okay?"

Elayne turned then and looked at Charlie. "I'm fine." she said calmly. "It's Jasen. He needs this now more than I do."

"*No, Elayne!*" I shouted. "*Don't!*"

But before anyone could react, Elayne tore the cork off of the vial and grabbed Charlie's hand firmly. She met his startled eyes with a fierce gaze and I could see her face darken.

"Charlie." she said. "Get out of Jasen's body... NOW!"

Then, there was an explosion of light as electricity shot out of the vial and surrounded us. I felt power surge through me, pulling me down hard. I heard someone screaming. It sounded like my voice... but it was far away. I was spiraling, turning and falling... and then there was nothing but blinding white light.

Chapter Twenty-Nine

An Unexpected Turn of Events

 was falling in the light. Lightning flashed violently around me, and with each flash I was pulled hard to one side or another. It was like being trapped in an electric barrel tumbling down a mountainside.

"Jasen! Go into your body now!"

It was Elayne's voice cutting through the chaos… her *real* voice… soft and melodic like I remembered it before her change. I could feel her with me in the storm of light.

"Go, Jasen. Now!"

There was a push, and then I hit the ground… hard. I felt it jolt through my bones as if I had fallen off a building and smacked into the pavement below.

There was a giant, trembling boom--- thunder, I realized. It shook the walls and floor. The towering glass ball in front of us started to roll and I stumbled out of the way just before it crushed me. Even before the wood stopped trembling, I heard the crash, like a bomb going off, as the giant glass ball shattered on the stone floor far below.

I heard people shouting. Corey and Emily were around us. Corey was helping me to my feet unsteadily. Even though there was no light anymore, I could still see bright spots pop in front of my eyes when I blinked. I smelled smoke coming from somewhere, and when I looked down at myself, I saw that my clothes were blackened and charred.

Then, even as Corey was asking me if I was okay, the realization hit me: I was back in my body again.

I looked at my hands as if seeing them for the first time. I moved my fingers and they actually moved. It was like a miracle.

Then, I looked up at Elayne and saw that she, too, was looking at her hands with wonder. The expression on her face, though, slowly turned to growing horror.

"*WHAT HAVE YOU DONE TO ME?*" Elayne screeched. She lifted her pudgy, calloused hands up to her face with horror.

Corey and Emily gaped at Elayne, struggling to understand what was happening.

Elayne's hands went to her wiry hair, then to her face, where she fingered the huge, hairy black mole there. "NO!" she screamed. "NO! NO! NO!"

She lunged forward and grabbed me by my shirt, pinning me roughly against the wall. She bellowed through yellowed teeth. "I WANT THAT BODY BACK! I STOLE IT! IT'S MINE!"

"Sorry. Looks like you're stuck with that one now." came Elayne's voice (her *real* voice again), clear and strong in my mind.

I stared into the pudgy white face of the woman who was holding me pinned to the wall in rage and I realized that I was looking at Charlie trapped behind those bulging, bloodshot eyes..

Elayne had used the vial to rip Charlie out of my body. I was back in control now and Charlie was trapped in Elayne's former body. That could only mean that Elayne was…

"Lookout." Elayne said in my mind. "He's going to try to hit you."

Corey and Emily were staring at us in shock, not understanding the drama unfolding before them. To them, it looked like Elayne was suddenly attacking me.

Charlie, shaking with rage, curled his pudgy, pale hand into a fist and swung hard for my face. Taking Elayne's warning, I ducked just in time and the punch landed on the wall behind me with a loud crack. Charlie's eyes opened wide in surprise and pain.

"Elayne, stop it!" Emily cried out. "Why are you doing this?"

"That's not Elayne anymore." I said with a grim satisfaction as Charlie howled in pain, holding his hand. "It's Charlie."

Corey and Emily looked at Charlie in shock.

"How could this happen?" Charlie was blubbering. "No! No! No!"

Corey looked at Charlie and his eyes grew serious. "*That's* Charlie?" he asked, pointing to the pudgy woman.

I nodded.

"Are you *sure*?" Corey asked me.

I nodded again.

Corey turned to the woman and raised his fist. "THIS is for kissing my girlfriend, you creep."

Emily grabbed his arm before he could swing. "Corey! Stop! You can't hit a woman!"

Corey looked at Emily in frustration. "What? But that's not even…"

"Let me do it." Emily interrupted. Then, she turned and swung, knocking Charlie in the jaw and sending him tumbling over the edge of the shelf.

We ran to the edge and saw him falling in Elayne's borrowed body. He bounced against some webs and slid down some more, getting tangled, but still falling. Near the bottom, he bounced again and we saw him land on the hard floor with a *thud* amid the shattered pieces of the glass ball.

Almost instantly, he was up again, looking up at us with a frightened and furious expression, then he ran for the open window and was outside, climbing down the vines.

"We need to go after her... or him... or whatever it is!" Corey said. "He's getting away."

"Where's he gonna go?" I said. "He's trapped up here on a cloud just like the rest of us. If he's smart, he'll stay hidden until we're gone. Otherwise, he's likely to get punched again."

Corey smiled and looked at Emily. "That's right! This is *my* girl right here! I didn't know you could punch like that!"

Emily smiled proudly. "Me neither. Hey--- is my hand supposed to be hurting this badly?"

"Good job Emily!" Elayne laughed in my mind in her sweet, soft voice.

"Elayne!" I said suddenly.

Emily and Corey looked up at me. "Where? Where is she?"

I held my hands up over my eyes. "Oh, man, Elayne. What have you done?"

"I saw a chance to save you and I had to take it." Elayne said.

"But that was our only way to get you back into your body!" I said. "You shouldn't have wasted it on me!"

"Jasen," she said. "I love you... and I would do it again in a heartbeat. You're the most important thing in the world to me. Nothing else matters."

"Elayne!" Emily gasped worriedly, looking around in the shadows as if she expected to see Elayne's spirit floating nearby.

"I'm all right." Elayne said. "Tell them not to worry. We can still stop Sidhera. Even if I don't get my own body back, we must not let Sidhera wear the Crown of Lions."

I remembered the terrible feeling of floating helplessly, tied like a balloon around the waist. "Don't worry, Elayne." I said. "We'll get you back into your own body."

"But if we don't, Jasen, then that is okay, too. I'm with you, and that is all that matters."

We slept on the shelf that night.

Even though she was without a body now, Elayne remained awake as she always had, and kept a watch for us. She promised to wake me up at the first sign of danger.

No more danger came our way that night, though, and when the sky outside the giant shattered window was just turning a shade of predawn pink, I heard Elayne whisper gently in my ear. "Wake up, sleepyhead."

I woke up with a start and I heard Elayne giggle softly, a beautiful sound that I had missed badly these past few weeks.

I smiled, stretching and pulling my aching and tired body up slowly. As I looked around the dusty and cobwebbed shelf that we were sleeping on, it all came back to me and my smile faded.

"Elayne…" I said quietly. "What are we going to do now? The coronation ceremony is today and we've got no plan. Nothing."

"Don't worry, Jasen. We'll work things out as we go. Right now, we just need to start our climb back down and meet Grendesh so he can carry us to the castle."

Grendesh. I had forgotten about him. There was still that terrifying ride ahead of us.

Absently, I reached into my shirt to pat the North Star that I had tucked away there. Instead, I felt only a damp spot on the cloth where the jewel had been.

I jumped up and patted my other pockets down quickly.

"What is it?" Elayne asked. "What's wrong?"

"The North Star." I said with rising panic. "It's gone!"

Emily and Corey, who had slept cuddled together against a giant leather book in the corner, stirred awake and squinted up at me.

"What's up, bro? What's with the dance?"

I scrambled around, looking to see where the gem could have fallen. "It's not here!" I said. "The North Star is gone!"

That made Corey and Emily's eyes open wide.

"What do you mean?" Emily asked. "Did Charlie steal it?"

I ran my hands frantically through my hair. "No. He can't, remember? If someone tries to steal it then it melts into…"

I stopped suddenly and reached back into my shirt, patting the damp spot there. I pulled my fingers out and sniffed.

"Eww, bro!" Corey said. "Get some deodorant."

"Salt." I said, rubbing my fingers together. "It's salt water."

"Oh… no…" I heard Elayne say. "This is very, very bad."

I stared, horrified, at Emily and Corey. "When Charlie stole my body, he was holding the North Star."

Corey's eyes grew wide. "So?" he asked slowly.

"So when he did that, he was stealing the North Star from me, too." I pinched the damp pocket on my shirt as proof. "It… melted."

Corey shook his head, his eyes scared. "No!" he said. "No. Your shirt is still salty and wet from being in the ocean. That's all."

"That was days ago, Corey. This water is fresh."

"No!" Corey insisted, looking truly panicked now. "It… fell out somehow! On the climb up here, maybe!"

"It's gone, Corey." I said, and I felt the terror of the situation rising in my chest.

Emily was staring at the lightening sky outside. "Grendesh is going to kill us." she shuddered.

We sat in shocked silence for a long time after that. My thoughts were racing in a thousand different directions, but every plan that I played out in my mind ended badly. I could see no way out of our situation now.

I saw my own worries and fears mirrored on Corey and Emily's faces, as well. Elayne remained as silent as the rest of us.

Then, when my mind had stopped playing out different plans and had started into a hopeless spiral of bad, bad thoughts, Emily suddenly jumped to her feet and dug the small leather pouch out of her pocket.

I realized with a faint glimmer of hope what she was getting.

Dryan's wood piece! We still at least have Dryan's wood piece.

"Jasen!" Elayne's voice came to me suddenly. "Jasen! Tell Emily to look out!"

Emily was untying the leather pouch now and was pulling out the piece of wood, which I saw was blank once again. I hesitated, not sure what Elayne was telling me to do.

"Jasen! Get Emily out of the way! It's coming... from up above. Do it now!"

Without hesitating, I dove forward suddenly and plowed into Emily. The wood piece in her hand went flying out of reach and I heard something land with a soft, heavy "thump!" right behind us as we fell.

Corey started screaming.

There was a skittering, scratching sound on the wood and I turned to see a giant, hairy spider... the size of a dog, scrabbling across the shelf towards us.

"Kick it, Jasen!" Elayne's voice rang out.

Sharp pincers moved hungrily right below its massive hairy body as its legs carried it in a jittery walk forward. I brought my foot up and kicked it hard, sending it sliding across the wooden shelf and leaving a long smudge in the dust.

Thump! Thump!

Two more spiders fell onto the shelf then, one to the left and one to our right.

I looked up in time to see even more starting to pour out through a gaping crack above us.

Without hesitation, I grabbed up Emily from beside me and started to run. As I ran, I grabbed Corey, who was standing frozen to the spot and still screaming. Holding them both tightly, I dove off the edge of the shelf, hearing the *thump! thump! thump!* of more fat, bloated bodies falling to the shelf behind us as we leapt.

Corey and Emily screamed then, and we hit the webbed netting and bounced. We fell twenty more feet, then bounced again, getting jostled and turned around. Three more bounces and we landed in a tangled heap on the wooden floor.

We looked up to see the spiders charging down the webs after us. Their pincers clicked hungrily and the webs shook under the weight of their jittery, skittish walk.

We ran.

Up a leaning chair and to the table beneath the window ledge. I was out first, grabbing the vines outside and starting to climb down.

I had not climbed the vines before, and the sudden feeling of the cold wind and the terrifying drop below made my head spin dizzily, but I forced myself to keep moving as Emily and Corey jumped out the window and started climbing down above me.

We all watched the window above us nervously as we climbed, waiting tensely for the spiders to come pouring out and continue their chase... but they never came.

Still, we climbed as fast as we could down the tangle of vines. I tried to ignore the wind and the height… and most of all the terrible pit in my stomach as I realized that Dryan's wood chip… our last good hope… was now lost.

Grendesh was going to kill us in a few hours and Elayne was trapped without a body. We now had absolutely nothing with us except an empty silver vial and the clothes that we wore, and Sidhera was going to be crowned queen in a few short hours.

I decided then, as we climbed down the side of that tower in the clouds, that things were as bad as they could possibly get.

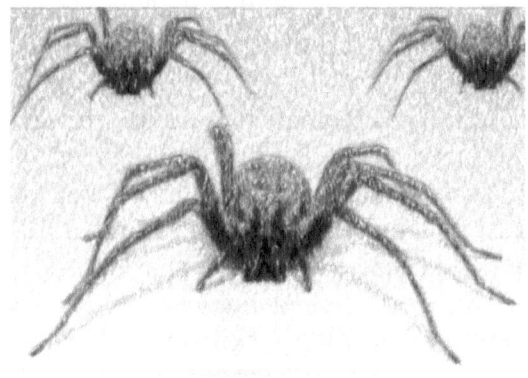

Chapter Thirty

Coral

he sun was much higher into the sky by the time we reached the bottom of the tower again. Grendesh would be returning soon.

There was no sign of Charlie, who I had half expected to be waiting at the base of the tower to attack us... but he must have wisely decided that staying hidden was his best choice right now.

Corey, Emily, and I collapsed on the enormous wooden drawbridge, breathing hard from the strenuous climb.

"All right." Corey said as he lay on his back beside me. "I've given this a lot of thought and... I think that we should hide from Grendesh when he comes back."

"I was thinking the same thing!" Emily quickly agreed. "He may tear the castle apart looking for us, but at least we would have a chance of staying alive."

"We'd also be stranded here." I said.

"Fine with me!" Corey said. "I'd rather be alive and stranded than dead and... well... dead."

I closed my eyes and tried to clear my mind of all of the fear and confusion swirling through it. "Sidhera's getting crowned today." I said finally.

"We won't be able to stop Sidhera if Grendesh kills us." Corey said.

I thought quietly about this. I waited for Elayne to say something, but she remained silent... perhaps waiting to see what I decided to do.

"You can hide when he comes." I said at last. "In fact, you should. But I need to try to get to Sidhera in time."

Corey sat up on his elbow and looked at me. "You're kidding me, right bro? Tell me that you're kidding."

I shook my head slowly. "I've got to try to get to the castle in time, Corey."

Corey threw his arms up. "What does it matter if you make it to the castle or not? The magic that could get Elayne back into her own body is gone now. Even if Grendesh spared you-- which he won't-- any guard there will arrest us on sight. Plus, I think that we made some of them mad enough during our escape that they might rather stick us with their sword than try to bring us in alive."

I pushed my hands through my hair. The sun was coming up fast. There was always a deadline... always the need to rush. If we had more time to think things through and come up with a real plan then we might have actually had a chance here. Time seemed to always be working against us, though.

"If lightning was what we needed to switch bodies, then maybe it would work again." I said. "If we could get a lightning rod or something..."

"Oh, right!" Corey scoffed. "And what, pray for a storm at just the right moment? Or hey--- maybe we could just get her to stick a fork in an electric socket or something. Think she would fall for that? How about putting her tongue on a 9-volt battery? That'll give her a good jolt. Maybe that'll do the trick."

"That was a special magic." Elayne said softly to me. "I don't think that regular lightning would have the same effect. It may even kill her."

I clenched my teeth in frustration. This was impossible. There was no way that we could...

I sat up suddenly. "Wait... what did you just say?"

"What?" Corey asked. "About a 9-volt battery? Yeah, that really hurts, actually. I tried it in second grade and my tongue went numb for three hours."

"Shhh! Not you, Corey. Elayne was talking. Do you think that would really happen, Elayne? It would kill her? I thought that fairies couldn't die."

Elayne was quiet for a moment as if considering. "No... you're right. I don't think that Sidhera would actually die. But... I was thinking about what Dryan told us... that Sidhera didn't just disguise herself... that she actually pulled her spirit into my body."

"Right." I said.

"What's she saying?" Emily asked.

"Hang on." I said. "Go ahead, Elayne."

"Well, if Sidhera is in my body, then she may be more vulnerable than usual. Certainly she cannot use some of her stronger magic."

"What do you mean that she may be more 'vulnerable'?" I asked.

"Her spirit is inside my body." Elayne said. "If my body died, Sidhera would be forced to come out of it."

Even considering the thought made my stomach turn, but I explained to Corey and Emily what I was thinking.

"What?" Emily gasped. "You're talking about killing Elayne!"

"It's just her body." I said. "Elayne is actually right here with us. And maybe, if Elayne can jump back into her body right after Sidhera is pushed out, then she could take over again."

Emily looked thoughtful. "There are ways to kill her that would still leave her body in good shape."

"Like what?" Corey asked.

"Poison. Strangling. Drowning." Emily counted off.

Corey looked startled. "Geez! That's pretty dark. Remind me never to fall asleep around you anymore."

Emily shrugged. "I like reading murder mysteries. Those are the classic ways to die. Very clean."

"It would have to be quick." I said. "Corey's right about the guards. They'll be on the lookout for us and it's going to be really hard to get close to her... especially on the day of the coronation."

"No kidding!" Corey said. "And you think those guards hated us before? They're *really* going to go bonkers if they think that we're trying to kill their princess."

"Poison would be our best shot." Emily considered. "We could try to slip down to the kitchen and put it in her food. That way we don't have to fight our way through the guards to get to her."

"Where would we get the poison?" I asked. "Something so deadly that it could kill her in an instant?"

We were all quiet for a thoughtful moment, then Corey's eyes grew suddenly wide. "Beautiful and dangerous." he said quietly.

I looked up at him. "Where have I heard that before?"

Corey stood up and dusted off his pants. "Come on." he said. "I think that I know what we can use."

Corey led us back inside the castle to the sitting room with the fireplace and the enormous upholstered chair. He stopped beside the giant glass fishbowl. Pressing his face to the dusty glass, he peered in at the dry sand inside. A moment later, he smiled. "Bingo!" he said, pointing through the glass. "Right there. Beautiful and dangerous, just like our big sister."

We looked to where Corey was pointing and I saw a cluster of coral there, half buried in the sand. Among the various bright colors, I recognized one very different cluster that was bright red with black stripes. I remembered seeing it back in Rhiannon's underwater palace.

The slightest touch will kill you instantly.

I looked at Corey and for the first time I felt a glimmer of hope in our hopeless situation. "You're a genius, Corey."

Corey flashed a crooked smile. "That's what I've been telling you for fifteen years now. Glad to hear you finally admit it."

We decided that I should be the one to go since I had the extra advantage of Elayne in my head. Just as in the room at the top of the tower, the cobwebs here were draped across everything and made climbing to the shelf above the massive bowl pretty easy. Once there, though, I had to strain and pull to tear some of the webs down so I could lower them into the gaping bowl beneath me. Every time I pulled on the webs, I held my breath, hoping that it wouldn't send an army of fat, hungry spiders skittering out at me from the dark corners and cracks.

When I had gathered a long enough web and secured it to the base of a towering candlestick nearby, I began my slow and careful climb into the huge fishbowl. About halfway down, I looked over my shoulder and saw Corey and Emily watching me anxiously through the smudged glass. When I finally got to the bottom, I let go of the web and landed with a muffled thump in the powdery white sand.

I stumbled through the thick sand towards the cluster of half-buried coral. I avoided looking at the white bones of the long-dead mermaid as I passed. My breathing echoed in the huge glass bowl and I started to feel a bit trapped, but I forced myself to stay calm and focused on the red and black chunk of coral that lay ahead of me.

"Remember," Elayne said softly in my head. "We only need a tiny piece… and whatever you do, do not touch it!"

I knelt down beside the cluster of coral and carefully reached into my pocket to pull out the empty silver vial. Pulling the cork out, I leaned forward and lightly tapped the edge of the poisonous coral with the bottom of the vial. The metal clink sound filled the hollow bowl and echoed back to me… but it wasn't hard enough to break off a piece.

Carefully, trying to make my hands stop shaking, I tapped the rock again… harder this time. A little jagged piece, the size of a pea, jumped off and landed in the white sand nearby. I reached forward and scooped it into the vial, pushing the cork back in quickly.

I didn't breathe easy again until I was well out of reach of the deadly coral cluster and almost back to the web.

An hour later, the sun was high above us and blazing down on the drawbridge outside. Corey, Emily, and I sat nervously working out our rough plan while Elayne joined in the conversation from where she floated invisibly somewhere nearby. I had my shoe turned up and was picking at a crusty and sticky chunk of green neon gum that was still stuck to the bottom from school a week ago. It was black with dirt and grit that it had collected, but when I pulled at it, it was still gooey underneath.

"So as soon as we land," Emily was saying, "Corey and I are making a run for the kitchen."

Corey nodded. "That shouldn't be a problem. That's one of the few places in the castle that I can get to easily."

Emily patted him lightly on the stomach. "Looks like all of those afternoon snack runs are going to pay off after all."

Corey smirked. "Told ya." He licked his lips. "Hey! Maybe I can grab a few cinnamon rolls while I'm down there…"

"You'd *better* not." I said, still plucking at the green gum on my shoe. "I'm going to need you back up in the Throne Room fast."

"It's still going to be hard to get there without a distraction." Elayne said.

"Oh, I don't think you have to worry about a distraction." I said. "Once Grendesh finds out that we no longer have the North Star, things are going to start getting real hot around there."

"So how exactly are you going to get close enough to Sidhera to make her touch that coral?" Emily asked me.

I pulled a long, slimy string of the bright green gum out from between the cracks in the sole of my shoe and held it up to the sunlight with a smile.

Corey looked at it dangling from my fingertips. "Er… bro? You planning on sharing that or what? We're all hungry here."

I took the long sticky thread and rolled it between my fingers into a little ball. Then, I pulled out the silver vial from my pocket, removed the cork and stuck the gum to the inside of the cork before putting it back in and giving the little vial a shake. The tiny piece of coral inside rattled for a moment, then was quiet.

"With Elayne's help," I said as I pushed the vial back into my pocket, "I'm going to try to work my way through the guards and get to…"

"He's coming." Elayne interrupted suddenly.

My heart started to pound instantly as I stood up. Without a word, Corey and Emily jumped up beside me. A moment later, a huge black shadow rose over the edge of the cloud and the giant, snake-like head of Grendesh appeared. His liquid-gold eyes locked onto us as we stood there on the drawbridge.

"Where's the fourth one?" he asked in a rumbling growl.

"She decided not to come." I said loudly, trying to keep my voice strong and steady despite my terror.

"Fine." he snapped, then shot forward in an instant, snatching us up without another word.

With one giant push from his massive leathery wings, we were up and over the edge of the cloud, then dropping fast. I closed my eyes and struggled to breathe in the torrent of wind and color and noise as we rushed headlong into our final confrontation.

Chapter Thirty-One

Coronation Day

 braced myself, knowing that when we landed, things would start happening fast. When I could finally open my eyes, we were already slowing down and Elayne's castle was directly below us. We dropped with terrifying speed and I had just enough time to see the hundreds of tiny guards milling about, their armor glistening in the midday sun. It looked like an entire army had assembled outside of the castle.

"Land on the drawbridge!" I yelled over the rushing wind.

Grendesh gave a rumbling grunt of disgust, but I felt us dip suddenly to the side and start dropping straight for the open bridge. We fell fast, and even as we were tossed roughly to the wood, the shouts and screams erupted around us.

I struggled to jump to my feet. My head was spinning wildly and I found that I could barely breathe after the dizzying ride. My shoulder hurt where I had been thrown down onto the wooden drawbridge and my chest was bruised and sore where Grendesh's claws had gripped me.

Bells began to ring and shouts of alarm were echoed from all around. Almost instantly, some of the closest guards ran at Grendesh with drawn swords. The dragon flicked his tail dismissively and sent them flying backwards.

Grendesh's head was down in front of my face at once. His golden eyes were right in front of me as my vision came into focus again.

"Give me the jewel!" he rumbled. "Our bargain is complete!"

Corey and Emily had just stumbled to their feet and I motioned for them to go quickly. They started running through the open drawbridge, past guards that were too busy gaping at the sudden appearance of Grendesh to notice the two of them running past.

A barrage of spears and arrows rained down suddenly from the high wall above the drawbridge. They bounced harmlessly off Grendesh's black glistening scales and he kept his eyes locked on me. Another whip of his tail sent two dozen guards sprawling back with a clatter of dented armor.

"I don't have the jewel anymore." I said, bracing myself firmly. "It was stolen from me and it melted into seawater."

In the chaos of the attacking army around us, I could hear only my heartbeat pounding in my chest and the slow, furious breathing of Grendesh as he glared at me.

"I will get you another jewel." I said quickly. "I will keep my word. I just don't have that one anymore."

"Get ready…" Elayne whispered behind my ear. "One… two… three… NOW!"

I jumped back as Grendesh shot forward and snapped his glistening sharp teeth into the air where I had been the moment before. He howled in fury, then opened his mouth to bite at me again.

"Get down!" Elayne said tensely. I dropped to the splintered wooden drawbridge just as his huge, serpentine head lunged forward again. This time, I heard the deadly snap of his jaws right above my head, then an instant later, there was a jarring "THUD" that made the whole drawbridge vibrate. I heard Grendesh let out a sudden wail.

I rolled out of the way just as two more massive "THUDS" rocked the bridge.

"Jump back!" Elayne yelled.

I stumbled back just in time to miss getting sliced by Grendesh's tail, which was suddenly thrashing about wildly. When I finally looked up, I saw the massive wet tentacles of the leviathan, reaching out of the moat and wrapping themselves around Grendesh. He roared and a jet of fire shot from his mouth, spraying the side of the castle walls and making the guards all run for cover.

"Run!" Elayne yelled. "Now! Go!"

I scrambled to my feet and started running hard for the inside of the castle. The battle of the giant beasts behind me had made the massive drawbridge start to sway alarmingly.

"Jump!" Elayne called, and I dove without thinking for the stone archway. In that second, there was a startling crash and the drawbridge behind me collapsed. There was a giant explosion of water as the leviathan pulled Grendesh down into the depths and the raging battle sank beneath the surface of the moat.

"Go, Jasen!" Elayne prompted, and I didn't have time to even catch my breath before I was up and running again, past the startled and shocked soldiers who had lined up at the threshold to watch the terrifying sight.

I started to run towards a nearby archway, but Elayne shouted for me to take a smaller doorway to the left. I dove inside and found myself in a long, narrow corridor. Now, I heard the shouts and alarm bells outside start up again. I ran as fast as I could down the long, shadowy stone hall, chased by the sounds of my own footsteps and the muffled sounds of chaos from outside.

"We have to get to the crown." I said as I ran. "We need to get to it before the coronation."

"I know." Elayne said. "Duck behind the tapestry on the left!"

I jumped to the side of the corridor and slipped behind the tapestry, trying to suck in my stomach and make myself as flat as I could against the cold stone wall. There was a sudden clamor as a group of armored men rounded the corner and ran past. I listened as the echo of their rattling armor disappeared down the long corridor, then I jumped out again and started running.

"Take the next right up here. The red room will be at the top of the stairs." Elayne said. "Be ready. The guards at the door have their swords drawn."

I felt a wild rush of fear as I ran headlong up the stairs. I had no armor, no sword, nothing at all except the voice of Elayne in my head to protect me... and I trusted her completely to keep me safe.

The guards were there. Six of them, fierce-looking and with swords drawn as Elayne had said. I ran up the stairs, sprinting full-speed towards them without hesitation. There was a moment of stunned surprise when they first saw me coming and I knew that it was the only advantage I would get.

"The third one from the right." Elayne said quickly. "The one with the red beard. Get the key off his belt!"

I slid to the polished floor like a runner sliding into home base, right through the cluster of soldiers. I grabbed the key from red beard's belt and yanked it off, pulling it free as I slid between them.

"Kick your left leg out behind you!" Elayne instructed. It ended up being a great move. I caught the two guards on the left of me right at the shin and they fell down with a loud clatter of metal.

Without hesitating, I thrust the key into the lock and heard the "click" as I turned it.

"Pull your arm back!" Elayne shouted.

I let go of the key and jumped back just as a sword came slicing down and smashed into the lock, sending sparks flying. The big golden door flew open and I could see the red room inside.

"Roll forward, then right!" Elayne said tersely.

I dove onto the thick red carpet, feeling something slice through the air above me. Before I even stopped rolling, I threw myself to the right and another sword sliced into the carpet beside me.

I got to my feet and ran, seeing the glass case on the pedestal in the center of the room. "Get down!" Elayne said quickly and I fell again just as I reached the pedestal. A soldier who had been running behind me stumbled suddenly over my crouched body and was sent sprawling into the pedestal. With his heavy armor, he ran into the marble pedestal with enough force to topple it over, sending it to the floor and smashing the glass case on top.

Scrambling forward, I snatched up the silver crown from the carpet where it had fallen and jumped to my feet again.

"He has the crown!" one of them shouted.

I struggled to my feet, backing myself into a corner as the six guards fanned out to block my escape. I gripped the crown tightly, listening for Elayne to give me some direction, but she remained quiet. The guards closed in on me slowly, watching me warily like a cornered lion.

"All right, now." the red-bearded guard was saying as he crept closer. "Let's all just take it easy. You've got nowhere to run now, Jasen. Hand over the crown so nobody has to get hurt."

I moved the crown behind my back. "I can't do that." I said, searching for a way past the guards.

The six guards stepped closer, their sharp swords raised and ready to strike.

"You're making a mistake." I said, breathing hard from the chase. I swallowed, trying to catch my breath. "The coronation ceremony has to be stopped."

"Enough!" a voice rang out suddenly.

I looked up to see the king and queen standing at the doorway with Elayne. More guards had arrived behind them, blocking off any chance of escape.

The king glared at me with a furious expression. "Enough of this, Jasen! You have betrayed this family for the last time." His voice boomed in the closed space of the red room.

"Your majesty!" I said quickly. "That is not Elayne! That is Sidhera in disguise! If you crown her today, you will be giving Sidhera the power to rule your entire kingdom!"

The queen looked for a startled moment at her daughter standing beside her. Elayne's cool blue eyes remained locked on me.

"Nonsense." The king said dismissively. "You helped Sidhera escape from our dungeon eight days ago, and a hundred of my men saw you do it."

"That's not true." I said frantically. "I helped Elayne escape from your dungeon. Sidhera has taken over her body."

"We'll hear no more of your lies." Sidhera said quickly. Elayne's beautiful face twisted into a contemptuous scowl. "We do not know if you are under a spell or if you have been a traitor to us since the beginning. We will decide these things later, though. For now though, you will hand over the crown or be killed."

"You're making a mistake!" I said to the king.

Sidhera's slender hand went up. "Five! Four!"

"Can't you see that she's not your daughter?"

"Three!" Sidhera continued to count in Elayne's voice. "Two!"

"Please!" I said, pleading now to the king and queen.

"One!" shouted Sidhera, finishing her countdown.

"Jasen, give them the crown." said Elayne's voice in my head.

"Kill him." said Sidhera, and the guards surrounding me began to move forward again, raising their swords to strike.

I quickly pulled the crown out from behind my back and held it out. The red-bearded guard reached a heavy gloved hand forward and snatched it up. While the others kept their swords directed at me, he carried the crown over to the queen and bowed down in front of her, offering it up.

I saw Sidhera's eyes watching the crown closely as the queen reached forward and lifted it lightly from the guard's hands. Once she held it, the king made a gesture and the guards fell upon me, grabbing me roughly and holding me tight.

Elayne's mother's eyes looked up at me with sadness as she held the crown in her hands. Sidhera stood beside her, watching me struggle with cold satisfaction.

"The ceremony is about to begin." the king said. "Take him to the dungeon and we'll deal with him later."

As the guards started to drag me forward, Sidhera raised her hand and laid it lightly on the king's arm. "Father," she said in Elayne's soft voice. "I think he should be made to watch the ceremony. It will be fitting justice for him to witness my becoming queen after all he has done to try to prevent it."

The king hesitated and watched me, still with a furious anger boiling in his eyes. "Fine." he said. "Carry him to the throne room where he can watch the ceremony before we lock him away."

A smile curled on Sidhera's lips, barely visible to anyone but me. I glared at her, hating that she could hide so completely behind the beautiful face of the girl I loved.

The three of them turned to go and a moment later, I was being dragged across the thick red carpet behind them.

Chapter Thirty-Two

The Death of Elayne

 layne remained quiet in my mind as we watched the ceremony in the throne room. I was sickened and horrified that the king and queen had been so completely fooled by Sidhera. Looking around the giant hall at the hundreds of onlookers, I saw that in fact Sidhera had *everyone* fooled. They watched her up there, radiant and beautiful, standing poised and smiling as her mother held the silver crown aloft and prepared to make her the new queen. Every face in the crowd watched in admiration and awe. They watched with joyous wonder as Sidhera's plan sealed their terrible fates.

The guards at my sides held me near the back of the room. Their iron grips on my arms made it impossible to even move. I could only watch in desperate silence as the queen's voice echoed through the throne room.

"Jasen," Elayne whispered quietly in my ear. "It's almost time. I want you to know... whatever happens... I love you. I don't care about any of the things that we fought about before. You mean more to me than anything in the world and I never want to lose you."

"I love you, too." I said softly. "I'm so sorry about the things that I said. I don't want to lose you, either. I love you so much."

The red-bearded guard that was holding my arm tightly looked down at me with a startled expression.

I looked up and him and smiled sheepishly. "Oh! Sorry. I didn't mean you. I was just... talking to myself."

The guard eyed me uneasily for a moment longer, then turned his attention back to the ceremony on the stage at the front of the room.

"It's coming." Elayne said. "When it happens, you will have a second when you can break free. I won't be able to help you after that."

"That's fine." I whispered. "Just go. Do you see Corey and Emily? Did they make it?"

"Yes." Elayne said. "They're in the crowd near the stage."

"Good." I said, clenching my stomach and trying to ready myself. "Here goes everything..."

Up on the stage, Sidhera had now knelt down in front of the queen and the queen was lowering the crown slowly down to Elayne's radiant blonde hair. The crowd watched in hushed awe and the crown was placed on her head. As it was laid down, I held my breath along with everyone else in the silent throne room.

The queen opened her mouth to speak the final words, but was cut off by a sudden shriek from the stage. I saw Sidhera jump up, tearing the crown from her head and pressing her hand against her ear as if she was in pain.

As she pulled the crown away, a long, sticky string of neon-green gum stretched to where it was tangled in her blonde locks. She reached into the gummy tangle and pulled something out in fury. She held it up for the crowd to see: A small jagged red and black spur of coral that had been stuck to the inside of the crown.

"Poisoned!" she wailed in fury. Her face was twisted in terrible rage, and she seemed to be glaring directly through the crowd and right at me. Then she collapsed upon the stage as the crowd watched in stunned silence.

There was an instant, before the chaos, when nobody moved. It was just too shocking and too unbelievable. Those in the crowd didn't know if this was some odd part of the ceremony or if what they were watching was real. I saw some of them turn to one another, murmuring questions, even as the king and queen rushed forward to Elayne's fallen body.

I watched that stage closely. I watched and waited, hoping...

Then, it was there.

A flicker.

A tiny flash of dark green light above Elayne's fallen body... so quick and so subtle that it would have been impossible to see if I had not been straining to catch it. And it was at that moment, when Sidhera's spirit was abandoning Elayne's body, that Corey and Emily jumped up from opposite sides of the stage. They each threw a handful of white powder at the same time. The queen screamed and the king fell back at the sudden movement. Instantly, guards rushed to the stage, even as the puff of white glittering powder was still falling over Elayne's body.

Then, somebody in the audience screamed.

Moments later, there was an eruption of shouting as a wave of shock passed over the gathered crowd. There on the stage, above Elayne's body, a twisted, black-robed spirit had suddenly appeared. Its arms were outstretched and unmoving. Its face, even from this distance, was horribly familiar.

It was Sidhera.

Emily and Corey had been successful in their kitchen raid. They had found some salt and had thrown it at just the right instant, trapping Sidhera's spirit as she escaped Elayne's body. Exposing her for all to see.

The crowd, realizing what they were seeing, broke into a terrified panic.

"It's Sidhera!" a woman screamed, and from all around came the sound of the guards drawing their swords suddenly.

The crowd turned and began to push wildly for the doors, even as the guards on the outside of the crowd tried to push forward to get to the stage. The resulting tangle of bodies and flailing limbs was a nightmare.

I used the opportunity to leap forward, pulling from the surprised grip of the guards beside me and diving into the swirling crowd.

As I fought my way through the chaos, I felt a tug in my chest, as if something were tied around me and pulling hard to break free. A moment later, I felt it snap as it was pulled loose. I knew that Elayne had left me then, and I prayed silently that she could push her way back into her own body.

I made it to the stage just as the cloaked figure of Sidhera began to shimmer and fade again. Her face, which I had known so many years as Ms. Locke, looked upon me with hatred in her oily black eyes. Then suddenly her arms were moving and I knew that the effects of the salt were wearing off.

The guards were upon her at once, swords raised and charging. She raised her hands and green light shot from her fingertips, sending the men flying back so hard that they smashed into the stone walls twenty feet away.

I gritted my teeth and ran at her blindly, hoping to catch her off guard and tackle her to the ground. Before I reached her, though, she twirled around in her black robes and disappeared. She reappeared in a flurry of smoke behind me and threw her hands up, knocking me in the back with a blast of magic that sent me sprawling face-down on the hard stone floor beside Elayne's body.

More guards came. Sidhera moved at lightning speed, shooting green bolts of magic in almost every direction at once. The guards were thrown back by the dozens, followed quickly by the king and queen who also had tried to charge at Sidhera in terrified desperation.

Corey and Emily were free again. I saw Corey throw another handful of salt in Sidhera's face, but she just turned on him furiously and sent him flying back so hard that he landed deep in the fleeing crowd, knocking over several of them in the process. Another green light hit Emily in the chest and she froze, unmoving, like a statue on the spot.

Sidhera's black eyes were filled with contemptuous rage as she threw back wave after wave of guards. Finally, no more came and the last of the fleeing crowd was pushing out the doors on all sides. The giant room was littered with armored soldiers, either knocked out or lying on the ground and moaning in pain. I saw Corey out on the stone floor, his face bruised and bleeding. His eyes were closed and he was not moving.

The queen was kneeling in the corner, holding the limp body of her husband in her arms. He was still breathing, but he was unconscious and bleeding badly. Elayne lay beside me, white as death, and not breathing at all.

Sidhera scanned the room one last time with her black, swirling eyes, then turned her terrible dark gaze on me.

"You have meddled in my plans for the last time, boy." Sidhera said, gliding across the stage towards me. "It is time that you joined your lovely princess here. I should have killed you the moment I saw you. I know now that it was a mistake to let you live. That oversight, however, can be easily corrected."

Sidhera glared down upon me and a smile of hateful satisfaction curled her lips. She raised her hands and green lightning began to arc between her fingertips.

I held my hand up to shield myself from the deadly blow, and she threw her arms forward, green fire arcing towards me.

I had just enough time to brace myself when suddenly the green bolt of magic exploded in the air, inches from my face, in a shower of purple sparks.

"Jasen is under my protection, Sidhera," a voice from out of nowhere. "The laws of magic forbid you from killing him."

Sidhera and I both turned at the same instant and saw a tiny purple spark of light floating in through one of the doorways. As it floated closer, I could just make out the tiny winged figure of Bridgette hovering in the light's center.

Sidhera spun back on me in an instant and threw both her hands up, sending two jets of green fire at me. A purple shield expanded around me suddenly, sending the green fire bouncing off towards the far walls.

"No, no, no." Bridgette said again calmly. "You never were one to follow directions well, were you? Even when all of the fairy tribes lived and worked together in peace, there was always something dark and twisted inside of you. Too much pride and so much anger."

"Do not dare lecture me, Bridgette!" Sidhera spat, and without warning, she turned and shot an arc of green magic at the tiny fairy.

Bridgette flicked it aside harmlessly as she flew nearer, but I saw her usually calm face darken as she watched Sidhera.

"And now," Bridgette said, "you have broken the most ancient of laws. You have attacked me, another fairy queen."

I looked at Sidhera and I saw a flash of fear cross her face… as if she had suddenly realized that she had just made a terrible mistake.

"Wait." Sidhera said, holding up her hands. "Bridgette…"

But before she could say anything else, a blinding flash of purple light filled the room. I shielded my eyes as it grew even brighter, and I threw my arms instinctively over Elayne's body to protect her.

In the bright light, I heard a sudden, terrible noise. A howling, piercing wail that made the hair on my neck stand on end. With a cold shudder, I realized that it was the sound of

Sidhera. She let out a long, horrified scream that crawled down my spine with an icy shiver. It was the most bone-chilling sound I had ever heard, and it seemed to go on and on and on in the blinding light.

When it stopped, there was sudden and complete silence. The purple light that had filled the room was gone in an instant. When I looked up again, Bridgette floated there alone, a tiny spark of purple light.

Sidhera was nowhere to be seen.

Some of the guards around the room had pulled themselves to their feet and were staggering forward, trying to shake the awful scream from their minds. Emily, who had been frozen in place by Sidhera's spell, suddenly collapsed to the stage. Taking only a moment to look around the room in surprise, she leapt up again almost instantly, running to where Corey lay bleeding on the floor.

It was then, as I lay there stunned and dizzy, with purple spots of light still floating through my vision, that I felt Elayne heave her first, heavy breath.

I lifted my head and looked at her face just in time to see her eyelids fluttering open. I felt a flood of disbelief as I watched her sparkling blue eyes lock on mine uncertainly.

"Jasen?" she asked carefully.

I reached up and pushed away her hair, which was still tangled with sticky green gum. After the terrible things that had happened in the past days, I felt my stomach clench with uncertain hope as I watched her face.

"Elayne? Is that really you?" I asked.

In reply, Elayne looked into my eyes and a warm smile broke across her lips. She leaned forward and kissed me, and that was all I needed to convince me that Elayne was back and that everything was going to be okay.

Amid the clatter and moaning of the guards around us, I heard a whoop of excitement from somewhere across the room. Corey was sitting up, supported by Emily. His face was cut and bruised, and his left arm lay limp in his lap, but even then, a huge grin spread across his face.

"That's right!" Corey shouted. "Take *that* you mean old witch! That'll teach you not to mess with my grandma! Woo-hoo!"

Chapter Thirty-Three

Sunset

lad you're home from your vacation." I said to Bridgette as I pulled Elayne up beside me.

Her tiny wings fluttered in a purple blur as she floated closer to us. "It looks like I returned just in time." she said.

"Ah, we had everything under control!" Corey said with a big grin as he limped across the room towards us, supported by Emily.

"I could see that." Bridgette said with a wry smile.

Some of the soldiers had made their way over to the king and queen now and the king had just begun to open his eyes, looking stunned and confused. Elayne's mother stroked his hair softly as she held his head in her lap.

Elayne looked at them worriedly. When she shifted herself to try to move towards them, Bridgette called out. "Princess! Don't move!"

Elayne froze where she was, looking at Bridgette uncertainly. Bridgette pointed a tiny violet finger toward the ground where Elayne had been about to lay her hand. There sat the tiny jagged piece of coral that had poisoned Sidhera.

Bridgette clapped her hands and the tiny shard burst into fine dust, scattering harmlessly across the floor.

Corey and Emily had made it back to the stage now and I could see that Corey's arm looked like it was broken. Still, he was grinning from ear to ear. "Alright!" he said. "Looks like we've got ourselves a happily ever after here, right? Now that we're out of mortal danger, I think that it's time we go down to the kitchen and…."

Corey was interrupted by the stone ceiling of the massive throne room crashing in on us. Bridgette shielded the king and queen and I had just enough time to pull Elayne out of the way before a giant slab of stone crashed to the floor where we had been sitting. There was a booming roar that shook the floor, and from out of the falling dust appeared Grendesh, tearing down one whole wall of the throne room as his glistening black body plowed through.

He moved with such terrifying speed that he was upon me before I even realized what was happening. His head moved in a blur towards me and in the next second there was a terrible pain erupting in my leg. I looked down just in time to see the dragon's razor teeth sinking into my thigh, then he was yanking me upwards.

Elayne grabbed out for me, but Grendesh was pulling me up and up, his teeth tearing through meat and bone in my leg. In one quick motion he tossed me up into the air above his head and opened his mouth to swallow me whole.

Instead of falling into his mouth, though, I froze in midair above him, floating helplessly. His teeth snapped closed, but when he realized that he had bitten down on nothing but air,

Grendesh opened one slitted, evil eye and fixed it upon me. He watched me floating above him for a moment, then opened his mouth again to snatch me out of the air.

"Stop!" Bridgette called from across the room.

Grendesh paused only a moment, casting a furious glance towards Bridgette. "Stay out of this, water fairy! This human entered into an agreement with me and broke it, forfeiting his life."

He reached his snakelike neck up to snap me out of the air and I floated a little higher, just out of reach. His teeth snapped down hard on the air directly below me. My torn and broken leg screamed out in pain as I tried helplessly to move.

Grendesh turned an angry eye back towards Bridgette. "The laws of magic forbid you to interfere here, fairy. This human's life is rightfully mine."

"What is this bargain you speak of?" Bridgette asked.

I struggled to keep from passing out from the pain in my leg. My heart raced, watching the enraged dragon breathing heavily beneath me.

"The North Star!" I said. "We promised him the North Star, but it melted into seawater before we could give it to him. I was going to keep my word--"

"Yet you did not and now your life is owed to me." Grendesh roared. He gave his huge leathery wings a flap and leapt into the air at me. This time, he almost snapped his teeth down on me before I was pulled out of reach by the invisible force that held me suspended.

Grendesh roared in fury, his giant body turning amid the rubble of the throne room to glare at Bridgette, who just watched him calmly.

"And yet," Bridgette said evenly. "If the North Star were to be given to you, then the bargain would be complete."

"ARE YOU DEAF, FAIRY?" Grendesh boomed. "The jewel is gone!"

Bridgette leveled a look at Grendesh. "I can hear perfectly fine, *dragon*. And you will watch your tone with me or find yourself turned into a salamander for a thousand years."

"Your magic is no threat to me!" Grendesh snapped, his golden eyes flashing with fury. Still, though, he grew silent, giving only a furious snort of black smoke from the slits of his nostrils.

Bridgette turned evenly back to me, where I dangled in midair above the dragon with a mangled leg. "Jasen," she said calmly, "When you entered into this bargain with the dragon, did you tell him a time that you would give him the jewel?"

A lump formed in my throat. "What? I don't…"

"I will not be taken in by fairy-double-talk!" Grendesh boomed. "We had a bargain and I will be satisfied at this moment! If not the jewel, then the boy's life!"

Bridgette just shook her head. "For an immortal dragon, you are far too impatient. By the laws, he has six months to fulfill the bargain if he didn't tell you otherwise."

"THE JEWEL IS GONE!" Grendesh raged. "What does it matter if I kill him now or six moons from now?"

Bridgette looked at me calmly. "Well, it matters very much to him, I should think."

Grendesh turned his shimmering eye carefully up at me again, watching me with sullen fury. "The laws compel me to wait." he said in a raspy whisper that was still loud enough to shake the remaining stone walls of the demolished throne room. "But in six moons, whether in this world or any other, I will find you and we will end this."

He closed his scaly claws into clenched fists, then turned and leapt into the sky. The wind from his massive wings sent chunks of stone sliding away and caused another crumbling section of the throne room walls to collapse. When the dust had cleared again, the dragon was gone and I was left hanging high in the air with my bleeding and broken leg dangling horribly beneath me.

Ironically, I ended up in the same bed in the same guestroom where I had been held prisoner only nine days before. Things were much different this time around, though.

I had expected Bridgette to heal my leg with a flurry of her fingers and a few magic words, but it turned out that she couldn't. She was able to stop the bleeding, at least, and Elayne had used some of her magic to ease the pain, but when they were all through, I still had a broken leg and a huge, jagged scar that wrapped around my thigh.

"You're lucky you still have a leg at all." Elayne was saying as she sat beside me, pushing up the pillows behind my head.

Bridgette, who had now returned to the human guise of Liz, stood nearby with my Grandpa. "It will be a few months before you completely heal," she said, "But if you exercise, you should be able to walk again."

I felt a stony pit in my stomach. "Great. On my feet just in time to be eaten by Grendesh."

"Not if you can give him the North Star before then." Bridgette reminded me.

"It's gone! I told you it melted when…"

Bridgette interrupted me with a small shake of her head. "Fairies always have a backup plan, young Jasen. I thought that you would have learned that by now."

Elayne looked at Bridgette hopefully. "You have a way to get the North Star back?"

Bridgette nodded thoughtfully. "I may know of a way for Jasen to complete his bargain with Grendesh without losing his life, but we will talk of these things later."

Corey, his arm in a cast and a sling, was watching the ugly scar on my leg. "Wow. Sucks to be you, bro. Wrecked car. Busted-up leg. A date with a hungry dragon. You got the stinky end of the stick if you ask me."

"What about you?" I said. "You've got a broken arm and your motorcycle is at the bottom of Terra Bog."

Corey's face fell. "Man! I forgot about that. That's depressing."

Emily rubbed his shoulder. "It's alright. We're alive and Sidhera was stopped. That's all that counts."

Corey was frowning. "Yeah, but my bike! It was such a sweet ride."

I looked at Bridgette. "So what exactly did you do to Sidhera?" I asked curiously. "Did you..." I hesitated, lowering my voice seriously. "Did you kill her?"

Liz looked at me with that unreadable expression that she always wore. "No, young Jasen. As you may recall, fairies cannot be killed. Let us just say that I made things... uncomfortable for her."

I shuddered. "By the sound of her scream, I think that she may have been a bit more than just 'uncomfortable'."

"She is a strong fairy. In a few centuries, she may be able to recover her strength."

I looked at Bridgette with a start. "A few centuries? You mean..."

Bridgette smiled lightly. "Yes, young Jasen. Sidhera should not trouble this kingdom again during your lifetime."

It was almost too good to believe. Even as the weight of Bridgette's words were sinking in, I saw her frown quietly to herself. "Of course, after her encounter with Grendesh last year, I did not expect her to recover as quickly as she did. How is it, I wonder, that she was able to regain all of her strength in so short a time?"

I didn't like the uncertain shadow that crossed Bridgette's face, but before I could ask about it further, we heard a small sound by the doorway and we all looked up to see the king and queen standing there. They were both battered and bruised as well, and the king had a bandage wrapped around his forehead. Their faces were dark and serious and I knew immediately that they had some bad news to share.

Grandpa looked at them, then looked back at me carefully. "Come on, guys. It's getting crowded in here. Corey, can you show me where the kitchen is in this place?"

Corey was more than happy to comply, and a few moments later, I was left alone in the room with Elayne and her parents.

The king looked down uncomfortably, his rough beard looking grey in the evening light streaming through the window. "Jasen," he began. "It is rare for a king to say this, but I owe you my gratitude as well as a sincere apology."

I shook my head. "It's alright. With fairies around doing all of these crazy things, I don't blame you for being paranoid. It's really hard to know who to trust."

The king nodded. "Truly it is." he said softly. "But you should know that we trust you completely. You have proven yourself for a second time to be more than worthy to take the throne beside my daughter."

Elayne looked at her father uneasily. "Oh! Father... don't. Jasen and I still have not talked about that yet..." She looked out the window at the setting sun. "I know that I have to be crowned before sunset, but Jasen and I still need some time to talk first."

The king scratched his beard uncomfortably. "Well, take all the time you would like, but there is another, graver matter that we need to discuss with you... both of you."

Looking at their faces, I wasn't at all sure that I wanted to hear what he had to say.

"What is it?" Elayne asked carefully, and I could hear the same uneasiness in her voice.

Elayne's mother looked at her father hesitantly, then looked carefully at Elayne and I. "The Crown of Lions is gone. Stolen."

Forgetting my broken and bruised body, I almost shot up out of bed, then winced and fell back suddenly as the pain overtook me. "Sidhera? She got the crown?"

The king nodded gravely. "We believe so, yes."

"But she wasn't coronated." Elayne said helplessly, terror in her eyes. "We stopped the ceremony before she could…"

The queen raised a calming hand. "No. It's true that the power of the crown was not bestowed upon her. However, by stealing it from us, she has also denied its power to you."

I clenched my teeth. "We can get it back!" I said. "We'll find her and---"

"It's too late." The king interrupted. "The sun is now setting on Elayne's seventeenth birthday. Since no one was crowned, its spell will be broken."

Elayne looked horrified. "There will be chaos. The kingdom will crumble…"

The queen shook her head. "No, Elayne. While it's true that the kingdom has been at peace for thousands of years under the crown's spell, kings and queens were ruling without it long before that."

The king took a deep breath. "Still, though, it is important that no one else know that the magic of the crown is gone. We are having another crown made and we will coronate you tonight. To the rest of the world, it must look like nothing has changed."

Elayne, her face white, sank slowly to the edge of the bed. "But without the crown, how can I rule? There will be corruption, war, dissent."

"All things that a strong ruler can overcome without magic." the king said firmly. "I have no doubt that you and Jasen together are more than capable of…"

The queen, seeing the sudden look of uneasiness on Elayne's face at the mention of my name, put her hand lightly on the king's arm. He grew quiet, then nodded hesitantly.

"It's late." he said finally. "You two have a lot to talk about. Elise and I will give you some time alone. Elayne… we will summon you sometime before midnight for the private coronation."

A moment later they were gone.

Now Elayne sat beside me, the rays of golden light from the setting sun streaming in through the window and across her face. Her expression was stricken and fearful, and there was a moment of thoughtful silence as we watched each other in that glowing light, each lost in our own uneasy thoughts. When I started to finally speak, Elayne opened her mouth to say something as well. We both stopped short and watched each other sheepishly.

"You may speak first, your highness." I said with a tilt of my head.

A tired smile pressed Elayne's lips. "What I was going to say was that it was wrong of me to assume that you would change your life's plans to suit mine. I know that before I came along, you already had an idea of what your future would be like and I have no right to take that away from you."

"Elayne…" I began.

"No, listen." she interrupted. "I must be crowned queen tonight. I don't have a choice… but you do. Things are going to get much, much harder in the years to come, and this is my burden to bear, not yours. Your life is wide open to do whatever you want with it."

I squeezed Elayne's hand. "What I want," I said, "is to spend my life with you. Your destiny is my destiny and I would never change that."

Elayne shook her head. "Jasen, honestly. You don't need to."

"I know I don't need to," I smiled. "But I want to. I want to marry you, Elayne Lionheart. I want to marry you and be king at your side."

Elayne's eyes watched me intently for a long moment, then a smile lit across her lips. She leaned forward and hugged me tightly, and although the aches and bruises in my body cried out all at once, I couldn't help but feel a sense of elation as I reached up and hugged her back.

A moment later, in the light of the setting sun, I held her hand and smiled up at her. "Listen," I said. "Before the sun goes down, there's one more thing I wanted to tell you."

Elayne looked at me curiously. "What's that?"

I looked up at her with a grin. "For the first time in over thirteen hundred years… happy birthday."

Epilogue

e had known that the fat mole-faced girl was up to something even before it happened. She had been casting him suspicious looks all afternoon. Then, when he had made the offhand comment about pixie dust, he had seen her eyes flash to him and he had known that she knew.

Still, he had not been expecting what had happened next. At the top of the tower, they had found the lightning...

Jasen had probably seen it coming... not that he would have said anything. That lying, two-faced traitor! After all he had done for that thankless boy... after all the times he had saved that boy's neck...

"Charlie, get out of Jasen's body, NOW!" the woman had shouted, and then there had been a flash of light and the world had spun. When Charlie opened his eyes next, he had found himself trapped inside the fleshy prison of the ugly one's body. It had been terrible and unexpected. A horrible nightmare that he couldn't escape from.

He had run, of course. There were three of them (four if you counted the ugly girl's spirit which now floated who-knows-where) and he hadn't liked those odds. They were angry at him, which Charlie resented, considering all he had done for them.

He had run and he had hidden on a bookshelf downstairs. He had watched as they came in the next day and peered into the fishbowl. He had watched as Jasen climbed up to where Charlie was hiding on the shelf right above the bowl. At first, Charlie thought in a panic that the boy was coming after him. He hid behind a candlestick and waited, ready to attack Jasen if he came after him.

Instead, Jasen had climbed down into the bowl to retrieve something while the other two watched. It would have been so easy for Charlie to loosen those webs and make Jasen fall, trapping the traitorous boy in the bowl forever. If Jasen had been alone, Charlie would have done it, too. His friends were watching, though, and Charlie decided to stay hidden until the boy had climbed back out and gone down to join his friends again.

After that, they never came back into the castle. Later, he heard the roar of the dragon outside and then it stayed quiet for a long time. He finally decided that they were gone and it was safe to come out again.

Later that day, the spiders attacked for the first time. Charlie had climbed up on the massive kitchen table to search for food, and had found nothing but dust and more cobwebs. While he was picking at a hardened, black stain that was stuck to a prong on a giant fork, he had heard a fat, soft "THUMP!" behind him and had turned to see the hairy brown spider skittering across the dusty table towards him. He had screamed and run, tumbling off the side of the table even as more of the bloated, hungry beasts landed behind him.

He had gotten away finally by hiding under a teacup. He had huddled in the shadows there, his heart beating fearfully in the bloated, fat woman's chest and had listened, terrified, for the skittering sound of the spiders to return.

He awoke sometime later to the terrifying sounds of explosions that rattled and shook the whole castle. The wooden shelf beneath him trembled with each monstrous boom, and one time he even heard a dish come crashing to the floor in another room, a sound like a building collapsing. Charlie soon realized that it was a thunderstorm that was shaking the cloud that the castle sat upon.

The next day, starving and exhausted, Charlie carefully climbed out from under the teacup and crept outside. He walked out onto the wooden drawbridge and peered over the edge of the cloud at the ground far below.

He could see the seashore now. The ocean stretched endlessly to the east and a rocky coast cut right up to the horizon. There, on the edge of the sea, Charlie saw something glittering in the morning sunlight. It looked like a collection of tin-roofed buildings built upon the rocks against the water. Charlie looked at them for a long time, and realized that he was looking at the seaside town of Lisette's Cove, which they had passed through on their travels.

Watching those glittering rooftops in the distance as his cloud floated by, he began to understand what it was he would have to do next.

The wind was blowing hard, and he knew that it was a crazy, reckless idea, but he also understood that if he didn't do something soon, he was going to die up on that cloud anyway. He would rather die trying to escape, at least.

He had seen some thin, cotton-like spider webs in one corner of the kitchen, and they had reminded him of a long-forgotten scene from a cartoon he had seen once when humans had lived in the Kasner house. Charlotte's Web. In the cartoon, a thousand baby spiders had burst forth from their eggs. They each had a tiny silk web parachute that caught the wind and carried them away, scattering them in all directions.

Now, Charlie grabbed up a double handful of the fine silk webbing and, without pausing to think of the horrible death that awaited him if it failed, he leapt off the edge of the cloud and into the wind.

Unlike the cartoon, the fine silk did not pop open into an airy parachute. Instead, it flapped uselessly in the wind as he shot towards the earth with terrifying speed.

If he had not been over the water, he would have been dead instantly. Instead, he landed with bone-jarring force in the waves and struggled upwards for breath. When he finally found the air again, he was far from shore and he had to push and struggle in the fat woman's body to make it to dry land.

Back on the beach, he lay in the sand for a long time, gasping and choking to pull air into his burning lungs. High above, in the distance, he saw the huge white cloud he had been on. It looked small and alone in the empty blue sky. Looking up at it, he could hardly believe that he was still alive after his foolish leap.

He walked along the coastline for the rest of the day until he came across Lisette's Cove towards the evening. Once in town, he found a dark alley off one of the busy streets. He waited until someone was foolish enough to try to pass through alone... then he clubbed him over the head and took the small pouch of gold from the man's belt. Whistling happily, he wandered into a tavern called "The Singing Mermaid" and ate until his stomach ached and his hands were covered with grease and gravy. He used the last of the gold to rent a small room for the night and collapsed face-first on the hard cot.

In the morning, he began walking west from the coastline. By midday the next day, he reached the line where the trees of the forest ended abruptly and the murky waters of Terra Bog stretched out in front of him. Despite his exhaustion, he forced his pudgy, fat legs to keep marching forward.

It was well past dark when he reached the small hut. The will-o-wisps bobbing nearby lit it with an eerie glow beneath the moonless sky. There was nothing he could make a fire from, so he just gathered up some old, moldy burlap sacks and laid down on the hard-packed dirt floor. After the exhausting hike, he found that sleep came to him quickly.

He was awakened before dawn by the sound of something crashing into the hut. He looked up to see a woman in black robes come stumbling in. Around her feet, four vicious-looking creatures circled and followed. At first, he thought they were trying to attack the woman, but then he saw that they were really carrying her... trying to help her as she stumbled in.

Her eyes locked on him the moment she saw him laying there. Her face was young and pretty, but her skin was pale white in the darkness and her eyes were black and sunken. She looked sick or hurt and swayed unsteadily as she faced him. In one hand she clutched what looked like a silver crown.

"Sidhera?" Charlie asked in the darkness.

She looked at him and her eyes narrowed suspiciously, perhaps recognizing the ugly woman's body that he was trapped in.

"Who are you?" Sidhera rasped. The dirty, impish creatures by her side all looked at him hungrily.

"You can call me Charlie." he said, pulling himself up.

Sidhera's black eyes watched him closely. Even hunched over and injured, she looked like a deadly viper.

"You know that I am going to kill you for being here." she said.

Charlie nodded. "I know."

Sidhera lifted her eyes curiously. "Are you not afraid?"

Charlie shrugged the big woman's shoulders. "I have been dead before." he said.

Sidhera seemed to consider this. The creatures by her side pranced from one foot to another, as if waiting anxiously for the order to attack.

"What do you want?" she asked at last.

"I want the same thing as you." Charlie said, leveling a cool gaze at Sidhera. "I want revenge,"

About the Author

Joe Tompkins has been writing since he was old enough to hold a pencil. *Sidhera's Revenge* is his second published novel. Although born in Georgia, he grew up in the small town of Monroe, New York... nestled in the secluded Catskills much like the fictional town in this story. He now lives in Covington, Georgia with his wife, Lisa, and their two wonderful daughters, Victoria and Michelle.

Joe is a full-time teacher and also writes educational software for students of all ages. You can find out more at www.gepetosoftware.com.

www.ingramcontent.com/pod-product-compliance
Lightning Source LLC
Chambersburg PA
CBHW050556260626
47157CB00002B/590